Stealing the Spanish Princess

Art Theft Mystery

Book 1

Bea Green

*ROUGH
EDGES
PRESS*

Rough Edges Press
An Imprint of Wolfpack Publishing
5130 S. Fort Apache Rd. 215-380
Las Vegas, NV 89148

roughedgespress.com

Paperback ISBN 978-1-68549-156-7
eBook ISBN 978-1-68549-155-0

For three talented artists, who always bring a smile and a laugh into my life:
Victoria Papageorge,
Cathy Hart
and
Coleen Little

Stealing the Spanish Princess

"That's my last Duchess painted on the wall, looking as if she were alive. I call that piece a wonder, now; Fra Pandolf's hands worked busily a day, and there she stands."

—*My Last Duchess* by Robert Browning

1

Richard

Chief Inspector Richard Langley was inspecting a mummified foot in his basement office at New Scotland Yard when the phone call from the Superintendent came.

The foot wasn't the most valuable item confiscated from an Egyptian traveller at Heathrow Airport earlier that week but it was certainly the most interesting. The toenails were still intact and the sole of the foot still preserved the puffy flesh of its owner, the palmar flexion creases criss-crossing from side to side. The top of the foot had an area where the skin had given way and the waxy yellow of the bone beneath it was visible.

A leather cord hung loosely between the two biggest toes and must have been at one time part of a leather sandal. Lifting it up, he could see colorful beads were sewn onto the thong in an intricate pattern, all of them threaded through with fine gold wire.

Looking at the delicacy of the foot, Richard guessed it had once belonged to a woman but he was no expert in mummified body parts.

The phone rang suddenly, startling him and shattering the silence in the office with its ringtone.

Richard quickly put the foot down on the sterile container in front of him, took off his white gloves and picked up the handset.

He gave a cursory look at the phone extension calling him and sat up a little straighter in his chair.

"Dick?"

Richard cringed inwardly at his Superintendent's colloquial use of his name.

"Yes, sir."

"Could you pop up and see us at Room 402?"

Surprised by this request, Richard began to rub at the five o'clock shadow on his cheek, and, as he felt the bristly hairs prick his fingers, he remembered he hadn't shaved that morning, or the previous one either, come to think of it.

He doubted he was looking presentable. Never one to preen himself, he had become sloppier than usual about his appearance in recent weeks. More so on days when he had no important meetings to go to. Given the nature of his job he was going to be summoned without notice at some point but this time, thankfully, he was lucky. Superintendent Lionel Grieves, who was on the other end of the phone, was unlikely to pay close attention to his outward appearance.

The request to head up to Room 402 came as something of a bombshell to Richard because Room 402 was a meeting room used by his colleagues in the Homicide and Serious Crime Command at New Scotland Yard and this was not a department he was at all familiar with.

On the other side of the phone, his boss cleared his throat, hinting at his impatience.

"Yes, sir," Richard answered at last, feeling he had no other option but to agree to go.

"Thank you, Dick."

Puzzled, Richard hung up and stared at the wall in front of him.

Facing him and attached to the grey wall with bright red pins was a large poster of Canaletto's painting *The River Thames with St. Paul's Cathedral on Lord Mayor's Day*. Flags, sailing boats and rowing boats crowded the surface of the river in Canaletto's painting but although the jovial picture was situated directly in front of him, Richard wasn't observing it and in any case, he wasn't in a celebratory mood.

Quite the reverse in fact. His mind was filled with a sense of foreboding as he mulled over Lionel's strange phone call.

In his entire career at the Art and Antiquities Crime Unit he had never worked with anyone from Homicide Command, for not only was homicide not his specialty, he had never actually dealt with any murders within the scope of a job that entailed protecting art and artifacts of value from those intent on stealing them.

It wasn't unusual for him to be involved in high profile cases because unlike other countries, like Italy or France, the Art and Antiquities Crime Unit in Britain was so underfunded they only had the resources to deal with stolen items of exceptional value. But it was rare for any homicides to be involved in the professional art theft world, even though it was often a deeply unpleasant criminal enterprise.

Realizing he had better get a move on if he wasn't going to irritate the hell out of the colleagues waiting for him along in Room 402, Richard nevertheless decided to store away the Egyptian hoard before he left the office, accepting that this new meeting probably meant his investigation into the small collection of Egyptian artifacts would have to be postponed until some other, much later, time or even abandoned altogether.

Putting his gloves back on, Richard stood up and placed the mummified foot carefully back into a large plastic box, where it had been keeping company with a gold, turquoise and carnelian neck-collar, two dented gold armlets, several glazed scarabs, a diminutive hippo made of lapis lazuli and a wooden figurine of an ancient Egyptian woman.

He sighed as he placed the lid on the box.

Looting had become rife in Egypt since the Arab Spring. The Egyptian specialists at the British Museum were going to look at these items and if they determined they were in fact genuine, the Egyptian embassy would have to be notified. Gone were the days when British archaeologists appropriated ancient Egyptian artifacts; nowadays they were only temporary custodians of such treasures, and rightly so.

After removing and returning the white gloves to an empty desk drawer, he then picked up and carried the plastic box over to a shelf where a number of similar containers reposed, each one meticulously labeled.

Turning back to his desk, he reached across and grabbed his grey suit jacket from the back of the chair, shrugging himself into it as he picked up his mobile phone.

Richard walked out of the large, windowless office,

which had shelves stacked from top to bottom with miscellaneous items connected to unresolved art theft cases and tugged firmly at the heavy keypad door as he left, making sure it locked securely behind him.

Making his way slowly down the enclosed corridor he checked the emails on his phone and then, once he reached the lift door, he pushed the button to call it down to the basement floor.

He smiled to himself as he bent his head backwards to look up at the lift shaft.

The lift was encased in glass and revealed within its innards the technical engineering involved in its daily function.

The building's design hinted at transparency. The upper reaches of the Curtis Green Building were light and airy, with plenty of shiny floors, large windows and a pale colour palette wrapping itself around the newly refurbished rooms.

In contrast the Art and Antiquities Unit was located in the basement area of the building and had been left in the shadows, windowless and drab. When he ascended in the lift, he always felt like he was emerging from the dark, ugly and hidden parts of the ocean, reaching up to the unfamiliar sunlit surface.

The basement was an apt metaphor for the general status of the Art and Antiquities Unit within New Scotland Yard. Even though his department might rank low on the Met's priorities, art crime was now estimated to be the third highest grossing criminal enterprise behind drugs and arms dealing, and recent figures suggested that thefts of art and antiquities in the UK alone totaled more than £300 million.

In Richard's opinion art theft was more than losing

cultural property. It was currency to fund arms, drugs and terrorism but unfortunately the general public didn't seem to recognize this. Inevitably, his was a lone voice in the wilderness, a wilderness in which his fellow police officers were also struggling with the burden of reduced staffing and resources as they desperately tried to tackle rising rates of knife crime, acid attacks and terrorism. All of which were considered more important than art theft...

2

Richard

Richard opened the door into Room 402 and when he walked through it, he found he was facing a window with a magnificent view of the river Thames.

It was two thirty in the afternoon and the river's boat traffic was brisk. The London River Bus, rammed full of tourists with their faces hidden behind cameras and mobile phones, drifted past. Little motorboats scooted dexterously up and down, freight boats loaded with containers chugged their way up the Thames and, in the distance, the traffic on Westminster Bridge was moving at a snail's pace.

"Ah, Dick. Thanks for coming. May I introduce you to our other colleagues?"

The rasping voice had a note of censure in it.

Richard reluctantly removed his gaze from the window and turned to look at the others gathered around the rectangular table.

Like many of the rooms in the Curtis Green Building, this room was small, and the four other people in it seemed to shrink it down even further.

"Dick, this is, as you already know, Chief Superintendent Matthews," said Lionel Grieves, in a morose tone of voice that always reminded Richard of Eeyore in *Winnie the Pooh*.

Richard reached over the table and shook the Chief Superintendent's hand, feeling momentarily surprised at the strength evident in his superior's handshake.

CS Alan Matthews was a large, powerfully built man, who seemed very uncomfortable in the shell of his police uniform.

He looked to be someone who would have been better suited to working as a brawny farmer, striding across his extensive crop fields, or as a ranger single-handedly managing a pine forest in an isolated patch of northern Scotland. He was fresh-faced despite being sixty-two years old, his head of thick, grey hair was intact and he had rosy-red cheeks. One thing was for sure, he didn't look in the least bit like a pen pusher.

However, after eleven years in the force, Richard was well aware that the Chief Superintendent's guile-less expression masked a formidable intelligence that managed the convoluted office politics at New Scotland Yard like it was a walk in the park and anyone who chose to underestimate his intelligence did so his or her peril.

Richard had no idea why Chief Superintendent Matthews was in their meeting as he was far too senior to waste time on Chief Inspectors and their day-to-day business. Chief Superintendents tended to be the behind the scenes philosophers in the police hierarchy, not the actioners. Unless in this particular case there happened to be sensitive, internal politics involved or the potential for a major international incident? Or maybe it was possible there was something extremely valuable at stake, thought Richard, like a Leonardo da Vinci or Picasso?

His day suddenly felt a little brighter.

"And this is CI Abdul Hazim and DI Eilidh Simmons," said Lionel, indicating the two other persons seated next to each other on the other side of the table.

Richard stretched out a hand to them, studying Abdul and Eilidh with interest.

Abdul's chiseled face was inscrutable as he shook Richard's hand.

He was a small man, approximately 5 foot 4, but with a charisma about him that was hard to ignore. Understated confidence radiated out of Abdul and because of this assurance Richard intuited he was in a meeting with a hand-picked officer of the highest caliber.

He started to wonder for the umpteenth time what kind of a case they were going to be presented with today.

Abdul's impenetrable black eyes stared steadily back at Richard, eyes that were sharp and intelligent, and despite Abdul's quiet demeanour Richard had a feeling he didn't miss much.

He smiled at him and in return received a minuscule upturning at the corners of his colleague's mouth.

Interestingly, Abdul appeared to have a wall of self-control built around him and Richard thought he could guess at a reason for this. In the past the Metropolitan Police hadn't been known for its openness to ethnic diversity and given the pockets of narrow-mindedness that still existed in the police force, Richard guessed if Abdul had reached the position of Chief Inspector he must have outperformed every other CI at New Scotland Yard on his way up the ranks.

In the process of climbing up the promotional ladder he must have taken care not to tread on any sensitive toes and, as Richard knew to his own cost, this required a high degree of self-restraint in a job as stressful as theirs.

Seated demurely next to Abdul, Eilidh's expression by contrast was open and welcoming. Her handshake was firm and she greeted Richard with a smile that had more than a hint of cheekiness about it.

She was young, he noted with surprise, guessing she had to be in her mid-to-late twenties. Eilidh had short blond hair, a freckled face with a broad, slightly upturned nose and a provocative bow-shaped mouth. She looked delicate and slim in her uniform but it was her large eyes that attracted his notice most of all. Her irises were a rich chocolate colour and surrounded with long, black lashes, enormous ovals in an otherwise small-boned, elfin face.

She would be good at interviewing witnesses, thought Richard, summing her up. He tried to ignore the fact she was also very attractive.

Richard himself was tall and slim but he was ruefully aware he was no Adonis.

He reckoned most people would describe him as an archetypal geek. He was sure his more robust and streetwise colleagues saw him as some kind of professor rather than a police officer; in part because of his expertise in art but also in part due to his appearance. He wore tortoiseshell, round glasses, had a long, pale face and looked permanently disheveled, even when in uniform. His floppy hair, which was always cut longer than his fellow officers, straightaway pinpointed him as a privately educated nerd.

On the positive side, he knew that his encyclopedic knowledge of art history had made him an invaluable addition to the Art and Antiquities Unit since he joined the department eleven years ago.

Truth be told, there were some days when he wondered if it wouldn't be more rewarding to work for a company such as Sotheby's or Christie's instead of chasing after unique stolen antiquities or artifacts that might never resurface again. But those days were few and far between and for the most part he found a reasonable level of job satisfaction in restoring cultural treasures to their grateful owners.

Seeing the others in the room were all watching him with varying degrees of warmth in their faces Richard looked around, spotted a free chair around the conference table and quickly sat himself down on it.

Everyone then turned to face Superintendent Lionel Grieves, who was tapping a pen impatiently on the top of his open file.

With his damaged and misaligned face, Superintendent Lionel Grieves was something of a character within New Scotland Yard.

As a young man he would not have looked out of place associating with any gang loitering on a street corner or negotiating shifty deals within scraggy, neglected parkland. His balding head was shaven, his crooked nose bore testimony to his street-fighting days and his cauliflower ears had been pierced several times.

He was covered in crude tattoos that reached up to his skewed jawline and right across his hands: all the work of a not-very-talented tattoo artist.

Brought up on a Hammersmith council estate with a mother addicted to heroin, Lionel had managed to accumulate quite an impressive résumé of minor criminal misdemeanors before turning his life around and joining the police force. He was always the one at New Scotland Yard who pushed the boundaries of official protocol and political correctness to their full stretch but often he did so in support of his officers so he was a popular, albeit unorthodox, boss.

"OK. Good. Let's get started," said Lionel briskly, looking down at the notes on his file.

The others waited in silence as he flicked the pages in his file backwards and forwards, flashing the bright tattoos on his hands as he did so.

He closed his file with a snap and, without saying anything, picked up the pile of vanilla-coloured folders in front of him, carefully separating three of them which he then pushed across the table.

Richard picked up the folder nearest him and opened it, looking down with curiosity at the topmost photograph.

Unaccustomed to dealing with murders, the first shocking photo of the victim would remain embedded in his mind long after the meeting was over. Unlike his other colleagues, he wasn't used to seeing dead bodies, let alone murdered ones.

The photo was of a pale face, the hauntingly beautiful face of a young woman. Her head was twisted round at a grotesque angle to her body. Her bobbed, ebony hair was splayed messily across the side of her face but you could still see her delicately penciled eyebrows, the thick, black eyelashes and the ruby-red lipstick on her mouth.

There were several more photos showing her body facing downwards on the floor of what looked to be a bedroom, with her graceful white hands raised to either side as though the woman had been sleeping peacefully before she was killed. A thick pool of wine-red blood soaked the back of her white shirt and spooned her body as it lay contorted on the pale blue carpet.

"Right. This case is top priority as far as we're concerned and we're expecting the three of you to work together. I've taken this case off CI Malvin for reasons that'll soon be obvious," said CS Matthews, as he watched the others rifling through their folders. "We initially thought we were just dealing with a murder but now it's a lot more complicated than that. An item of great value has been stolen and the repercussions are potentially massive. We can't afford to screw this one up."

He clasped his hands together and then waited while the others continued to read through their dossiers, refusing to speak until he had their full attention.

He didn't have to wait for long.

Within a couple of minutes, they were all looking towards him, eager for more information on the case because there was precious little to be gleaned from the folder's contents, other than several crime scene photos and a couple of typed sheets with some basic facts listed on them.

All three of them had now taken pens out of their pockets and were ready to scribble down notes.

"The housekeeper notified the police of the murder at 9.35 on the 24th, which was shortly after she came into work," began CS Matthews. "She also reported in that call that a painting had been taken from the main bedroom. We'd no idea of the painting's value until we spoke to its owner but we've now been informed by him that it was priceless. So to be clear, what we now have is a murdered woman of Russian nationality, who was stabbed to death, and a missing masterpiece by an artist called El Greco. Apparently his pictures are worth a small fortune. Know of him, Richard?"

Transfixed by his surprise, Richard was staring open-mouthed at the Chief Superintendent and it took him a few seconds to answer the question.

His dossier had made no mention of the artist so it blew his mind to find out they were dealing with one of the most illustrious painters of the sixteenth century. El Greco was a painter who had influenced scores of artists from cubists to expressionists to abstract impressionists.

Richard lifted a hand to his forehead and brushed his fringe away from his eyes as he tried to pull himself together.

"Yes, of course I know the artist," he replied, not in a boastful way but as though stating a fact. "He's very famous. He's a genius painter from the latter half of the sixteenth century and he was the forerunner of nineteenth-century art. Paintings by Manet, Picasso, and Cezanne were all influenced by El Greco's work. I take it this stolen painting has never been part of a public collection then?"

"As far as we know it has always been privately owned," said CS Matthews. "Before it was stolen it was hanging up in a flat in De Vere Gardens, Kensington. It belongs to a Russian oligarch called Igor Babikov. At the moment it seems he spends most of his time in St

Petersburg with his business interests but he has this pad here in London. He also has two Picassos and a Manet currently on permanent loan to the National Gallery."

Ah, thought Richard, suddenly understanding why it was of the utmost importance to pursue this case. Three famous, prestigious paintings on permanent loan to the National Gallery would mean more to the British government than all of Igor's obscene wealth and possessions. Nobody would want Igor Babikov to remove those paintings from Britain.

"And the murdered woman, sir?" chipped in Abdul, obviously feeling they had discussed the least important aspect of the case for long enough.

"Yes, the woman... She's Igor's girlfriend, Irina Kapitsa. Russian national. There's no sign of the knife and no handbag or mobile phone either. Initial observations have concluded there wasn't a struggle with the victim, which begs the question as to whether the woman was sedated or given some other drug. Pathology report isn't out as yet. Igor Babikov arrived in London two nights ago and is at the flat as we speak."

CS Matthews stopped talking and glanced across at Lionel Grieves.

Never one to be rushed, Lionel studied his expensive Omega watch, assessing how long he should talk for. Lengthy meetings were anathema to him.

Lionel liked his toys and had a penchant for the latest innovative gadgets, which was why he was often nicknamed *"Flash"* behind his back by the people working for him. Richard knew Lionel was aware of his derogatory nickname but his superior had a skin as thick as a rhino's and seemed totally unfazed by it.

There had been many times during the last six years of working for Lionel when Richard had felt himself to be diametrically opposite to his Superintendent.

Often he felt like he was a ballet dancer performing with finesse alongside a hardened footballer with every trick in the game up his sleeve.

Due to the nature of his job, Richard's head was generally stuck in the past alongside the artworks and artifacts that required his attention whereas Lionel's tempestuous, volatile character was firmly rooted in the here and now.

Richard's posh, stable background couldn't have been more different to Lionel's either but surprisingly the two of them had a good working relationship, Lionel having a grudging respect for Richard's intellect whereas Richard, who was something of an eccentric, tended to appreciate Lionel's unconventional, irreverent attitude towards his work and bureaucrats in general.

"I suggest the three of you make your way there after this meeting and interview Igor while he's still fresh and new to the situation," Lionel remarked at last. "It's a strange case this one and not straightforward at all."

While CS Matthews nodded in silent agreement, Lionel took center stage in a well-rehearsed double act between the two of them.

"Igor's housekeeper is Filipino and her name's Rosamie Torres," stated Lionel, now on autopilot. "She was the one who found the body and is therefore a person of considerable interest to us. Works there for three hours every weekday morning. She says she wasn't there at the time of the attack and she has a solid alibi for that afternoon and evening. Seems genuinely shaken up by what's happened but we need to have a more in-depth interview with her as she has an inside track on what was happening at the flat prior to the murder."

Lionel coughed, a thick rasping cough that reminded everyone in the room that he was a heavy smoker.

From what he knew of Lionel, Richard suspected he spent a substantial part of his working day out of the office and on external duties for that reason alone. Richard wasn't one to underestimate the addictive nature of nicotine having witnessed as a young boy his grandfather smoking outside of the hospital where he was being treated for pneumonia.

He watched Lionel as he battled with his lungs, his face turning puce as he did so. At last the coughing fit stopped and Richard released a deep breath of relief.

"The attack occurred, according to the initial opinion of the pathologist, between four and six in the afternoon of the 23rd," persevered Lionel in a slightly choked voice. "A few of the houses around the corner at Canning Place have privately paid security but Igor didn't. Might be worth checking them out in case they saw anything unusual that day. There's a porter by the name David Shelton. The porter apparently heard absolutely nothing but some of the neighbors might have seen something."

Lionel opened his file and studied the paperwork in front of him.

"There are two doors at the entrance to the flat. The external one has a deadbolt lock and the internal one has a keypad. Pretty much invulnerable, I would say. The internal door could be hooked open but according to their housekeeper this only happened when there was a drinks party or a formal dinner at the flat," Lionel said, still reading from his notes. "At the back of the flat, in the main bedroom, there is a solid steel fire door but again this was bolted and locked in three places from the inside and there's no possible form of external entry. There are no signs the flat was broken into, which suggests Irina knew her assailant. Either that or they managed to get hold of the keys and the keypad code because there's no other way to get into the flat. The windows were all locked and bolted, too."

"How was the painting removed?" asked Richard, curious.

"Sliced clean out of the frame by all accounts," said Lionel blandly, ignoring Richard's pained grimace. Lionel was a philistine towards all artwork although he had a healthy respect for their value.

"And sorry, lastly, what's the name of the painting? We should begin taking steps to get it registered on Interpol's Stolen Works of Art database, as well as the Art Loss Register's database."

For the first time, Lionel looked a little unsure of himself.

"There's a slight problem. As far as I'm aware the painting doesn't have a name and it hasn't been officially recognized."

"What?" exclaimed Richard in a disbelieving, high-pitched voice that brought a smothered giggle from Eilidh's side of the table.

Unlike the others, Richard was flabbergasted. What was the point in treating the painting as a priceless masterpiece when it wasn't even recognized by the art world? Major artwork or not, it was next to worthless unless the owner had proof that several leading experts had independently verified it.

"Igor Babikov says he's only had the painting and its artist verified very recently by experts at the Prado Museum. For whatever reason, he didn't want their findings to be made public. His great-grandfather apparently bought it at a bargain price from..." Lionel looked down at his notes again. "The Grand Duchess Olga Constantinovna, just before the Russian revolution kicked off. She was married to George I of Greece and apparently the painting was in the Greek royal collection before they were deposed...". Lionel lifted his eyes from the page and glared defensively at Richard. "I didn't really get all the details."

Richard assimilated this interesting piece of information and then shook his head. Deliberately ignoring Lionel's hostile demeanour, which was signalling he was more than ready to move on to other things, he started to voice his misgivings.

"I can't understand why an El Greco painting would've been in the Greek royal family's collection... I mean the artist didn't become really famous until the nineteenth century. During his lifetime he fell out with the Spanish King and after that he moved to Toledo, mainly earning a living doing commissions for the nobility in Spain. His work was seen as a bit of a joke after he died."

Richard scratched his chin, lost in his private reflections.

Seizing the moment, CS Alan Matthews opened his mouth to speak but before he could say anything,

Richard decided to jump in and finish his intriguing train of thought. He hoped the others would understand how important it was to establish the provenance of the painting as it was essential for its authentication.

"You know, the interesting thing is that El Greco lived in Spain for most of his life and died there but he always remained a Greek at heart. He was friendly with the Spanish intelligentsia but most of his close friends were Greek; in fact two of them witnessed his will. The painter signed his paintings with Greek letters and he never actually learnt to speak Spanish properly, so he was Greek through and through."

Richard leaned forward eagerly and clasped his hands. Complete silence reigned as he studied the stony and implacable faces on the opposite side of the table from him.

"It's possible a painting of his was brought back to Greece during his lifetime, or shortly after his death, but only because of the artist's emotional attachment to his country of birth. As far as we know the artist himself never went back to Greece. In other words, it's not entirely implausible for a painting by El Greco to end up in the Greek royal family's collection, but it would be very unlikely I'd say," he reasoned, conscious as ever that he wasn't among art history enthusiasts and trying to wrap things up quickly.

They are more like *Line of Duty* enthusiasts, he thought bitterly to himself as he watched them. The others stared vacantly back at him, totally disinterested in discussing the artist or the premise for the painting.

Peeved, Richard shrugged and gave up.

Ignorant sods the lot of them, he thought, as he took

his glasses off and rubbed the lenses clean. It was obvious he wasn't about to get any art converts today.

CS Matthews cleared his throat.

"I'm sure Igor will supply you all with more detail about the painting *and* his girlfriend. I imagine he'll be around for quite a few days. He'll have to make the funeral arrangements for a start."

Abdul looked at his watch and then glanced across at Richard.

"Assuming Igor's willing to see us today shall we aim to head out there, say, in half an hour's time?"

Richard nodded. That would give him time to tidy up his desk and attend to the few items still needing to be logged in.

Everyone stood up and Richard peered longingly out of the wide window. The boats had disappeared, apart from one small tug. It was the 27th of September and already the leaves on the trees in front of their building were starting to change colour, thinning down as they started to shed their summer coat.

With a sigh, Richard picked up his file and prepared to descend once more into the nether world of the Curtis Green Building.

3

Richard

As Abdul, Eilidh and Richard exited the building and approached an unmarked car, there was a moment's awkwardness while they decided the pecking order. Needless to say Richard ended up in the back seat, the other two up front. The homicide squad always had more prestige than the art crime unit. Policemen who chased after valuable paintings or antiquities were generally considered expendable in the natural hierarchy of the police force. Art detectives were often seen as lily-livered policemen, who never put themselves at risk and hardly ever achieved any major results.

Richard had bucked the trend in recent years, achieving an enviable success rate, but if he was honest with himself he had to admit this had a lot to do with his friendship, and at times partnership, with a private investigator called Mike Telford. Mike, who was an art aficionado like Richard, could cross smoothly into the murky underworld of the criminal art scene and mix with criminals in a way that Richard, stuck in the confines of the official police force, could not.

Mike had a network of connections throughout London and these contacts went from the smallest pawnbroker who might deal in stolen coins and jewelry to a couple of shady art galleries in Knightsbridge and Chelsea which had contacts with the highest echelons of the mafia. It was a veritable network of Chinese whispers but often enough to secure a lead in a seemingly hopeless case of stolen artifacts or art.

Richard looked out at the rush hour traffic building up on the road ahead of them and started to think about the case. There were many things that confused him about this one.

High-level art thieves generally didn't like to leave a trail behind them and many would consider a murder just that. It instantly raised the case from "theft" to "murder" and meant more police resources would be dedicated to it. Right from the start of this case he'd felt out of his depth because he had never once come across a situation where people were prepared to murder in order to steal a priceless painting or artifact.

There were, of course, plenty of cases where small-time thieves murdered in their desperation to get their hands on some petty cash or jewelry but often these murders were unpremeditated and spontaneous. As far as Richard was aware, any organized, high-level museum or residential theft in the last ten years had been done without the complication of dead bodies.

Another aspect that troubled him was the thought of the El Greco painting hanging in a flat with minimal security. Surely a man who also owned two Picassos and a Manet would have had better security than that which seemed to be protecting his prized Greco painting. He would have to check it out but it seemed as though there'd been no sensors, no intricate alarm system that would have been set off if someone had tampered with the painting.

"Here we are. Number 40," said Eilidh, looking out of the car window and pointing up to a large building as they drove slowly down a street of what had once been humongous five-story Victorian houses but was now a street of prestigious flats in the center of London.

Richard had spent a little time browsing De Vere Gardens on his phone before they arrived there.

Apparently, De Vere Gardens had at one point been considered the fifth most expensive street in England. Directly opposite the entrance to De Vere Gardens the neat, colorful flower beds of Kensington Gardens could be found, and a short distance away the cheerful, red brick facade of Kensington Palace.

His mobile also informed him that this part of London was a constant reminder of Queen Victoria's legacy.

Kensington Palace, the birthplace and childhood home of Queen Victoria, was the relatively homely looking palace they had driven past barely a moment ago, and just ten minutes" walk away stood the Albert Memorial, with the golden statue of Prince Albert immortalized as an arts enthusiast by the well-known painters, poets, musicians, sculptors, and architects carved into the frieze at its base.

Across the road from the Albert Memorial also stood the rotund shape of the Royal Albert Hall, looking smug with its reputation as one of London's most iconic buildings.

They parked in an empty parking space, not far from the pillared entrance to number 40.

Abdul walked up the steps and pressed the doorbell for Flat 5, asking the officer securing the flat to give them access.

The door buzzed, Abdul clicked it open and all of them walked into a warm, carpeted hallway. Once he was inside the building Richard started to look around at the decor appreciatively. A red, thick pile carpet led the way up the curving flight of stairs and directly in front of them, much to his delight, was an antique Art Deco lift that seemed to have remained intact since its insertion in the 1930s.

By tacit consent all of them started to walk silently up the carpeted stairs to the second floor.

As he waited to be admitted into Igor's apartment, Richard glanced down absent-mindedly at the red carpet by the front door and noticed the little dots of silver powder that speckled the floor.

Fingerprint dust.

It was clear forensics had thoroughly combed the flat for fingerprints after using an alternate light source to examine the surfaces and applying cyanoacrylate. The police were working with unaccustomed speed in this case and Richard wondered at the influence Igor Babikov seemed to wield over his superiors.

They were clearly hoping for an early breakthrough.

Technology was advancing all the time in police work and it was sometimes hard to keep up with it all. Recent announcements at New Scotland Yard had declared that new trials were now running at Stratford train station using scanners to detect if people were carrying hidden weapons on them, all in a bid to reduce rampant knife crime.

The latest rumor in the office was that police forensics would soon be using colour-changing fluorescent films to capture latent or hidden prints. Given that at present only 10 per cent of fingerprints from crime scenes were good enough for court use, this had to be a positive development.

However, as Richard knew well, professional thieves would always use gloves, so chances were the police would only capture the opportunist or the amateur using the latest fingerprint technology, not the professional. As one retired art thief Richard had been familiar with would say *"make sure you've got your turtles on so you don't leave any dabs"*.

The heavy door of the flat opened and a young sergeant with a red, shiny face and black greasy hair motioned for them to enter. Once they were all in the spacious hallway, he pointed to a door at the end of the long corridor.

"Igor Babikov's in the sitting room," he whispered conspiratorially. "He's badly shaken up and can't seem to stop crying." He grimaced with typical Anglo-Saxon horror towards extreme emotion. "I think he blames himself for his girlfriend's death, thinking that if he hadn't had the painting in the flat in the first place she wouldn't have been murdered."

Abdul nodded his thanks for this superfluous forewarning and then marched sanguinely to the door at the end of the corridor, Richard and Eilidh following close behind him.

Abdul had seen all this before, too many times to count.

Ironically, Richard too had seen similar emotions when dealing with the victims of theft because when people had their prized possessions stolen, they often mourned them as they would the loss of a cherished relative. Some artworks or antique valuables were the only connection someone had to their ancestors or their past. These unique items were often as much a part of their identity as the special people in their life. Richard found they would cry with the same anguish and vehemence over the loss of an antique necklace or a china ornament as someone who had lost a beloved partner or family member.

They walked into Igor Babikov's spacious sitting room, with its impressive high ceiling and ornate plasterwork.

It was an opulent room and it was not to Richard's fastidious taste.

Too much gold and fabric, he thought to himself as he looked around. It was as though the owner wanted to make a statement about his wealth and make sure that every person entering the sitting room was aware of it.

Billowing gold-coloured silk curtains ballooned at the large floor-to-ceiling windows. Patterned, gold fabric wallpaper covered the walls and a huge gilt chandelier hung down from the ceiling, its multiple layers of rococo metalwork almost too big for the space enclosing it.

Several large oil paintings, again all in gilt frames, covered the walls. Most of them appeared to be floral still lifes in the style of the Dutch Golden Age and Richard found himself devoutly hoping that they weren't originals from the seventeenth century because it would be a huge risk to have them hanging up in a building with so little security.

Stately, gold-upholstered pieces of antique furniture were arranged neatly around a large marble coffee table. Glancing at the unusual rococo design of the eight-legged sofas, Richard wondered briefly if they were Chippendale antiques.

Richard then turned and scrutinized the coffee table with interest.

He recognized it straightaway as the Muso cocktail table, created as part of Laura Kirar's collection from the American brand Baker.

Reposing on the table, among other miscellaneous objects, was an exquisite Chinese red porcelain jar with the delicate design of a golden dragon encircling it under a cracked glaze finish.

Enthralled, he inched himself closer to examine it.

"It's from the Jiajing period in the Ming dynasty," said a deep-throated voice.

Richard nodded in silent agreement and looked up.

He found himself staring at a compact man of average height, smartly dressed with a stylishly cropped and gelled head of grey hair.

Igor Babikov.

His face was aquiline and aristocratic-looking. Reddened eyes with blue irises were surveying Richard with intelligent curiosity. The man certainly had a presence; it emanated from Igor without him saying a word or making a single gesture.

A crumpled handkerchief and a glass, heavily weighted with whisky, were reposing unashamedly in front of him as he sat on one of the sofas.

"Hello, I'm Chief Inspector Richard Langley of the Art and Antiquities Unit," said Richard hurriedly, keen to explain their presence. "And these are my colleagues, Chief Inspector Abdul Hazim and Inspector Eilidh

Simmons, from Homicide Command at New Scotland Yard."

He extended a hand to Igor and without bothering to stand up, Igor shook it.

He signaled to the sofas and chairs beside him.

"Take a seat, please," Igor said with quiet assurance, further fuelling Richard's impression that this was a man used to being in command of every situation and possibly now even the investigation into his girlfriend's death.

Eilidh settled herself on the sofa next to Abdul, who was nearest Igor, and then took a notepad and pen out of her bag.

Richard positioned himself comfortably on the sofa opposite them.

"Mr Babikov, firstly may I say how sorry we are for the loss of Irina Kapitsa," said Abdul quietly, his hands on his thighs as he leaned forward.

At the sound of his girlfriend's name a spasm crossed Igor's face but otherwise he remained impassive.

"We can assure you we'll do everything we can to track down the perpetrators but we'll need your help and cooperation to do so."

Igor bent his head in assent.

"Of course, I'm willing to give you any help I can to track down the *mudaks* who did this," he stated implacably.

"And we'll do our best to recover your stolen painting. Richard Langley is one of our most able detectives in this field," continued Abdul, much to Richard's surprise.

Igor didn't even glance at Richard but kept on listening to what Abdul had to say, unnervingly quiet.

Richard felt his lips twitch and had to bite his cheek to stop himself laughing out loud. He was pretty sure Abdul knew next to nothing about him and was just trying to butter Igor up. As he leaned back on the soft and plump sofa cushions, he hoped Abdul wasn't setting the bar too high as far as recovering the painting went. A virtually unknown masterpiece wasn't going to be easy to find.

"Igor, do you know if there was something on your girlfriend's mind before all this happened? Was she behaving differently at all? The fact that the murderers were let in, or had a key, suggests they could have known Irina."

Another grimace appeared on Igor's face at the sound of his girlfriend's name.

"No, there was nothing different. Everything was as it always was. She was due to join me in St Petersburg at the end of the week..." Igor said, his voice cracking with emotion.

He paused and drew a deep breath. The others waited in silence for him to continue.

"She was staying here for a little longer so she could go to a friend's hen party," Igor informed them, as though it was costing him a huge effort to speak.

"Would you mind telling us what her friend was called?"

"The one whose hen party it was? She's called Natasha Macklin. She lives at 74 Baker Street. They've known each other for about the last three years, I would say."

"Thank you. I appreciate this is difficult for you.

Any piece of additional information might help us uncover a motive or a perpetrator and the quicker we move the better are our chances of success," stated Abdul, his face earnest as he moved himself on the sofa so he was directly in Igor's line of sight. "Are there any other significant people that you know of, involved in her life here in London?"

"My God! Many, many people. I'd have to write out a long list. She was a social butterfly, my *kotyonok*. She was an extrovert. Whatever she did, it was always with friends. She was at her happiest out at parties, at lunch, dinner or shopping."

"Do you know if Irina had a laptop or some other such device with her?"

"No laptop. She usually had her iPad with her when she came to London with me."

"There doesn't seem to be an iPad in the flat," noted Abdul matter-of-factly.

Igor put his hands out with their palms facing upwards, his face perturbed.

"I've no idea where her iPad has gone. She usually left it on this coffee table or on her bedside table. Maybe they took that as well?"

Igor shrugged despondently and looked down at his glass as though tempted to take a drink from it.

In the ensuing silence the others looked at each other covertly, wondering who was going to speak next.

"Did she have family?" asked Abdul suddenly.

Igor face clouded over as he shook his head.

"She mentioned a sister to me but as far as I know she hadn't been in contact with her for years."

"And how did both of you meet, if you don't mind me asking?"

"Irina and I?" asked Igor rather pointlessly, smiling sadly to himself. "We met in Russia, four years ago, at a business conference in the ballroom of the Renaissance Monarch Centre in Moscow. She was accompanying a businessman who was showing no interest in her at all and was busy trying to talk with another colleague. I was drawn to her from the moment I saw her. She was so unusual looking, pale white skin with dark blue eyes and black hair. She was tall and graceful but also strangely defiant. Queenly almost..."

Igor picked up his handkerchief and held it tightly as though willing himself not to cry.

"Eventually she ended up at the bar on her own, sipping a gin and tonic, and I approached her before the other men who'd been eyeing her up had a chance to speak to her. She was working in Moscow as a translator. Her English... it was impeccable."

Igor closed his eyes for a moment and took a deep breath. A tear formed and dribbled down his cheek. Before long another had appeared. As Igor opened his eyes again he started to wipe away the tears using his crumpled handkerchief, his movements unselfconscious and brusque.

Richard started to feel a great deal admiration for this man, who somehow retained his dignity even when crying openly in front of them.

"She grew up in Vladivostok, by the Sea of Japan. She didn't talk much about her background or childhood," he continued. "That didn't bother me. She got on well with my family, my mother and father, and my sisters. My friends all liked her too. She fitted into my life like she'd always belonged there. We were happy." Igor shrugged his shoulders. "She wanted us to buy a house in Paris and start a family. Those were the kind of things we discussed. The future..."

"Did Irina have a job?"

Igor shook his head.

"No, if she'd worked we would've never seen each other. I have to travel a lot in Russia with my business so it worked out best for both of us to not have her working."

"And forgive me for asking this, but if something had happened to you would she have been looked after financially?" Abdul asked slipping the question in as though he'd been asking a neighbor what shade of paint had been used to paint the front door.

Igor didn't say anything for a long moment which instantly led to the others tensing up as they realized this was the first question in the interview that Igor was having problems with.

"Sorry Igor, would you mind answering the question? It could be important," reiterated Abdul, smoothing down his black hair in a gesture that spoke of his nervousness.

"I think that's a question you should put to my lawyers and accountants in St Petersburg, to be honest with you," replied Igor apologetically, looking Abdul in the eye. "It's their job to protect my wealth and me. They did get her to sign a legal document so she wouldn't be able to make a claim on my assets in the event we split up."

Igor rubbed his forehead as he pondered this.

"I really don't know exactly how things stood financially," admitted Igor. "But she was fine as far as money went. I mean this flat, for example, is in both our names. I've given her so many expensive gifts and she had a number of credit cards that she could use freely so she wasn't under any financial restraint at all."

Gold digger, thought Richard callously to himself.

"If we'd split up I would've been very generous to her but I loved her, you see. That thought never crossed our minds," added Igor, the tears starting to trickle down his cheeks again. He wiped his nose and sat staring down at the coffee table as though already thoroughly exhausted by the interview.

4

Richard

"Igor, I wonder if you could give me some details about this painting by El Greco," said Richard quickly, before Abdul came up with any more questions and Igor decided he had had enough questioning for the day. "My superiors say it was verified by experts at El Prado recently but apparently it wasn't registered or generally recognized? Is that right?"

Igor nodded, his eyes looking sad still but he also seemed relieved at the change of subject.

"Yes, that's right. Do you know the painting by El Greco that's in Pollok House, Glasgow? The one called *Lady in a Fur Wrap*? It's very famous."

Richard nodded, wondering what kind of a connection Igor was trying to make with one of Scotland's most famous paintings.

"There's always been speculation about that painting. Who's the lady in the picture and who was the artist? Recently experts have questioned whether the artist was El Greco and they've had formidable debates as to who the subject of the painting is. Many people say the woman in the picture looks like Catalina Micaela, the daughter of King Philip II of Spain but again other experts argue that El Greco fell out with the King of Spain so the artist wouldn't have painted his daughter."

Igor stopped talking for a moment and pulled gently at the cuffs of his shirt, choosing his words with care.

"Art historians who don't believe *Lady in a Fur Wrap* is of the Spanish princess say that a royal princess in those days wouldn't have been portrayed so informally. For example, she wouldn't have been dressed in such a way and with her hand clutching at her fur wrap..."

Igor looked around at them all as though trying to create a dramatic moment.

"My painting proved to the experts gathered in the Prado that beyond a shadow of a doubt, El Greco had painted portraits of Princess Catalina Micaela. My painting was yet another portrait of her. Stylistically, *Lady in a Fur Wrap* and my painting are very similar."

Igor stood up and went across to a beautifully inlaid desk at the corner of the room. A Sheraton Revival desk from the early twentieth century, thought Richard musingly. And with eight legs again... Igor clearly had a thing for eight-legged furniture.

Igor opened a drawer and pulled out a large file. He brought the file to the coffee table and pushed away a few coffee table books to make space for it. He then pulled out a number of photographs and laid two of them down on the marble surface in front of Richard.

Richard peered eagerly down at them.

The photographs were of a portrait. It was an

accomplished painting, showing the upper half of a striking young lady, who had black hair and intense ebony eyes, and was sitting on a velvet turquoise chair. She was dressed in what looked to be a sixteenth-century burnt-orange silk dress with lace right up to her neckline and ornate jeweler sewn on to the edging of the bodice and sleeves. Pearls were hanging abundantly from her ears and neck. Her delicate hands were clasped demurely at her waist and she had many jeweled rings on her long white fingers. On her black hair a lace cap could be seen under an elaborate headgear.

"Excuse me, do you mind if I have a closer look at the photographs?" asked Richard.

"Isn't she beautiful? Yes, yes, of course. Have a good look at them," Igor said, waving his hands towards the photos.

Richard picked up an 8 by 10 photo and studied it avidly while the others kept a respectful silence.

The painting was captivating and showed considerable artistry, thought Richard, examining it carefully. The way the artist had portrayed the shine of the silk dress, the delicate lace at the breast in contrast to the white, pink-tinged skin and the texture of the fur edging on the sleeves demonstrated whoever had painted the picture had considerable skill as an artist.

The expression on the young lady's face was startlingly unconventional. She gazed at the viewer with naked allure, her lips slightly parted and her eyes watching the viewer with a bold and inviting expression in them. It was clearly a provocative portrayal of an aristocratic lady, tempting the viewer to stare longingly at

the painting just as the Mona Lisa tried to do, unsuc-
cessfully, to millions of tourists every year.

It was disappointing, but Richard knew from
research that most viewers looking at the Mona Lisa
only spent an average of fifteen seconds looking at her.
People's perception of beauty has changed with time.
One only had to look at Ruben's work to see that.
"Grotesque, fat women" was how Richard's sister had
described Ruben's portrayal of *The Three Graces* when
she saw the painting hanging up in the Prado.

Richard put the photo down and picked up the
others. One by one, he inspected the photos, looking at
the enlargement of the signature, the detail of the
hands, the face and the clothing.

Finally, with a sigh, he put the photos down.

"So this is the painting El Prado Museum verified
was by El Greco. It's astonishing."

"Yes, indeed. They were very excited by it. You see
it proved beyond doubt that El Greco *had* painted
Princess Catalina Micaela. There's a Greek inscription
on the back of the painting that says: *"For Catalina
Micaela, my soulmate, Doménikos Theotokópoulos"*.
And there's a cameo pendant of Philip II which is still
in the royal collection today, hanging on her bodice."

Igor rummaged through the photos and plucked
one out of the pile, which he then passed over to
Richard to look at again. It was a close up of the bodice
in the portrait and sure enough, in the painting a
distinctive cameo was hanging on a small chain,
partially hidden by the pearls hanging from the lady's
neck.

But even so, Richard wasn't going to take Igor's
word for the painting's authenticity. It looked like he'd

have to make a short trip to Madrid to verify this intriguing tale. Right now, though, he had other questions he wanted Igor to answer.

Igor took a swig from his tumbler and then, as if realizing he hadn't been hospitable, asked if the others would like a drink.

The others declined politely.

"I've been told that you have two Picassos and a Manet on permanent loan at the National Gallery. Is that correct?" asked Richard.

"Yes," said Igor calmly.

"And yet your business interests are all in Russia and you seem to spend the majority of your time in Russia. Would it not make sense to have the paintings there?"

Igor sighed. He leant back on the sofa and looked at Richard with some amusement.

"You do not fully understand the situation in Russia," he stated bluntly, stretching out his legs and tucking his hands into his pockets.

"Don't get me wrong, I'm a patriot and I love my country," he added after a moment, placing a hand over his heart. "But all of you here in the UK have had democracy for over a hundred years now. That is not the case in my country. Even today there is censorship and the government has a tight control on our society..."

Igor coughed, raising a hand to his mouth.

"I'm not making a judgement on which is best," he said. "Democracy has its shortcomings too, you only have to see what a mess your democracy has made of Brexit." Igor shrugged, nonchalant and blasé about the problems facing the UK. "Countries like mine have had an autocracy for a major part of their history; it's the way it has always been. But with private enterprise and wealth after communist rule, corruption and the mafia have flourished and the wolves are always circling, picking off the weakest."

Igor gazed out of the sitting-room window as though visualizing his home in Russia.

Abdul and Eilidh were listening to Igor with a great deal of interest, so much so that Eilidh had stopped taking notes.

"Any art collector will tell you that collecting art is addictive. I have a large collection of artworks in Russia, mostly by contemporary artists. But having the Picassos and the Manet in the National Gallery, here in the UK, is probably the best security I could have for them. Certainly it's paid for by the tax payer but then their beauty is shared with everyone."

"And the El Greco painting? You didn't think of also securing it in a gallery?"

"No," confessed Igor, sadly. "I didn't. I thought because it wasn't internationally recognized or known, it would be safe. Nobody knew of it. I specifically asked the experts, the ones who met at the Prado Museum to study my painting, not to make it known to the public. They kept their records confidential. They were reluctant to do so but they did. I loved that painting and I wanted it in my home."

"But not in Russia," interposed Richard.

"No, not in Russia," agreed Igor. "Why would I risk it? Here I'm not in the spotlight, over there I am."

"What's the provenance of the painting?"

"My grandfather, Alexander Babikov, bought it from the Grand Duchess Olga Constantinovna. She was Russian. She became Queen of Greece through marriage but after her husband died she came back to Russia for long periods of time. She only just managed to escape falling victim to the Bolshevik firing squad. She survived thanks to the help she was given by the Danish government, they intervened on her behalf and secured her release. She sold the painting to my great-grandfather before she left Russia for good. He was her doctor at the time..."

Igor grasped his tumbler of whisky and took another large mouthful, savouring it before swallowing.

"Olga Constantinovna was a special woman, the only member of the exiled Greek royal family to receive a pension from Greece, and she was Russian!" he said proudly. "She was loved by the Greeks because of all the charitable work she did and the hospitals she founded."

"El Greco wasn't internationally recognized until the nineteenth century," commented Richard, trying to focus on the painting again. "Do you have any idea why Olga Constantinovna would own a painting by El Greco?"

"No, I've no idea. The portrait is of a member of the Spanish royal family, isn't it? That had to mean something to them. Or maybe Olga just fell in love with it, as I did... I don't know if El Greco's family or friends brought the portrait to Greece at some point and then sold it to the Greek Royal family or if the painting came directly to the Greek Royal family. I really don't know, I'm afraid. It's quite a mystery."

"Do you have any documents showing that Olga Constantinovna sold the painting to your great-grandfather?"

"I don't have a receipt, if that's what you mean,"

said Igor, with his mouth twisted in an ironic smile. "But I do have all the correspondence between the two of them and in one letter Olga asks about the painting and my great-grandfather replies to her, telling her that the painting is hanging up in their dining room."

"Could I possibly borrow these photographs and get copies made?" asked Richard.

"Of course, help yourself. They're of no use to me now," replied Igor bitterly, pushing them across the table towards Richard.

"Did Irina know the painting's potential worth?" interposed Abdul, seizing his chance to ask a question during a momentary lull in conversation.

"Possibly, but I doubt it. She wasn't really interested in art and I certainly didn't tell her anything about it. It was personal to me only."

"OK. This has been very helpful, thank you," said Richard. "Can I ask lastly, has anyone recently shown an interest in the painting at all? Is there anything at all that might have made you concerned for its safety?"

Igor shook his head.

"I've only had one offer for that painting and that was about a year ago. It was from a friend of Irina's. The lady saw it when she came to a drinks party here. Irina must have shown her it because it was hidden away in the main bedroom. This lady obviously had no idea who the artist was and offered a ridiculously small amount of money for it. A pittance. I refused to sell it and that was that."

Igor leaned forward and stared compellingly at Richard.

"I'd do anything to get that painting back. It has a special place in my heart. Please, let it be known I'll offer a reward of a million pounds for its safe return. Please do whatever you can to bring it back to me."

"Ahem, well, I'm afraid the police force can't offer huge rewards like that for stolen goods," replied Richard, unaccountably embarrassed. "It would be seen as rewarding criminals and encouraging crime. But I've a good friend who's a successful private investigator, with many contacts in the art world. He could get the word around on your behalf."

"Yes, please do give me his contact details. That would be very helpful."

"That'll not be a problem I'm sure, but let me run the case by him first. He's a very busy man these days, often as not chasing down missing paintings abroad. Don't worry; I'll try to get in touch with him and let you know as soon as I can. I just wonder, before we go, could you show us where the painting was hanging?"

"Certainly," said Igor, standing up straightaway and making his way to the door.

Eilidh scrambled to put her notebook away and then stood up, waiting for Abdul to precede her. Abdul stopped Richard in his tracks by holding up a hand and then bent his head towards him.

"Richard, I'm going to speak to the sergeant at the door and have a look around with Eilidh," he said quietly. "We'll meet you at the front door."

Richard nodded. It was always easier for detectives to have a look around without the owner of the property there, supervising their every move.

He walked behind Igor down a long corridor and into the main bedroom right at the end of it.

The first thing he saw was a dark wooden frame,

hanging above the king-size sleigh bed with the painting missing from the center of it.

He took his shoes off, climbed up onto the bed and inspected it closely. A few delicate canvas threads hung down from the inside edges of the frame but otherwise it was just an empty hollow with the blue patterned wallpaper showing through it.

It looked incongruous and odd but what was left after the canvas had been cut out could almost pass muster as a work of art by Magritte or some other surrealist artist, he thought to himself.

He jumped back down to the floor.

"So the frame was left on the wall?"

"Yes, exactly like that. They think someone must have stood up on the bed to extract the painting. Irina, poor darling, was found by the window, over there," said Igor, pointing to the floor by the window, his eyes welling up again with tears.

Richard nodded sympathetically.

He was busy looking around, trying to get an impression from the room of its owners.

The team would be trawling over the crime scene photographs later on but for now he wanted to absorb the atmosphere of this house and get a feel for the personality of its owners, a little like in the program *Through the Keyhole* but without the comedic factor. His initial thoughts were that unless forensics uncovered something, it looked to be a very cleverly orchestrated job, certainly not one that would be easy to solve.

He continued to walk slowly around the room, trying to see if there was anything unusual or out of place.

He liked the decoration in this room better than the

sitting room. Apart from wooden mahogany, everything in the bedroom was a shade of sky blue except for a red Venetian glass chandelier that hung from the center of the ceiling and a vase filled with sweet-smelling red roses, their large, bulbous heads drooping a little. In another day or two they'd need to be replaced.

"Your housekeeper, Rosamie Torres, have you known her for a long time?"

Igor turned to Richard in surprise.

"Rosamie? I've known her ever since I bought this place eight years ago. She's an angel. She couldn't hurt a fly."

Richard nodded as he continued to scan the room.

He walked across to the bedroom window, noting it was double-glazed and had metal-locking fixtures screwed into its wooden edges.

Then he looked down at the floor and observed someone had done an inexpert job at removing the bloodstains from the thick pile carpet. No doubt this carpet was made of the finest natural fibers, making it all the harder to clean.

Richard had plastic, bleach-proof carpets in his little flat and had discovered that with tough PVC flooring you could even remove Irn-Bru stains from it. But here on the luxurious pile, rust-coloured stains were smeared across a large area with their uneven edges stretching from under the bed all the way to the sash window. Given the amount of red staining it would be starkly obvious to anyone looking at the floor that Irina had bled to her death. Igor was going to have to replace his expensive bedroom carpet to bring things back to a semblance of normality.

Richard turned to Igor.

"Have you identified her at the morgue?"

"Yes." Igor shuddered. "She was always pale but I've never seen a human being as pale as she was in the morgue. She didn't even look human... My poor little *lapochka*."

Igor wiped his eyes and then reached out and grasped Richard's arm.

"Tell me, do you think they're going to find who did this?"

Innately truthful, Richard tried to not show his doubts on his face and was relieved to be interrupted by Abdul and Eilidh entering the room a few seconds later.

5

Eilidh

It was mid-morning, so Eilidh found it easy enough to find a parking space at De Vere Gardens. She reversed slowly and carefully into an empty parking space on the left-hand side of the road (no wonder she'd failed her Emergency High Speed Driver Training).

She switched off the engine and took a sip of her Americano, bought on the way there at Kensington High Street. Parking on the double yellows outside Costa that morning hadn't given her even a twinge of guilt. No doubt shoppers and commuters would have assumed it was another case of shoplifting.

As she swallowed her hourly caffeine fix, she glanced across at her tan leather satchel and the case file sticking out of the top of it.

She did not feel remotely optimistic about this case. Irina's handbag had vanished with the painting. No handbag meant there were no phone records or bankcards to look into and forensics had come up with up with absolutely nothing suspicious or incriminating.

Meanwhile, the pathology report said they

suspected use of GBL tranquilizers or other sedatives but unfortunately the body was found too late to verify this with a blood sample. The position of the body and the fact there were no signs of a struggle suggested to the pathologist that the victim had been attacked while incapacitated.

The other notable fact in the pathology report was that the victim had an interesting tattoo between her breasts, an image of a circle with a triangle in the middle, suggesting possible addiction recovery.

The pathologist estimated the knife used in the attack to be a five-inch knife, repeatedly plunged into the back and neck of the victim to puncture the chest cavity and the neck. There were eleven puncture wounds in total and the force used suggested it could have been either a female or male wielding the knife. The pathologist went on to state that she personally would be inclined to suspect a female assailant as the knife on a few occasions had barely managed to cut through the surface layer of muscle, which suggested in turn a certain weakness in the assailant's blows.

Eilidh sighed despondently.

Knife crime was a regular feature of police work nowadays yet there were so few convictions made. Whoever had concocted the motto prevention is better than a cure knew what they were talking about. Yet with so many cuts to the police force there wasn't a hope in hell of getting to grips with the current knife crime epidemic. It was impossible to have zero toler-ance when there were zero officers out on the beat, making connections with the local community as in days gone by.

Eilidh's feelings were ambiguous. She recognized

that the UK had a huge deficit to overcome. Cuts had to be made but where were the public's priorities? How could anything be more important than a life?

It was impossible to be in the police force for a few years without becoming slightly jaded. Some days surpassed expectations; others lowered them. She'd been with New Scotland Yard for six years now and, weekly, she was looking at job adverts online. The fire service appealed although she was pretty sure she would fail the fitness test; it had been a very long time since she last set foot in a gym.

Eilidh finished the last dollop of her coffee in one big mouthful and put the empty plastic cup back into the cup holder, ready to be washed when she was back at the office. As far as the environment was concerned, she had a healthy social conscience.

She plucked her satchel from the car seat, turning the folder around so it fitted neatly into it, and got out of the car with caffeine-induced zest, hoping that the buzz would keep her going during the interviews. Richard would be discreetly following up leads with the painting too, of course, but her priority was figuring out how Irina had ended up bleeding to death on the carpet of the main bedroom.

So far she had not been able to fathom CI Richard Langley out. Like a young professor out of a highbrow university, he seemed to be completely detached from his fellow humans and only beautiful objects seemed to bring a spark of interest into his eyes. She had not missed the way he had stared at the furniture and objects in Igor's flat. The man was the most visually driven person she had ever met.

As she started to climb up the stairs to the main

door she briefly tried to imagine what Richard's home looked like...

Eilidh looked at the numbers in front of her and pressed the first door buzzer, planning to work her way up the stairs.

There was the irritating hum of the intercom and then a shrill voice said, "Hello?"

"Hello, I'm Detective Inspector Simmons. I was wondering if I could have a word with you."

There was a pause.

"Yes, of course. Come in."

The door buzzed and Eilidh pushed it open. As she walked into the warm hallway she saw the front door to the left of her was open and a small woman wearing a white hijab was peering out at her.

Eilidh lifted up her badge and the woman, who looked to be in her late fifties, inspected it carefully before making way for her, allowing her to walk into the spacious, cream-coloured hallway of her flat.

The mouth-watering exotic smell of spices assailed Eilidh as soon as she was in the flat, making her wonder where this lady's cooking came from. Her stomach grumbled with hunger.

The lady led her into a sitting room that was crammed full of white leather sofas, all facing towards the big screen television on the opposite wall.

"Can I get you a drink?" asked the diminutive lady hospitably, as Eilidh sat herself down alongside her.

"No, thank you. I'm sorry to disturb you but no doubt you're aware that a murder happened at number 5"

The lady drew a deep breath, her soft brown eyes glistening with emotion.

"Yes, it's horrible. We're all so shocked. It seems there's nowhere safe anymore," she said, shaking her head disapprovingly.

Eilidh couldn't have agreed more, even though she couldn't say so.

"I've a few questions to ask you, if you don't mind," she said instead. Seeing her hostess nodding her head vigorously, Eilidh clicked her ballpoint pen so it was ready to take notes. "Could I take your name please?"

"Zara Farooqi. Zara Hania Farooqi."

Eilidh quickly wrote this down.

"And how long have you lived here?"

"About eight years. We moved here from Pakistan."

"I see. And could you tell me if you were here on Monday?"

"Yes, I was. The 23rd of September," added Zara helpfully, holding her nicely manicured hands together in a tight clasp.

"And did you see or notice anything that was out of place that day?"

"No, nothing. I'm sorry but I didn't hear or see anything."

"Nothing at all? I mean anything that might've appeared strange or out of place that day."

Zara shook her head as she thought this over.

"Did you see Irina that day?"

"Yes, yes I did. Several times. Come, let me show you."

Zara got up and went to the front window, pulling aside the greying net curtains. She pointed to the steps leading to the building's main door.

"See, I can see everyone from here. Sometimes, when I'm bored I sit on this window seat and do my crochet. I watch the world go by as you British would say. I saw Irina at least three times that day. She was with her sister."

"I'm sorry, did you say her sister?"

"Yes, it was definitely her sister."

"Had you met her sister before?"

Zara shook her head impatiently.

"No, the people who live here, we don't have much to do with each other," she said sadly. "It's very hard because in Pakistan we have tight communities. Everyone there knows one another and yet here nobody wants to talk to each other. I wouldn't be surprised if old people here died and people didn't find out about it until weeks later. Nobody seems to care about their neighbors in this city."

Having seen ample evidence of this lack of neighborly feeling, Eilidh again felt she couldn't have been in more agreement with Zara. Only two weeks ago she had heard from canteen gossip that police officers had been called out to a flat near Regent's Park because the neighbors were complaining about a foul smell emanating from the apartment next to theirs. Nobody had answered the doorbell but when they managed to break down the front door they found out what was causing the terrible stench. It turned out the smell was caused by the decomposing body of an old man who had been lying in his bed, dead as a dodo, for at least a couple of weeks. Sadly, nobody had noticed his absence.

Somehow Eilidh doubted the same thing would happen at 40 De Vere Gardens because Zara, along with her crocheting, seemed to be the embodiment of neighborhood watch.

Eilidh looked at Zara curiously.

"So tell me, how did you meet Irina's sister?"

"I didn't meet her, *I saw her*. She had thick hair to her waist, like mine. She was walking with Irina in the direction of Hyde Park."

"Did Irina tell you she was with her sister?"

"No, no. She never said more than a polite hello to me. She never had the time to stop; she was always rushing in and out of the building... Always with other people too."

Eilidh felt confused.

"So how do you know she had her sister with her?"

"Because they both looked the same as each other... Identical."

"Identical twins?"

Zara nodded.

"Yes, they were twins. But their hair was different. And the sister had different clothes on. You know black jeans, a worn leather jacket. Irina didn't wear that kind of stuff. She was always dressed in expensive designer clothing."

"Did they seem to be getting on?"

"Oh, yes. They were laughing when I saw them. They seemed very happy."

"Can you remember, approximately, what time you saw them?"

"It was in the afternoon. Irina usually never went out until lunchtime. I think the first time I saw them it was just after two o'clock. They were coming into the building. The second time, I'm not sure. Could been three or four o'clock they left. They came back shortly afterwards, carrying a bag of groceries from the Gloucester Road Deli."

There was a silence in which Eilidh's stomach made a loud complaint.

Zara looked at Eilidh with motherly concern and placed a plump hand on her arm.

"Would you like some samosa? Please, let me bring you some food."

Eilidh gazed into Zara's lonely face and nodded.

"That would be delightful, thank you. I missed breakfast today."

Later on, revved up by several samosas and a strong espresso, Eilidh covered the ground, first and second floors in record time. Two of the flats so far were regrettably empty, which meant she'd have to come back another time.

Ms. Mariana Hill, the glamorous lady living in Flat 3, directly beneath Igor and Irina's flat, was the only one of the residents at number 40 who knew Irina on a personal level. They had apparently attended yoga together on Wednesday nights when Irina happened to be in London. This Tuesday she'd wondered why Irina hadn't answered her phone, or turned up on her doorstep, as was her usual custom before they went to yoga. In the end Mariana had gone to yoga by herself.

She had been utterly horrified to find out that poor Irina had been murdered and wasn't even sure she wanted to stay in De Vere Gardens any more.

She hadn't seen anything suspicious and she hadn't seen Irina herself on the Monday. When asked about Irina's sister, she said she knew Irina had a sister but had never met her. And as far as she was aware there was nothing worrying Irina, or anyone bothering her.

The two retired solicitors in Flat 4, also on the first

floor, were very keen to share gossip about Irina's scandalously noisy parties but had little else to offer.

Flat 6, opposite Igor's flat on the second floor, did not respond to the doorbell so Eilidh made a note to come out one evening and try and catch the residents at home.

Igor had said he would be staying at the Baglioni Hotel further up the road because, reasonably enough, he was unwilling at the moment to reside in his own flat.

On the third floor she had greater success.

The two flats on this floor were smaller than the others, with lower ceilings, and were obviously meant as the servants" quarters in days gone by.

She rang the doorbell at number 7 and waited.

A teenage boy with a handsome, although spotty, face opened the door. Eilidh estimated him to be about sixteen years old but later found out he was studying at Imperial College and was actually a nineteen-year-old.

"Hi," she said, sticking out one hand abruptly while holding up her badge with the other. The boy took her hand and shook it limply.

"I'm Inspector Simmons. Would you mind if I asked some questions regarding Irina Kapitsa? The lady at number 5"

The boy nodded and silently stood aside to let Eilidh in. The way his face had clouded over at the mention of Irina's name and the melancholic look in his eyes automatically hinted to Eilidh that this boy had had something of a crush on Irina.

She didn't for a moment think Irina would've reciprocated his feelings. Irina seemed to be someone who was attracted to powerful, older men, not teenage boys in the throes of calf love, even if they did have all the allure of Italianate looks like this one had.

"Do you live here alone?" asked Eilidh, as she studied the tastefully decorated, well-appointed flat. Having sat themselves down in the sitting room, facing each other across a small glass coffee table, Eilidh felt it was important to break the awkward silence.

"No, I live here with my parents. They're out at work at the moment."

"And may I have your name?"

"Rollo Masuri."

"And your age?"

"I'm nineteen years old."

"OK. Fantastic. Thank you. Did you know Irina at all?"

"Not really. We used to chat a bit sometimes if we bumped into each other on the way in or out of the building."

Eilidh nodded, wondering if those chats would've been the highlight of his week.

"Did you see anything suspicious at all on the day she was murdered?"

Rollo held his breath for a moment, looking sideways at her like a startled deer and pressing his hands down on his jean-covered thighs. Observing the tension in him, Eilidh prudently waited for him to speak.

"No, nothing at all."

"And you didn't see her either?"

"No. I *did* see her but I didn't see anything strange... She was the same as always."

Rollo shifted uncomfortably on his chair.

"Sometimes when my parents are out, I like to go into the stairwell and open the window so I can have a smoke," he confessed. "My parents don't like me doing it in the flat, you see. On Monday at around midday, I saw their maid leaving the flat. She's the lady who usually comes in the mornings to do the housework for Irina. She came out of the flat on Monday, with a few envelopes and a long parcel. And a short time later, at around two o'clock I think it was, I saw Irina going into the flat with someone who must've been her sister."

"Yes, the neighbor downstairs says that they looked identical. Would you agree?"

"Yes, it was kind of weird. I've never seen identical twins in real life before but they were the same. I mean her sister had longer hair and looked scruffier but they were so alike. It was incredible."

"Have you seen her sister here before?"

"No, I haven't. But they seemed to be pretty familiar with each other. That's to say, they were laughing together. And talking in Russian, I think."

"Thank you, you've been very helpful. I might be back at some point to try and see if your parents have anything to add to this."

Rollo looked panicked and started to rub his hands nervously together.

"Please don't tell them about me smoking in the stairwell."

"I won't," replied Eilidh reassuringly, not wanting to add that if it came to it all of this would have to be admissible in court. Still, she wished she could inform Rollo's parents of the other hair-raising exploits teenagers Rollo's age got up to. Little though they might realize it, they'd been let off easy with Rollo smoking fags in the stairwell.

Flat 8 had a retired doctor from Harley Street, who

knew nothing whatsoever about the other neighbors in the building, and in fact seemed to positively resent the inconvenience of Irina's demise and Eilidh's intrusion into his hermitic life. There would clearly be no tears shed by this cantankerous doctor who seemed to have eschewed human society generally, if the state of his flat was anything to go by.

Eilidh left his stuffy and disordered flat with relief and made her way downstairs to the porter's flat in the basement of the building, looking at her watch and noting it was nearly lunchtime.

This was the nature of the job. Loads of grunt work, looking for the proverbial needle in a haystack so the police force could then have its eureka moment.

She waited patiently outside the porter's flat, wondering for a moment if he, too, was out for the day, when she suddenly heard the latch move and the door opened.

"Mr. Shelton?"

"Yes, yes. Do come in. It's a terrible business this murder. Never ever did I think I'd be dealing with something like this! Though of course, with the Russians you never know what you're going to get, do you? Half of them are involved in the mafia, aren't they?"

Eilidh stared at the rotund porter with overt fascination. It was always intriguing for her to see how in such a multicultural, multiracial place as London you could still find isolated pockets of prejudice and ignorance.

"They've told me she was poisoned," continued Mr Shelton, nodding. "Sounds just like that Skripal case, doesn't it?"

Eilidh's heart sank as she listened to him. He looked to be the kind of man who'd come up with any number of ludicrous theories with the benign intent of helping her out with the case. She could see straightaway that he was going to get lost in his sleuthing fantasies and find it hard to separate fact from fiction. She had come across quite a few of these fantasists in her line of work.

If the young sergeant was responsible for this poisoning rumor, he was going to be in deep trouble.

"I'm sorry, Mr Shelton, who told you she was poisoned?"

"The neighbors opposite their flat told me. Personally, I think a secret lover of hers must have committed the murder because I know Igor was away at the time. Whoever it was, Irina must've let them in as there were no signs of a forced entry."

Eilidh noted Mr Shelton was slyly covering his lack of supervision by commenting on the fact that there was no forced entry but she probably would have done the same in his position. After all, what was the point of having a porter if they didn't catch sight of these things? Under his watch a woman had been murdered and a valuable masterpiece had been stolen.

"That's an interesting theory," replied Eilidh reassuringly. "As far as the poisoning goes, I wonder where they got that from, because as far as we know she wasn't poisoned."

"Really? That's a surprise. They seemed so sure too," said Mr Shelton, looking disappointed. "Anyway, do come in and have a chat. It's best not to talk about these things out here."

He looked around as though expecting a masked murderer to jump out at them, then turned and led the way down a narrow hallway to a room at the end. Eilidh shut the front door behind her and followed him.

They walked into a neat little television room at the back of the flat, the windows giving out to a dull grey courtyard at the rear of the building, full of concrete and brick, with not a stem of grass in sight. No vegetation could survive this far down; the towering walls of the surrounding flats seemed to cast only darkness and shadow into the back of this London enclave.

Eilidh took a seat on the cane sofa and declined the offer of a drink. The heavenly smell of bacon emanated from the corridor but Eilidh, replete with samosas from the hospitable neighbor at number 1, was able to ignore it.

"Mr Shelton, how long have you been living here for?"

"Well, let me see. It'll be six years this January. I was very lucky to get this job as a porter, and the flat with it, when I retired from the council. It's such a fantastic location."

"Yes, it is. Lovely and central. Do you live here alone?"

"No, I live here with my wife. Let me give her a call."

He stood up and walked to the doorway.

"Katie! Katie! Police are here to speak to you."

Eilidh waited while Katie shuffled down the corridor, her slippers scratching unpleasantly on the rough, tufted runner outside the room.

A woman in her fifties entered the room, with wisps of grey hair drifting down across her face from a loose bun at the back of her head. Her face was a kindly one with crows" feet at the edges of her eyes and her facial skin creased in all the benign places. The laughter lines on her face were defined and intact.

Eilidh stood up and shook hands with her.

"Hello Mrs Shelton. Nice to meet you."

The woman nodded, smiling broadly at her. She sat next to her husband, a picture of domestic docility.

"I'm Inspector Simmons and I'm here to see if anyone noticed anything on the day Irina was murdered."

"Yes, we were expecting to be interviewed by the police. Awful, isn't it? We feel terrible that we weren't able to stop it or do anything to help her. We were here all that afternoon. The policemen told us it happened on the 23rd, isn't that right?"

Eilidh nodded. The couple seemed to have shown a good deal of interest in the murder compared to the other inhabitants.

Mrs Shelton shuddered.

"I still can't sleep at night thinking about it all."

"That's true," grumbled her husband. "She's in and out of bed like a damn yo-yo. Keeps me up too."

"On the day it happened did you hear or see anything unusual? Anything that surprised you?" asked Eilidh.

"No," said Mr Shelton adamantly. "I was on duty all that day. Which basically means I was available in case anyone needed me for anything: whether it be for repairs, waiting in for workmen or simply to help with their errands and messages. I do things like dealing with the bins and making sure the stairwell is clean and in order."

He sniffed disapprovingly.

"As far as the building's security goes, it's a bloody

joke. The stupidest thing is that the porter's flat is down here in the basement and so of course you don't get to see anything that's going on really, up where the other flats are."

"So, what did you do exactly, that Monday afternoon?"

"We had lunch and then I cleared up in the kitchen afterwards," said Mrs Shelton, scrunching up her forehead in the effort to remember. "David went outside with our rubbish and was back here shortly afterwards. Then he watched the bowling on television while I did my tatting."

"No, Katie, I went and had a look at the lift door, remember? Folks were complaining that it was getting stiff and difficult to pull across when they shut it. I then came back here to get my WD40 can and sprayed some oil onto the hinges. The bowling didn't start until three o'clock."

Katie Shelton nodded in agreement at this, obviously used to being corrected by her husband.

"Did you see or notice anything while you were out of the flat?" asked Eilidh, feeling desperation get a silent grip of her.

"No, nothing. Saw Mrs Farooqi from Flat 1 but she always pops out when I'm around. She's bored most of the time, I think. And lonely..."

Mr Shelton scratched his chin as he thought about this, his finger rasping loudly against the profusion of grey hairs sprouting out of his unshaven skin.

"She's a funny one, that Mrs Farooqi. Never seems to go out much. Never see her husband around much either... Do you think she could've seen the ones who did it?" asked Mr Shelton enthusiastically, latching on to this notion with sudden gusto.

Eilidh smiled wearily.

"I'm afraid I really don't think she did, Mr Shelton."

As his eager face dropped she added, "All I'm doing at this stage is collecting as much information as I can about that day. Do you have any idea when Irina usually went out in the morning? Nobody seems to have seen her going out early that morning so I'm assuming she was at home."

"I've no idea when she went out that day. Usually, she didn't get out and about until late morning. Too much partying if you ask me," said Mr Shelton with a censorious sniff.

He glanced uncertainly at his wife, who was watching him with an anxious countenance. Mrs Shelton gave her husband a look that Eilidh could only surmise was a silent warning. Maybe she was worried that her husband was sharing too much and could get them into trouble. Either way, he subsided quietly, letting his wife take over the conversation.

"We didn't see anything, I'm afraid. I'm sorry we can't be of more help," said Mrs Shelton, gently but with unmistakable firmness.

Eilidh gave up. She wasn't going to get anything of interest here. It was incredible how people could live in the same building and yet know next to nothing about what went on in their neighbors' lives. She was sure if this murder had happened in a quiet suburb or in a country village, it would have been a different matter altogether.

6

Richard

Rosamie Torres leaned back on her uncomfortable metal and plastic chair and beamed with friendly good humor at CI Hazim and CI Langley. Her shoulders were down and her hands were resting loosely on her lap.

Straightaway, Abdul and Richard relaxed a fraction.

If Rosamie could be this at ease in the spartan interview room at New Scotland Yard, with its cell-like walls and floor, then it was likely she had little to hide.

Rosamie studied the two men in front of her with blatant interest; her large brown eyes were warm and her facial expression was both open and friendly. Her silvered black hair was neatly tied back in a tight bun and she wore a little mascara and pink lipstick. She had on a smart white blouse for the occasion and a pair of black trousers tapering to a pair of high-heeled, black ankle boots. It was very formal attire but obviously chosen carefully to fit in with what she perceived as the importance of her interview at New Scotland Yard.

"Right, Rosamie. Thank you for coming in to see us today," said Abdul.

Rosamie nodded in acknowledgement of his thanks.

"We've read through the transcript of your statement to the police on the 24th. From what we understand, you found Irina's body in the main bedroom at around 9.30 a.m. and straightaway called the police. You didn't touch or move the body as you could see Irina was dead and you said that you also noticed the painting on the wall was gone."

"Yes, that is correct."

"Irina's handbag was missing too. Is that correct?"

Rosamie Torres snorted dismissively.

"I didn't see a handbag. I was concerned only with what had happened to Irina."

"Of course. We understand. Have you anything to add to your previous statement, with the benefit of hindsight?"

"No, I have nothing more to add. Everything was as I said."

Abdul nodded as though he'd expected this response and was merely asking as part of standard procedure.

"You live at 35 The Crescent, New Malden. Is that right?"

Rosamie nodded.

"I wonder if you could tell us a little about yourself before we start talking about what happened at the flat in De Vere Gardens," said Abdul quietly.

The complacent smile was wiped off Rosamie's face.

"What do you want to know about me, officer? I'm a British citizen. I've lived here now for forty years," replied Rosamie, sounding offended and defensively putting a hand on either side of her waist.

Abdul smiled and raised his hands in an unspoken apology.

"Rosamie, we are just interested in your general background and what your history is with Igor Babikov and Irina Kapitsa. I can assure you we're not looking into your citizenship. It's standard procedure to ask the people we interview these questions, especially in important cases like this one."

Rosamie exhaled slowly and loosened her stance, crossing her arms in a protective, self-comforting way.

"Well, I don't really know what you want to find out about me. I've lived here in London for forty years. My home's in New Malden, as you know already, and I live there on my own since my husband died three years ago. I have plenty of friends and relatives close by."

Rosamie stared at Abdul and Richard, uncertain and wondering what else they wanted her to say. The two detectives remained mute and smiled encouragingly at her.

"I came to Britain originally to work as a nurse but twenty years ago I started to look for work as a housekeeper to the wealthy," she said at last, in a tone of voice that suggested she had decided to humor her interrogators. She crossed her ankles and leant back on her hard seat. "It was better pay, easier work, and also better hours than nursing. I've worked with seven families in that time, but for Mr Babikov the longest. I've worked for him since he bought that flat."

Abdul nodded.

"It sounds as though you've had very loyal employers in that space of time," he said with a smile.

"They must have valued your work greatly. I understand you worked at Igor's flat for three hours on weekday mornings, is that right?"

"Yes, sometimes I was asked to cook meals for them if they were here, which wasn't very often, or else I would deal with their post or food shopping for them. Mostly, my work involves cleaning the house and checking everything's in working order."

"Isn't cleaning three hours, five times a week, a little excessive for a flat that's empty most of the time?"

Rosamie grinned mischievously and shrugged.

"Mr. Babikov's very rich. He sets the terms and I just do what I'm asked. Simple as that."

"I suppose with so many valuable things in the flat he liked having someone there to keep an eye on the place," suggested Richard, speaking for the first time.

The housekeeper eyed him up with approval.

"Oh, yes. Mr. Babikov has many beautiful, lovely things in his house."

"Yes, we had a look around. The flat does seem to contain some very nice pieces. Do you have any idea why the only painting stolen was the one in the back bedroom?" asked Richard, with the casual tone of polite enquiry.

Rosamie shook her head vigorously with a look of disgust on her face.

"No, I don't understand it. I didn't like that painting at all," she said emphatically, at the same time waving her hands in front of her with horror. "It must have been valuable or Mr Babikov wouldn't have it hanging up in his flat but I didn't like it. The lady in the painting looked too much like a *puta*. Sorry, I mean a hooker. Irina didn't like it either."

"Really? Did she say that to you?" asked Abdul.

"Yes, many, many times. She was delighted when they took it away to be cleaned for a month. She tried to convince Mr Babikov to put another in its place, but he wouldn't hear of it. He loved that painting."

"When did it get cleaned?" asked Richard, leaning forward slightly as if to catch her words.

Rosamie pouted as she tried to remember.

"It was about half a year ago. February? Yes, I think it was sometime in February."

"And do you know who cleaned the painting for Mr Babikov?" asked Richard interestedly.

"No idea. You'll have to ask him that," replied Rosamie with unmistakable firmness, clamming up loyally on her employer's behalf.

Richard paused for a long moment as he thought about this, during which time Rosamie watched both detectives with an amused expression on her face. The two men could see she didn't feel at all intimidated by her surroundings and was thoroughly enjoying the drama of attending a formal police interview.

Abdul cleared his throat. He was the lead interrogator in the interview and it was his turn to take over.

"OK, Rosamie. Could you tell me what your relationship with Mr. Babikov and Miss Kapitsa was like?" he asked.

For the first time Rosamie started to look distressed and her eyes began to shine with unshed tears.

"My relationship with them? It was very good. Very good. We had no issues. They were nice employers, courteous and kind. Irina always gave me an extra week's pay on my birthday and at Christmas."

"But you say they were also away most of the time?"

"Yes, most of the time they were in Russia. She sometimes came back to meet with girlfriends on her own but she never stayed very long."

"Did either Mr. Babikov or Miss Kapitsa look worried or concerned about anything recently?"

Rosamie pondered this, her forehead creasing in a way it customarily did not, as there were no permanent lines etched across her smooth brow.

"No, I can't say I've noticed anything like that with either of them. They seemed the same as always."

Abdul leaned forward on his chair.

"I'd like you to tell me what you did on the morning of the 23rd, in as much detail as possible, please."

"The 23rd?" repeated Rosamie, swiping away a tear that had trickled rebelliously down her face. "On the 23rd I arrived at my normal time, nine o'clock. The porter was downstairs, so I said hello and took the lift up. The lift door wasn't working right and I decided I'd speak to the porter later about it, the next time I saw him. When I went into the flat, Irina was having breakfast in the kitchen. We chatted while I collected my cleaning bottles from under the sink..."

Rosamie took a deep breath, gripping her hands tightly as they rested on the table.

"She didn't say anything strange or out of the ordinary. She was the same as always. She said she was going to be heading out for lunch with friends and wanted me to post some things for her. While I was dusting in the sitting room, she brought me four letters and a big poster tube. She wanted the letters sent first class and the poster tube sent by special delivery. She left them next to me with a fifty pound note and went off to get changed."

Rosamie stopped talking, but when Abdul and Richard didn't say anything she carried on.

"After that I cleaned the bathrooms and vacuumed the hallway. I did all of the ironing that had been left in the spare bedroom. Irina said a quick goodbye to me from the end of the hallway when I went out at quarter past twelve. I know it was that time because I was looking at my watch. I left with the things she'd given me to post... I still can't believe that was the last time I spoke to her."

The tears were coming thick and fast now and Richard helpfully placed a box of tissues in front of Rosamie. She grabbed one and started wiping her face carefully, dabbing under her eyes in case her mascara had smudged.

"Just out of curiosity, where were the letters and the poster tube addressed to? Can you remember?" asked Richard nonchalantly, once Rosamie had composed herself.

"Two of the letters were addressed to British Gas and the DVLA. The other two looked like cards and they were going to addresses here in London. One was in Baker Street, and the other was to an address in Chelsea. The poster tube was the strangest one; it was addressed to an address in Madrid. A lady called Victoria Bretanzos Forentin."

There was a short silence.

"I don't suppose you remember the exact addresses, do you?" asked Richard, feeling for the first time that this might lead to something relevant.

Rosamie paused while she considered this.

"I remember the card going to Baker Street because it was addressed to Natasha Macklin and I've met her before at a drinks party in Irina's flat... Number 74 Baker Street is where she lives. The other was addressed to a Mrs Fionnella Bianchi, in Chelsea. I think it was addressed to number 6 Wisteria Mews but I'm not a hundred per cent certain... The poster was addressed to a place called El Viso, Chamartín, in Madrid. Addressed to Victoria Bretanzos Forentin. I can't remember the number or the postcode, I'm afraid."

"Thank you. That's very helpful. Lastly, can I ask if you went into the main bedroom on the 23rd?" asked Richard.

"No, I didn't," answered Rosamie with assurance. "Irina asked me not to. When I arrived she only had a dressing gown on. She was getting herself ready in that room for most of the morning and by the time she came out dressed I was getting ready to leave."

"OK. Thank you very much, Rosamie. If we need anything else, we'll be in touch. I think that's all we need for today, don't you, Abdul?"

Abdul nodded and both men stood up, signalling the interview was at a close.

Abdul went and opened the interview room door.

Rosamie, looking grievously disappointed that everything was at an end, picked up her handbag from the floor and flounced out of the room.

Richard sat in the interview room twirling his tortoiseshell glasses with one hand, waiting patiently for Abdul to return from escorting Rosamie Torres out of the building.

It wasn't long before the door of the interview room opened and Abdul walked in with his decisive stride and took a seat where Rosamie had been sitting earlier.

The two men looked at each other.

"What do you think?" asked Richard, deciding to be the one to break the silence.

Abdul shrugged.

"Personally, I think she didn't commit the murder. She has a cast-iron alibi for the afternoon and evening before. And she must be... What? Five foot one? She's tiny. Can't see her having the strength or arm length to stab Irina in the way described in the pathology report."

"Remember Irina was incapacitated."

"Even so. As for the handbag and the painting... I don't know what to think. She could, of course, have taken them the morning she came into the flat, put them somewhere safe and then called the police."

"After the murderer had left? I suppose so. But Rosamie is a woman who has worked for wealthy people for last twenty years. Don't you think she would have tried to steal before now if she was that way inclined?"

"Depends if someone was offering her money for it. We could look into her employer history in more detail."

"Yes, that would be useful."

Weary, Richard rubbed his eyes.

"That painting isn't going to be easy to sell. Someone wanted that picture and I'm sure it was stolen to order. But the strange thing is not many people knew about it. It wasn't verified until recently. And it isn't a painting that would instantly attract the average onlooker. It's a striking and enthralling painting but most people would see it as old-fashioned and not nearly as attractive as Greco's other portrait of Princess Catalina Micaela, *Lady in a Fur Wrap*. You heard what Irina and Rosamie's reaction to the painting was."

"I think the murder and the painting are tied up together," said Abdul, quietly but assertively. "But it's not going to be easy to figure out what went on in that flat, not easy at all."

"Well, there's two things that struck me about that interview. How about you?" asked Richard, focusing on the little information they did have.

Abdul nodded, his face guarded and inscrutable.

Abdul would make a good poker player, thought Richard with amusement, because when he chose, the man was a closed book. Richard started to wonder what made this man unwind and loosen up. For a moment he tried to visualize Abdul chilling out at his local pub in South Kensington but then quickly dispelled the bizarre image from his mind. It seemed completely wrong somehow to think of Abdul in such a setting.

"Yes, several things stood out for me too," volunteered Abdul.

"Like the fact Rosamie says she never went into the main bedroom the day before Irina was murdered."

"Yes. And the fact that the painting was sent to be cleaned six months before it was taken."

"Yes," agreed Richard. "That's very significant. We need to find out from Igor where it was sent for cleaning. A professional at the height of their career would be able to see the potential value of that painting, no doubt about it. Besides, who knows who else could be working in that workshop? Word gets around."

Abdul was busy making notes, notes that were punctuated with bullet points.

Richard smiled. He preferred to retain snippets of information stored away in his head, to be pulled out as and when needed. As an art historian, memorizing facts and figures came easy to him.

Once Abdul had finished writing, Richard decided to bring up another fact.

"The poster tube. That's a strange thing to decide to post on the very day a painting goes missing and a woman's murdered..."

Richard could see he had Abdul's full attention.

"I cannot believe that a valuable painting would ever be put into such a tube or get posted by special delivery," Richard said. "However, I do think to cover all aspects we need to locate Victoria Bretanzos Forentin and find out what was in that poster tube. And also find out what was written in the cards that Rosamie posted that day. It could be innocuous but equally it could be a window into Irina's state of mind."

"Yes, but all of that will be very time consuming."

"I know. But at the moment, we have no leads at all in this case."

Fleetingly, a pensive look crossed Abdul's face. Noting it, Richard waited to hear what he had to say, picking up his glasses and cleaning the lenses with the edge of his jacket in the meantime. When Abdul did speak again it was an unexpected bolt out of the blue.

"Eilidh has discovered that Irina was with her twin sister on the afternoon of the 23rd."

Richard stared at Abdul, surprised.

"On the day Irina was murdered, she was with her sister?"

"Yes, apparently so, according to the couple of residents who saw them. Irina's sister was described as having long hair and scruffier clothing, but both witnesses are absolutely adamant they were identical twins."

"Has anyone told Igor this?"

"No, as yet we haven't spoken to him. Eilidh's trying to contact him as we speak, in order to arrange another meeting with him."

Richard nodded.

"OK, I'll leave you two to sort that one out. In the meantime, I think it's time I contacted Mike Telford."

Abdul's face showed the respect that the name of Mike Telford engendered.

For many years Mike's mythical reputation had caused ripples throughout New Scotland Yard because he often made the impossible happen, enabling priceless works of art to be returned to museums unscathed under his competent hands. He was someone who always liked to work in the shadows, so very few members of the police force had actually met him.

Mike Telford, like Richard, had an obsessive passion for artwork and antiquities and fortunately for the police force he liked to work on the side of law enforcement. Had he decided to become a career criminal many museums would have needed to beef up their security.

"I want to make a brief trip to Madrid in order to speak to the specialists at El Prado Museum," added Richard. "I want to speak to any of the experts who saw and identified the painting and check their version of events. I have them listed in the file Igor Babikov gave me. At the same time I'll see if my other half working in Madrid can locate Victoria Bretanzos Forentin for me."

Abdul grinned boyishly at Richard.

"I'm jealous. Your remit is more international than mine."

"Has it ever crossed your mind that we might have to liaise at some point with the Russian side?" asked Richard as Abdul stood up, picked up his briefcase and started filing away his notes.

Abdul paused for a moment as he thought this through. Then he grinned humorously again, flashing his even white teeth at Richard.

"I'd love to see the gaffers" faces if it came to that. Can you imagine their reaction? Especially after the Novichok affair in Salisbury... We'd be lucky to get the Russian police to even pick up the phone."

7

Richard

Following the steady stream of people flowing out of Highbury and Islington Station, Richard soon found himself engulfed by the chilly air outside.

He put on his thick overcoat, relieved to be out of the hot and stuffy underground train.

He had spent most of the journey standing next to the door of the train, heated up to sweltering point by the people crammed up against him which hadn't been an enjoyable experience. At least he was tall and so was able to look over most people's heads but he did wonder what it was like for the others who were shorter than him.

On the journey to Islington his fellow passengers had behaved like typical Londoners, meaning that they had all avoided eye contact and instead of interacting with anyone else, they had studied their phones, gazed at the floor or stared up at the train adverts with bogus interest. Thinking back to the discomfort of the train ride, Richard questioned if this was how sheep and cattle felt when they were transported cross-country. Somehow he suspected livestock had more access to fresh air than Londoners did on the Tube.

He walked briskly down Holloway Road with its busy lanes of early morning traffic, turned right at Highbury Corner and then made his way towards Compton Avenue.

A few minutes later he reached Islington Park Street and came to a stop at an empty driveway with a dark grey three-story building at the end of it. 102–104 Islington Park Street was the premises of Oliver Newton's Old Master Restoration Services.

Richard studied the building in front of him with interest. All its windows had a white security grille on them and there were three black CCTV cameras positioned at different angles on the facade. He was certain there would be more cameras positioned out of sight at the sides and back of the premises.

He rang the buzzer next to the bright yellow front door, noticing there was no plaque advertising the workshop as a place of business and thinking to himself this was a sensible choice given the value of the illustrious paintings that regularly made their way to Oliver's company.

"Oliver Newton Restoration Services," sang out a voice.

"Hello, it's Chief Inspector Richard Langley. I'm here to meet Oliver Newton."

The door buzzed open and he walked into a narrow vestibule. At the end of it, sitting behind a desk, was a bored-looking security guard in black uniform.

Richard showed him his identification.

"If you could sign in please, sir," said the security guard, pushing a book across the table to Richard.

Richard filled in his name, time of arrival and the purpose of his visit.

The guard lifted a badge attached to a metal chain out of his desk drawer and wrote Richard's name on it. Handing it over to Richard he indicated the door adjacent to him.

"If you go through this door and wait there, sir, someone will attend to you shortly."

"Thank you," said Richard, obediently putting on his new badge.

He walked into a bright cavernous room that had three emerald-green Chesterfield sofas and a long console table with a number of magazines arranged in neat and symmetrical rows, as well as glass vase filled with yellow lilies.

It looked like a plush dentist's waiting room except for the imposing metal doors of a lift on the right-hand side.

A sizeable area at the front of the elevator doors had been left clear of furniture or any other obstacle and Richard suspected this was to make it easier for the paintings to make their way in and out of the building, because if the artworks were packaged professionally their protective crates would add substantially to their size.

He sat himself down on one of the Chesterfield sofas and began to browse the news websites on his phone as he waited for someone to come and fetch him.

Glancing up at one point, he saw there was a CCTV camera watching him at the far corner of the room.

Five minutes later the lift doors opened with a ping and a young lady popped out with such speed she seemed to lose her balance. Young and blonde, she was wearing a smart, navy suit and tottering on a high pair of bright red platform shoes. Looking down at the extraordinary height of her shoes Richard was surprised she could walk in them at all and assumed she must have picked them up at a vintage shop stocking gear from the 70s. He was pretty sure very few people would have the guts to wear such precarious and outrageously tall platforms.

"Hello. I'm Alice, Oliver's secretary," she said, shaking his hand. "If you come with me, I'll take you up to his office."

Without waiting for his reply, she turned around and went back to the wall to push the lift button. Richard quickly slipped his phone into his jacket pocket and joined her.

The elevator doors slowly opened again and they both walked in, side by side as the lift was so capacious. Industrial-sized, the lift was long and high enough to have comfortably carried several pieces of large furniture in it and as such was ideal for a restoration business. A painting packaged securely within its solid container could easily take up as much space as a sofa or cupboard. Most valuable artworks were transported with sensors on the frame and the crate, so that the temperature and the movement of the crate could be monitored, and this in turn tended to reduce the insurance costs involved in moving precious items from one location to another.

At the center of the lift's ceiling Richard could see there was yet another camera.

"Is it a nice day outside?" asked Alice courteously as they ascended to the third floor.

"Yes, not bad for this time of year."

"I'm hoping to get out for lunch later so I hope the rain stays off."

"I'm sure it will," reassured Richard, just as they reached the top floor.

When the lift doors opened again they found themselves in a dark hallway lit with the ghostly luminescence of a single light bulb.

Following Alice, who was stumbling occasionally as she walked, Richard made his way down a long, curving corridor. At regular intervals they would pass by a hanging lightbulb but as often as not it wasn't lit, so their shadows would dance and sway eerily against the wall in front of them.

There was not a window to be seen and he was starting to feel the place was similar to Fort Knox. Never a hundred per cent comfortable with enclosed spaces, he liked even less to find he had completely lost his bearings and at present he had no idea where they were within the building.

He did his best to shake off the tendrils of claustrophobia that were threatening to engulf him and ignored the voice within him which was urging him to make a break for the outdoors. Before Richard had time to change from an anxious state of mind to an agitated one, Alice was knocking on a door situated on their right-hand side.

As they waited for Oliver to let them in, Richard began to think about the kind of artworks Oliver Newton's company dealt with and, almost drooling at the thought, visualized in his mind's eye the treasures that had made their way there from exclusive collections around the country. Judging by the security he had observed in the building the insurance premiums for Oliver's business had to be phenomenal and yet, despite this, it was such a privilege to be able to rescue and restore paintings by some of the best artists in the world.

"Hello Chief Inspector Langley, I'm delighted to meet you," said Oliver affably, as he opened the door into his office.

He was a tall, elderly man with half-moon glasses and a thick thatch of white hair. Dressed in worn brown corduroy trousers and a red tartan shirt, he didn't look like the proprietor of a prosperous business. Like its owner, the room they were in wasn't in the least bit pretentious and looked more like a homely study than the office space of a managing director, with several framed family photos on the wall and bookshelves stacked with well-used paperbacks.

Oliver shook Richard's hand and offered him a seat while Alice exited the room, closing the door behind her.

"I understand you're interested in finding out some information about the restoration of Igor Babikov's Catalina Micaela painting? We've restored quite a few of his paintings in the past."

"Yes, that's right. I've a few questions to ask you, if you don't mind," said Richard, seating himself on an armchair and glancing briefly through the window at the back garden with its small collection of fruit trees.

"Of course not, go ahead."

Oliver sat down on an adjacent chair and smiled at him.

"We're wondering how long Igor's painting was here for and who did the restoration work on it," asked Richard, cutting to the chase. "And what happens to the paintings at the end of the working day? By that I mean do they get stored at the close of business or are they left out on the workroom floor?"

Oliver crossed his legs and leaned back on his armchair.

"My, what a lot of questions! Let me see, the man who did the restoration is a chap called Max Hofmann," he said cheerfully. "He's absolutely brilliant at what he does. I think he's the best conservator-restorer I've come across in the forty years I've worked with the industry. I'll take you along to speak to him in a minute. I've had a look at our records and that painting was here for three weeks. It was in a surprisingly good condition. Antique artworks have often been restored or retouched several times during their lifetime but Mr Babikov's painting only needed an in-depth surface clean."

"That's quite unusual, isn't it?"

"Yes, it is, actually. We use an ultraviolet light scan to check for prior restoration work but there was nothing. Which is excellent news for Mr Babikov because a well-preserved painting is always worth more than one that's had a lot of meddling over the years."

Oliver leaned forward and looked closely at Richard.

"You asked what happens to our artworks when the building's locked up for the day," he said with his voice lowered, as though he were imparting trade secrets. "They stay in the workshop. We don't move paintings once we've begun working on them. As far as I'm concerned, the less we move a painting the better as they can easily get damaged in transit. Also, we use solvents to remove the surface dirt and the paintings need to dry out properly once we've used them. After we've done the restoring and cleaning, we then reapply varnish to protect the work and again that needs to dry out... Nowadays we mostly use an oil-based semi-matt finish to lower reflections and minimize the glare but it's a question of preference for the clients."

Richard nodded, thinking through all this information.

"Do you have a security guard at night?" he asked.

"Yes, we do. We're very security conscious. We handle paintings worth millions and I can't afford for anything to happen to them. It's my reputation that's at stake."

"In terms of security, I'm wondering how many of your employees have access to the workshop and to any information there might be on any of the paintings?"

Oliver frowned at him and crossed his arms, a defensive gesture that wasn't lost on Richard. Oliver didn't say anything but then again he didn't have to. It was obvious he was unhappy with Richard's question.

Unfazed by this, Richard continued to wait for his response, maintaining prolonged eye contact with Oliver until Oliver was forced to look away.

There was a shift in the ambience of the room as the tension between them accumulated and the silence stretched onwards.

Richard did nothing to break it.

Eventually Oliver sighed in defeat and said, "So this is where we're heading. I've heard Igor's picture was stolen from his flat."

"Yes, I'm afraid so, although up until now we've managed to keep that under wraps. May I ask who told you?"

Oliver snorted.

"Well, for a start, we don't normally get Chief Inspectors visiting us with questions about our work and safeguards. But if you must know, it was Igor's secretary who informed me."

"Ah."

"Yes, he's a remarkable man, Igor. I've known him for a long time. You see, from time to time we do get stolen paintings in our workshop. I tend to keep an eye on the databases for missing artworks. However, as I'm sure you'll appreciate, we tread very carefully."

"I do understand the need for caution when you're dealing with your clients. I can also see that you're very security conscious so I won't offend you by asking if you thoroughly vet the people working for you. I'm sure you do. But as you'll know the best of people can give in to temptation and that's why it would be helpful to know who in your business knew of Igor Babikov's portrait."

Oliver Newton grimaced.

"You're right. I don't like to think of it because I trust my staff implicitly and I've worked with them for many years. But when an art restorer is paid an average of thirty thousand pounds a year it's stupid to not see the temptation. Some of these paintings are worth millions..."

He rubbed his forehead with his fingertips, as though the possibility there a crooked employee working for him was yet another heavy burden to carry in the running of his firm.

"I've seven full-time conservator-restorers working

for me here," explained Oliver. "The business also employs two fine art consultants, who go out and assess the artworks at our clients" houses. They figure out transport arrangements, set expectations and discover what the client is looking for when they hand over their paintings to us. Of course, many unexpected things turn up in the process of restoring an old painting so we often have to call our clients up at different stages, informing them of any new developments, and take it from there."

"And are these seven conservator-restorers and two consultants the only ones who'd have access to information about the painting?"

"My secretary, who you met just now, knows all about the paintings here as she deals with all my correspondence. I have, as well, two transport workers who are specially trained in the packaging and transporting of valuable artworks. And then of course we have the security guards and the cleaners too. We subcontract our office cleaning to an agency so you'll have to contact them directly. I don't think any of the security guards or cleaners would have a clue as to the artists or value of the paintings we work on."

"Even so, could I have a list with all their names, please? We're going to have to speak to them all at some point."

Oliver's eyebrows twitched together and a furrow appeared on his forehead.

"There's no doubt in my mind that will set the cat among the pigeons here. My employees aren't going to relish being questioned by the police. Is this really necessary?"

"I'm afraid so. You see, we're not just dealing with the disappearance of a very valuable painting. Igor Babikov's girlfriend, Irina Kapitsa, was murdered at the same time."

"What? That's horrific!" exclaimed Oliver, clutching at his knees, the thick veins on his hands bulging outwards as he leaned forward on his chair. He appeared genuinely devastated, his face a shade whiter as the implications of this sunk in. "How awful! Poor Igor, I'd no idea."

Richard nodded in agreement.

"Nobody expected something like this to happen," he remarked. "I can honestly say I haven't had to deal with a homicide in the eleven years I've been in this job."

He fell silent for a moment, choosing his words with care.

"We've two serious crimes on our hands... Hardly anyone knew about the painting so that narrows down the field substantially, and I'm afraid since this painting was restored here six months prior to its theft we'll have to look into your employees too."

"Yes, I can see that now," agreed Oliver despondently, rubbing his forehead again. "That's fine, go ahead with your interviews. Anything we can do to help, let us know. I have to say that I sincerely hope none of my staff have been involved in this. My business up until now has had a spotless reputation and I'd like to keep it that way. We work as a close team and it's not good for cohesiveness when people feel they could be possible suspects in a heinous crime."

"There's no need to tell anyone about the murder

and I can promise you we'll try to be as discreet and unobtrusive as possible. It won't take us long to speak to your employees and then we'll leave you in peace. I'm sorry to bring such bad news to your firm. I'm sure, though, that as you work with old masterpieces you'll be aware of the risks involved with these artworks. The security in this building is evidence of that."

"Indeed. But the security here is meant to be preventative," remarked Oliver wryly, getting up from his chair. "Let me start by taking you down to the workshop and introducing you to Max."

Richard stood up and followed him out of the room. They walked along the corridor back to where Richard had exited the lift.

They took the lift down to first floor and walked into the workshop where five conservator-restorers were sitting on chairs, working intently.

In the background a radio was playing at low volume.

Completely engrossed, two women were seated in front of a huge pastoral scene and were dabbing their brushes on its surface with a lot of care and precision.

Gazing at the picture for a moment, Richard wondered if it was a Claude Lorrain original. If it was, what must it feel like to restore a painting by one of the true masters of landscape art? Both women seemed to feel the responsibility of their restoration because they plied their brushes with an almost religious reverence, one small brushstroke at a time. They were holding their brushes in a white-gloved hand, with their colorful palettes clasped in their other as they worked. Like a couple of cave explorers they had head torches on and bright portable lights were blazing onto the canvas from behind them.

Further along the room a balding man was staring through a microscope at a painting on the table and a young man, his black hair tied back in a ponytail, was scraping away at a canvas with a thin, metal instrument, wearing a face mask and gloves as he beavered away.

The last restorer drew the eye because his tousled hair was dyed a shade of what could only be described as Smurf blue. He was dressed in black and had intricate tattoos encircling both his arms.

"That's Max," said Oliver with a benign smile.

Max lifted his head when he heard Oliver's voice, and looked at them.

He had large, dark eyes framed by preposterously thick eyelashes, a wide nose and full lips. He would have attracted notice even if his hair hadn't been dyed bright blue because he was a very handsome young man.

He was holding in his hand what could best be described as a giant cotton bud.

Oliver and Richard walked across to Max's easel.

"Max, this is Chief Inspector Richard Langley. He's here to make some enquiries about the Catalina Micaela picture you worked on."

Max's eyes immediately became watchful.

He wasn't the most talkative of individuals, thought Richard, but then again spending hours working alone on paintings wasn't going to suit a convivial, extrovert character.

"You'll be interested in the painting Max is working on just now," commented Oliver, turning to Richard.

"It's a Gainsborough. The fascinating thing about this particular artwork is that at some point in the past, its owner decided the girl in the portrait wasn't pretty enough and gave the painting a makeover."

Oliver went up to a ring binder lying on the table next to them and opened it.

"We take photos at every stage of our restoration. If you look at this you'll see what this portrait looked like before we started to work on it."

Richard peered down at the photos Oliver was showing him and then looked up at the portrait in front of him. The portrait on the easel looked completely different to the one in the photos.

The ring binder photos revealed how a previous restorer had painted over the original to make the girl prettier and more suited to the tastes of a different generation. The nose had been straightened, the skin had developed honeyed tones instead of being porcelain white, and the face and neck were depicted as longer and more delicate than the original.

Richard turned to the easel.

The girl that stared back at him from the canvas looked just like a Habsburg princess with a rounder face and a prominent forehead. She had bulbous eyes and a slightly drooping nose. She might not be as beautiful as she was after her past makeover but she was now an original Gainsborough, gazing out at them as she had when the artist first painted her.

"Max has had his work cut out with this one. The varnish was badly cracked under the repaint so he's not only had to carefully remove the restorer's layer of paint but he's also had to take off the layer of varnish beneath it without disturbing the original painting."

As Max was now standing to one side, Richard bent down and looked closely at the canvas.

The work on it had been done sensitively as far as he could tell. He could see parts where the original layer of paint was still hidden beneath its historical touch-up.

"It's very impressive," said Richard admiringly, unable to take his eyes off the portrait.

"Do you enjoy what you do?" he asked, turning towards Max.

Max smiled.

"Yes of course. As conservator-restorers we could be described as frustrated artists. With this work we can at least have the credit of giving some of the best artists in the world a helping hand with their paintings. It's basically honoring the dead. This painting, for example," he said, pointing at the Gainsborough. "I'm restoring the work back to the original picture painted by the artist. Can you imagine what Gainsborough would have felt if he'd seen what that other restorer did to his portrait?"

Richard nodded in agreement.

"I agree," he said. "It's very worthwhile, and exciting too. You must have a lot of patience to do this kind of work. Did you like working on the painting of Catalina Micaela?"

Max's face suddenly closed up again. Watching Richard, he shrugged.

"There wasn't a lot needing to be done to it. We only had to remove the old varnish and then add a layer of fresh varnish to it. It wasn't too challenging," he said dismissively.

"Were you the only one working on it?" asked Richard.

"Yes, he was," interrupted Oliver, seeing the hostility entering Max's face at this question. "Igor Babikov wanted the best conservator-restorer in my firm."

As a result of Oliver's timely intervention Max's face relaxed a tinge.

Richard felt like kicking himself. He knew he was making a complete mess of it. Oliver had given him a chance to chat to Max and instead of establishing a rapport with him, all he'd managed to do was alienate him with his heavy-handed questions. Foolishly he'd let his feelings get the better of him and all because he sensed Max knew a lot more about Igor's painting than he was letting on.

So much for his assurance to Oliver that they would be discreet.

"I'm sorry to ask you these questions, Max," said Richard, deciding it was probably best at this point to be upfront. "But unfortunately the painting of Catalina Micaela that you worked on has been stolen and it's important we find out as much as we can about it. I'm not sure we'll ever be able to recover it but we have to try. It's a very valuable painting."

The other restorers had stopped their work and were staring over at them with interest.

Max continued to glare at Richard, his face mutinous. His posture, as he leaned in towards Richard with his hands in his pockets, was aggressive.

"I don't understand what you want from me," he said angrily. "I work here in the workshop with my other colleagues and security here is tight. I haven't done anything wrong."

"I'm not suggesting that you've done anything

wrong. All we're wanting at this stage is to find out exactly who knew about the painting. This narrows things down, because by all accounts not many people knew Igor Babikov had a masterpiece in his flat. Did you happen to speak to anyone about it?"

"You've got to be kidding me. Why would I want to talk to anyone about a painting with a sixteenth-century harlot in it? I do have a life, you know."

Looking at him, Richard decided he should leave things for now. It was only going to incense them all to have to answer police questions and he'd be better interviewing them individually at a later stage, possibly with Eilidh's calming presence there, once the police had exhausted all other lines of enquiry. Besides, if Max's Smurf-blue head had appeared in De Vere Gardens at some point, he was pretty sure the residents would have remembered.

The problem was he needed a trail to follow and as yet they had nothing solid to work on. At the moment everything seemed to be a smoke-and-mirrors illusion, leading absolutely nowhere. He decided he had to make a call to Mike Telford because the swashbuckling private investigator had helped him out of many such dead ends.

He turned to Oliver, who was watching him with a worried look on his face, and smiled at him.

"I think we can leave things for today. I'll be in touch."

Oliver looked relieved.

"Certainly, Chief Inspector. Let me walk you out."

"Thank you, Max," said Richard before he left, but already Max had turned his attention to the Gainsborough painting and didn't hear him.

They both strolled out of the room, Oliver chattering enthusiastically about a Raphael they'd worked on a year ago. Richard noticed all the conservator-restorers were fully focused on their work once more.

Oliver seemed to be a hard taskmaster.

8

Richard

Richard kicked off his shoes and lifted his feet up onto his desk, letting his office chair lean back as far as it would go. His long legs stretched out pleasurably. Next to him was a double shot latte from Starbucks and a half-eaten chocolate muffin. That day his work space was empty of people and he was indulging himself for staying on late at the office on a Friday evening.

Richard had the telephone to his ear and to his irritation it had been ringing out for the last three minutes, but he continued to persevere with it because he was sure Mike Telford would still be in his office at this late hour. Many of Mike's contacts liked to communicate in the evening, after the business of the day had concluded.

Suddenly the ringing stopped.

"Hello, Mike Telford speaking."

"Hi, Mike."

"Let me guess. Richard Langley?"

"One and only."

There was a long, frustrated sigh at the other end of the phone.

"Please don't tell me it's another Millais."

Richard chuckled.

"Not this time, Mike, no. Although, for your information, there's a reward of a million pounds up for grabs."

Mike whistled.

"So it's not a government request, then. Interesting... a private collector, no less. What's your department doing with a private collector?"

"He might have a few paintings hanging in the National Gallery."

"I see. Right, out with it. What's the painting?"

"It's a Greco painting that's been verified recently, but because its owner wanted things kept under wraps it hasn't been formally registered as such and isn't on any database."

Mike snorted derisively.

"Verified by who?"

"Prado."

"Mmm. Still doesn't sound right to me. Are you sure it isn't a fake?"

Richard pulled Igor's folder towards him and opened it up.

"According to the collector's file, the Prado Museum had it sent to Orion Analytical for testing. They concluded it was real, not a fake."

"Impressive. If it has been checked out by the Orion lab for authenticity I'll have to give the painting the benefit of the doubt."

"The owner, Igor Babikov, wants the painting back.

Any chance you could get the word around? As I said, the reward stands at one million."

"I'll be able to get my little bottom feeders sniffing around, that's for sure."

"I imagine this might be a crime at a higher level than a bottom feeder, Mike. There's a dead body involved, too."

Mike whistled again, his attention clearly caught.

"This gets stranger and stranger, my friend. The sharks might have taken it, but even so you're always better starting with the bottom feeders or even the pilot fish. There's always one of them that knows what's going on. I doubt the pond scum will know anything about this one."

Richard smiled to himself. For some absurd reason Mike Telford liked to analogize the criminal world as a marine eco-system. It was one of his many idiosyncrasies.

"Send me photos of the painting and I'll get my contacts to have a nose around," continued Mike. "I'll take the usual cut, of course."

"Of course," agreed Richard blandly. "Igor will have no problem with that."

The two of them chatted amicably about Lee Krasner's current exhibition at the Barbican and then cordially signed off.

Richard stretched out the tension in his shoulders, swallowed some of his now tepid coffee and then went across to look at the many outstanding cases that were stacked up on the shelves in the office. It was time he went back to monitoring progress on the other cases needing his attention.

Art theft was of such low priority in the police force

that he knew many of the cases sitting on his office shelves would remain unresolved. Many unique artifacts and paintings that had been reported stolen might well have disappeared forever. Today these items could be in any number of places, temporarily hidden under someone's bed or else lying at the back of someone's cupboard, gathering dust. It was possible they had been used as collateral in organized crime or they could even have ended up displayed in some very wealthy person's house, for them to gloat over in secrecy. Precious objects that by their very beauty should be a gift for everyone to enjoy and learn from...

He was busy losing himself in an art theft from the Fitzwilliam Museum the month before, when there was a tentative knock on the door.

Cursing the interruption, he jumped up from his chair with a frown and walked to the door.

He pulled the heavy door open only to find he was looking down at Eilidh Simmons" pixie features.

"Sorry, am I disturbing you?" asked Eilidh in her unmistakable Essex accent.

"No, not at all," lied Richard politely. "Please come in and take a seat."

Richard sat himself down and swiveled around to look at Eilidh.

She was dressed in casual clothes and looked stunning as usual. She had all the appearance of someone who was dropping by for a brief moment before heading out for a boisterous night out, as her face was done up with bold-coloured make-up, which looked almost garish under the strip lighting in the room. She was wearing tight jeans that hugged her legs attractively, a baggy black jumper that did a good job of hiding her curves, and a pair of knee-high black leather boots.

"You're not disturbing me at all," said Richard honestly, suddenly realizing he'd much rather be talking to Eilidh than reading a report on a museum art theft.

Eilidh walked over to the chair next to him and sat down. She crossed her long legs, gently bouncing her restless, airborne foot up and down.

"We've managed to arrange another interview with Igor Babikov for Wednesday morning next week," she commented. "He's heading back to St Petersburg after that. We were wondering if you felt you needed to be there too?"

"No, I think the three of us again would be overkill. If I need to speak to him I'll arrange it separately. These things tend to work better when they're less formal."

Eilidh nodded in agreement, looking pensively at him.

Richard began to wonder what was on her mind. She could have emailed or called him with her query but instead she'd made her way all the way down to the basement of New Scotland Yard.

"Richard, I wanted to run something by you but it's so bizarre, I'm struggling to get my head around it."

"Don't worry about that. There's nothing about this case that's normal. In fact, I shouldn't even be working with you guys. I've never had a case where a murder was tied into an art theft."

Eilidh smiled, her chocolate eyes narrowing in genuine amusement.

"Yes, we deal with the dirty, mucky side of humanity," she said. "You deal with beautiful objects. You must get so much more job satisfaction because you get to restore priceless, beautiful items to where they belong. With us, even when we put someone behind bars, nothing's bringing back the dead to the lives they've missed out on."

Richard was surprised by her attitude. Eilidh sounded as though she was one of the many long-standing officers who were jaded, disillusioned and burnt out by the job. There were many such officers around but he'd met none that were as young and beautiful as Eilidh. Maybe she was here to get a pep talk.

"We have to deal with some pretty ugly customers when we're trying to track down missing or stolen artifacts," he argued. "It's really not as glamorous as it sounds. How many unresolved homicides are there in England and Wales this year?"

Eilidh seemed surprised by this unexpected question.

"We had 571 unresolved homicides last year."

"OK. At least you have a number. We can't even begin to monitor how much art theft is going on."

Richard sighed with frustration when he saw Eilidh looking confused.

"With minor robberies, museums sometimes don't realize artifacts are missing until years later," he explained patiently. "There's pathetically poor practice in many council-run institutions. Inventory taking is often haphazard and the smaller museums and galleries are especially rubbish at it. Many museums and galleries have priceless works buried in storage but rarely do they get checked or monitored."

Eilidh was watching him closely, which was making him feel distinctly uncomfortable. It was the kind of look he knew, the look of someone coming across a rarity. Richard had always felt he was a bit of a freak, which was why he preferred not to be the center of attention, even now when he was the sole focus of Eilidh's attention.

Eilidh was still silently observing him, so despite being unnerved by this, Richard decided to continue to vent his grievances. At the very least, he thought, she would realize that not everything was hunky dory in the art world either.

"Now and again, for example, we might get a call from an honest dealer, who suspects that the coins he's bought might be stolen. When we trace them, we find that the museum they were stolen from was completely unaware they'd gone missing. It's an absolute surprise to them when they see us bringing back their coins. This is what we're dealing with and I find it utterly depressing. A great deal of art theft cases are unresolved because with the passage of time it gets harder and harder to locate missing items. And don't even get me started on the quality of the fakes flooding the market these days."

"I've heard that every gallery is estimated to have a few fake masterpieces in it."

Richard nodded morosely.

"Yes, unfortunately at certain points in history the forgers were far ahead of the experts in their specialism, but I don't think the situation's as bad as people make out. At least not yet, but who knows what lies in the future?"

Eilidh didn't answer Richard's question.

She glanced at her watch dial and then leaned forward.

"Richard..."

"Yes?"

Richard felt himself losing his train of thought as he stared into Eilidh's warm, brown eyes. Feeling singed by the intensity of her expressive eyes, he tried to pull himself together.

"I've been thinking about the murder and I'm wondering if it's possible that the victim might not be Irina."

Speechless and bemused, Richard stared at Eilidh as she squirmed uncomfortably on her chair.

"The witnesses are adamant they were identical twins. Could Irina be the twin that wasn't murdered?" she explained.

There was a long silence during which Eilidh started to look around the room, as though disassociating herself from the question.

"But one of the twins is described as having long hair and was scruffier, wasn't she?" asked Richard feebly, trying to gather his thoughts.

"Easy enough to alter her hair length, don't you think?"

"But why would Irina be the one to leave? What incentive would she have to leave her wealthy partner and lovely home?"

"I don't know. I've no idea. But we've always assumed the dead woman was Irina."

"Igor identified her though."

Eilidh crossed her arms impatiently, flicking her foot up and down again.

"Do you really think that, stricken with grief at her death, he was in any state to observe her closely?"

"No, he wouldn't have been in a good way," agreed Richard.

"I've been wondering if it's worth asking Igor about

the tattoo that woman had on her body. He would know if Irina had that or not."

"Yes, of course it would be worth it. That's an excellent idea. But if I were you, I would take another look at the body in the morgue first and check the hair. If it has been cut after her death, I imagine it'll be jagged and crudely done. Might be a better option before you stir up a hornet's nest of problems."

Eilidh looked relieved and nodded.

"Yes, that would be a sensible thing to do. I'll do that before I make a case. I just thought I'd best run the idea by you first and see what you thought."

"What about Abdul? What does he think?"

A sheepish expression crossed Eilidh's face.

"Abdul's so sharp; he's actually quite intimidating. He doesn't suffer fools gladly. One big blunder by me and he'll dismiss anything else I have to contribute."

"As far as I'm concerned, I see nothing wrong with your idea. You can tell him that, if it helps. It's a very worthwhile point. And it shows you're thinking outside the box, which is what we need with a case like this one."

"Thanks Richard," said Eilidh, with a bright smile, bouncing up and giving him a friendly pat on the shoulder. "I'd best get going now or I'll be late to meet my friends. See you next week."

She made her way out of the room with her long stride as he held the heavy door open for her.

She left a faint whiff of jasmine and musk lingering in the air.

Richard stared at the closed door for a few moments, before sighing and turning back dutifully to his caseload.

9

Eilidh

Eilidh was feeling pleased with herself.

Dr. Celia Finch, the forensic pathologist at 109 Lambeth Road, had further corroborated her hunch. The victim's hair, on close inspection, had shown unmistakable signs of having been roughly cut with a pair of nail scissors.

What was even more satisfying to Eilidh was that Abdul had complimented her on this surprising discovery and so, for a short time at least, she felt all was right with the world.

As they made their way along the thick-carpeted corridor to Igor's room at the Baglioni Hotel, she finally felt they had a new and positive lead on the case. A lot depended on what Igor could tell them about Irina's sister.

They stopped outside Room 142 and knocked politely.

"Come in!" said Igor's gruff voice.

Abdul opened the door and walked into the room.

Igor was standing by the window, talking in Russian

to someone on his mobile. He gestured towards the two sofas on either side of the coffee table and Abdul and Eilidh obediently sat down on a cream sofa, which happened to be the one facing the window.

Eilidh stole a look at the room while Igor continued his conversation, taking note of the plush furnishings, a heady combination of gold, black and cream decor.

She itched to look at the bathroom.

Eilidh had developed a fetish for posh bathrooms ever since her grandmother had taken her as a young girl to the Ladies" Room at Harrods. Bored by the endless display of consumer goods in Harrods and irritated by the crowds that jostled her rudely as they made their way to the food department, she found the Ladies" Room an absolute haven of peace and tranquility and was soon lost in admiration at the pristine, vintage quality of its decor.

From that moment onwards Eilidh had always taken an obsessive interest in everything related to plush bathrooms: the decor, fixtures, the soaps, hand creams and towels. Two years ago, an ex-boyfriend had shown he had noted her secret passion when he had booked them a memorable long-weekend break at the five- star Ellenborough Park Hotel in the Cotswolds. Needless to say, he booked the room which had the most stunning bathroom attached to it.

Before Eilidh succumbed to her madness and was tempted to stand up to take a sneaky peek at the bathroom in Igor's hotel room, Igor finished his call and then turned to face them, his expression remorseful.

"I'm sorry to be so rude, but it was an important phone call from Russia. It's very hard to run the business from here."

"We totally understand," said Abdul, as Igor sat down heavily on the sofa opposite them. "We're grateful to you for giving us more of your time."

"I'm very happy to do anything I can to help," confirmed Igor, leaning back on the sofa cushions and crossing his legs.

It was a strangely relaxed posture for a man being interviewed about his dead girlfriend but it also hinted at openness and transparency. Certainly the impression Igor had given them, Eilidh thought, was of a man who was habitually blunt and honest without losing that finesse that was clearly a by-product of his upbringing.

"Igor, would you be able to tell us the name of Irina's sister?"

Igor's eyes sharpened with interest.

"Irina's sister? Why?"

"We think she might be in some way involved in what happened."

Igor's face showed his disappointment and scorn.

"That's an utterly absurd supposition. I've never met her and I'm pretty certain Irina wasn't on speaking terms with her sister."

This off-putting comment didn't deter Abdul in the slightest. Eilidh could almost see Abdul brushing off Igor's blatant lack of faith in them as he prepared to repeat the question.

She admired his tenacity. It wasn't easy confronting a man of Igor's stature with a few unpleasant truths about his girlfriend.

"Even so, sir, we'd be grateful if you could supply us with the name of Irina's sister."

Clasping his hands together, Igor frowned at Abdul.

"Her sister was called Tatiana. Tatiana Kapitsa," he said reluctantly.

Abdul nodded and smiled his gratitude, hoping to encourage him to open up a little more.

"Thank you, sir. That's very helpful. I believe you said Irina originally came from Vladivostok?"

Igor nodded.

"I'd like to ask you if Irina had any tattoos on her."

Igor looked surprised.

"Tattoos? No! Tattoos are so... plebeian. Horrible," said Igor, his lips curling in disgust.

There was a poignant pause as Igor stared in confusion at them. Eilidh could see by the expression on his face that Igor was struggling to see where they were leading him but he was still trying hard to figure it out.

"Are you absolutely sure? No tattoos on her chest at all? For example, in between her breasts?"

"No, no, no and no!" growled Igor angrily. "I'm absolutely sure. What on earth are you on about?"

Eilidh placed a close up photo, taken of the chest of the dead body, in front of Igor. The strange circular tattoo was clearly visible between the two breasts.

There was a heavy silence as Igor bent forward and studied the photo.

"What's this?" he asked finally, in a bewildered voice.

"It's a photo of the dead body. That tattoo was on it."

There was another long silence as Igor sat immobile, looking down blankly at the photograph. After a while Igor averted his eyes from the photo and glowered angrily at Abdul and Eilidh.

"Are you trying to tell me that someone tattooed

Irina? She would have never allowed that to happen. A crass symbol like that? Never. Some maniac must have done it after she was killed."

Eilidh cleared her throat.

"Did you know Irina's sister was an identical twin?"

Igor shook his head silently, his piercing eyes unwavering as they watched her. Eilidh began to feel the sweat prickling at the back of her neck, gathering under her armpits and beneath her short fringe. God, she hated this job sometimes.

"Well, it turns out Irina did have an identical twin and she was with her sister on the day of the murder," she continued. "We now have three people at number 40 De Vere Gardens who are willing to testify to that. It turns out Irina's sister wasn't as well dressed as her and had long black hair but otherwise they were identical."

Eilidh came to an abrupt stop, hoping Abdul would come to her rescue.

"The thing is, sir," said Abdul smoothly, sensing that Eilidh was weakening. "Inspector Simmons asked the forensic pathologist to have another look at the hair of the victim and the pathologist subsequently confirmed the victim's hair had been crudely cut with what seems to be a pair of nail scissors."

"Go on," said Igor grimly.

"It led to Inspector Simmons wondering if maybe the victim wasn't actually Irina. She thought the victim might be Irina's twin sister, Tatiana. There's also the tattoo of course, which you yourself were unable to identify."

"Are you suggesting Irina might actually be alive?"

"Yes, sir," agreed Eilidh quietly. "That's what we're now thinking."

"So someone has kidnapped Irina and has imprisoned her somewhere?"

Eilidh didn't miss the hopeful note in Igor's voice and her heart sank. Igor still hadn't clocked it, and whose fault was that? She had no idea.

"No, sir," replied Abdul firmly, as ever keeping his cool. "That's not what we're thinking. Forensics have been through your flat thoroughly. There's no other DNA or forensic evidence suggesting someone else was involved or was even in the flat that day. There's been no sightings of any stranger entering the building or of anyone else accompanying Irina, other than her sister."

Igor's face drained of colour.

For a moment Eilidh was convinced he was going to faint. She got up quickly and grabbed a glass tumbler from the sideboard. Opening up the mini bar, she grabbed two miniature bottles of whisky and poured them into the glass.

She walked over to where Igor was sitting frozen on the sofa and passed him the tumbler. He took it in his hand and looked dazedly into it for a moment, before lifting it to his mouth and emptying it in four gulps.

Being Russian, vodka might have been more to Igor's taste but Eilidh remembered Igor drinking whisky during their first interview with him. She herself had a weakness for a tipple of whisky and felt it was bound to be beneficial, opening up his capillaries and other blood vessels and in doing so preventing the poor man from fainting.

"We've managed to track down a flight to Moscow with Tatiana Kapitsa on it... Leaving London the day after the murder," added Abdul softly.

Igor stubbornly shook his head in denial. Abdul

moved forwards so he was sitting close to the edge of the sofa.

"If you don't mind me asking, do you have a joint bank account with Irina? We're wondering if there was any unusual activity on it in the run up to the murder."

Igor put down the tumbler on the table, his hands shaking slightly.

"Yes, we did have a joint account but she also had an account in her name only, with Barclays. I have, of course, had a look at our joint account. It's fine, nothing unusual. I'll have a look at her bank account, as I know all her passwords. I've not shut any of them down yet. What you're both implying, though, seems utterly fantastical to me. I mean, why would Irina ever do anything like this? It doesn't make sense. She had everything she could have wanted with me."

Everything except possibly her freedom, thought Eilidh. It seemed a cruel jest to be disillusioned at the most vulnerable point in one's life but unfortunately this now seemed to be the case for Igor.

In the silence that fell over the three of them Igor shook his head from side to side in disbelief but it wasn't long before blazing anger replaced the firm denial in his face. Then moments later the fury in Igor's face was replaced by an expression of terrible, utter desolation, so much so that Eilidh had to look away.

Abdul folded his arms across his chest.

"This is a complicated investigation," commented Abdul, a neutral expression on his chiseled face. "It's going to take some considerable time to make any headway."

Igor eyed him scornfully, not refuting his conclusion.

"We also have a problem in that any further research is going to be extremely difficult. We've no cooperation with, or access to, the Russian police. Diplomatically things are tense. So tracing Tatiana Kapitsa, or Irina as we are now assuming she is, will be tricky."

Igor sighed heavily. He then leaned forward and rubbed his eyes.

Was he wiping away the tears that were threatening to form? Eilidh couldn't tell.

"I can help you with that. When I get back to St Petersburg I'll get my people on to it and see what they can find out from the police in Russia," he said in a tired voice.

Eilidh admired the sheer stoicism of the man. Endurance seemed to her to be a very Russian trait and she had always thought of Russians as a hardy people. One only had to look at their history to see it.

Three years ago, Eilidh's aunt had gone on a trip to St Petersburg and Moscow. She had described in horrifying detail the tragic mass war graves from the siege of Leningrad (now St Petersburg) at the *Piskaryovskoe Memorial Cemetery*, as well as the magnificent palaces the tsars had built for themselves on the back of impoverished and suffering serfs.

Eilidh was no intellectual but her father had always told her that you only had to read *One Day in the Life of Ivan Denisovich*, a book describing a Soviet Labour camp, to have a true understanding of human suffering.

Suddenly the sofa creaked noisily and Eilidh came back down to earth with a jerk, losing her melancholic thoughts in the process.

She glanced up and saw that Abdul was already standing and shaking hands with Igor.

She hurriedly got up from the sofa.

"Thank you very much again for your help, Igor," said Abdul. "We're sorry to bring you so much bad news. Hopefully, between us, we'll be able to make inroads into discovering what really happened on the 23rd."

Igor smiled, but there was no warmth in his face and he said nothing.

Five minutes later Eilidh and Abdul left the room with an uneasy conscience.

Igor had assured them he'd be fine and didn't need any further support, so there was little else they could do for him. However, he hadn't looked in great shape. His facial expression was tense and immobile as he waved them off from the door of his hotel room.

For what it was worth, they had already left Igor with a Victim Information Pack on their previous visit but Eilidh was sure it had quickly found its way to the nearest wastepaper basket.

Back in the patrol car Eilidh gazed out of the front window but all she could see was Igor's ravaged face, bravely trying to conceal his doubts and his broken heart.

"You're not cut out for this," said Abdul in a dispassionate voice.

"I'm sorry?" asked Eilidh in surprise.

"You're not cut out for this kind of work, Si. You're too soft."

Abdul had always called Eilidh "Si". Eilidh suspected he found her name too difficult to pronounce on an everyday basis and he certainly wasn't the type to start using the public school boy mannerism of addressing people by their surnames.

"Maybe," she admitted, not being someone who took offence readily. "But it's better that way than the other way round. I might be soft on the victims of crime but I'm not in the least bit soft on criminals."

10

Richard

Richard came out of the double doors at Barajas Adolfo Suárez Airport in Madrid and felt the warm air outside caress his sun-starved skin and envelop him in a bubble of relaxation.

He looked ahead at the clear blue sky on the horizon. Back in London he had left a grey cloudy day that had been drizzling constantly from the early hours of the morning.

He walked down the long taxi rank outside the airport and when he reached the foremost taxi, the taxi driver opened the door for him and asked him for the destination.

"El Prado, por favor," Richard said in his heavily accented Spanish.

The tedious ride to the Prado Museum was done without any interaction with the driver.

Sensing straightaway with the skill born of experience that Richard was a foreigner with a limited vocabulary, the taxi driver hadn't bothered to engage him in polite chit-chat and instead put on the car radio at top volume.

Incomprehensible Spanish babbled vigorously out of the car's speakers as they drove at a slow pace along the motorway towards the city center. The traffic was surprisingly heavy and Richard could only surmise commuters were heading out early for lunch.

Once outside the Prado, Richard paid the taxi driver the fixed sum of thirty euros. The Spanish government, in order to protect guileless tourists, had determined that all taxi rides from the airport to the city center were to be charged a maximum of thirty euros.

For a brief moment Richard thought the taxi driver was going to try to convince him that the taxi fare was in fact more than this but the knowing look in Richard's eye clearly put him off and, much to Richard's relief, the taxi drove off without an altercation happening.

Richard turned and looked at the neoclassical facade of the Prado in front of him.

A statue of the famed Spanish artist Diego Velázquez, holding a paintbrush, was situated in front of six large Doric columns which were located in the center of the building. The columns spanned both floors of the Prado. Needless to say this was known as the *Velázquez* entrance to the museum, and it wasn't open to the general public.

The Prado was one of the ten most visited museums in the world and today the building in front of Richard was shining like a dazzling, bleach-white monument to grandeur, gleaming brightly like a precious jewel in the warm Spanish sunshine.

Richard turned to the left and began to make his way to the *Jerónimos* entrance as instructed by the secretary who worked for Isabel Perón, the deputy director of the Prado Museum.

He skirted around the *Goya* entrance to the building with its queues of visitors standing outside and entered the more modern *Puerta de los Jerónimos*.

Although he was here on police business, there were a few paintings in the museum he wanted to see before he left the premises.

One of his favorite artists was Diego Velázquez.

Las Meninas was perhaps the artist's most generally revered painting but Richard had a soft spot for the *Equestrian Portrait of Prince Balthasar Charles*, with its ridiculously barrel-bodied horse, and also *The Surrender of Breda*, a blatant propagandist painting that not only showed off the might of the Spanish troops but also their magnanimity towards the defeated enemy. Richard was certain that in another life Velázquez would have been a renowned public relations executive.

The Prado also had a large collection of Francisco Goya's paintings and Richard planned to stop briefly by some of the most treasured paintings by this late eighteenth- and early nineteenth-century artist.

Instead of the two famous and voyeuristic *La Maja* paintings by Francisco Goya, Richard infinitely preferred Goya's *The Third of May 1808*, an emotional portrayal of Spanish resistance to Napoleon's armies. It was a painting that evoked such universal horror and suffering that it could apply to any war or armed conflict.

He also somehow could never forget Goya's farcical, cartoonish portrayal of the Spanish royal family in his painting *Charles IV of Spain and His Family*. Honored by the royal family as a court painter, the cheeky artist still managed to make them look like complete imbeciles.

Goya and Velázquez both had a sense of humor and that was one of the main reasons why Richard liked them so much as artists.

In a comical Velázquez painting, *Apollo in the Forge of Vulcan,* Apollo tells Vulcan his wife Venus is having an affair with Mars, the god of war.

The artist seemed to relish the theme and portrays the statuesque figures listening to the news with ludicrous expressions on their faces. Apollo's posture and face reflects his overblown ego, Vulcan looks as though he is about to explode and the other three men, positioned to one side like a male version of *The Three Graces*, appear gormless and stupefied by Apollo's message.

Trust a Spaniard, thought Richard, to know how to best convey extreme emotion and humor.

The very last stop on his wish list, on this whirlwind tour before departing the Prado, was going to be the room with the paintings by the impressionist Joaquín Sorolla. Widely described as the master of light, the Spanish artist managed to capture the enjoyment as well as the beauty of the outdoors.

The Prado owned two well-known paintings by this artist, *Walk on the Beach* and *Children on the Beach.*

Richard's favorite Sorolla work, however, was *The White Boat, Jávea.*

In that masterpiece Sorolla had painted two naked boys holding on to a boat as they swam in the sea, with a skill that in Richard's opinion rivaled that of David Hockney in his swimming pool paintings.

Sadly, *The White Boat, Jávea* belonged to a private

collector and therefore could only be seen on the rare occasion there was an organized exhibition of the artist's work.

For now, though, Richard knew he was going to have to concentrate his mind on only one painting, El Greco's painting of a Spanish princess...

Richard strolled into the main entrance of the museum and waited patiently behind a group of Chinese tourists to speak to one of the retail attendants at the front desk.

When he reached the front of the queue he was confronted with a diminutive and pretty brunette whose angelic face was marred by an expression of utter boredom.

"Por favor, tengo cita con la subdirectora Isabel Perón. A la una. Soy Richard Langley," he said to her politely as she looked at him with impatience written all over her face.

A tinge of reluctant respect crept into the receptionist's large brown eyes.

"Espere un momento," she said, lifting up her index finger at him in a patronizing way as she picked up her phone.

Richard surmised this girl was now on some kind of a power trip but he had learnt to have plenty of humility as a result of working within his undervalued and underfunded department. Throwing an infantile strop was not his style.

Refusing to be riled by her pompous attitude, he looked around the crowded hallway and studied with pleasure the white marble statue that was situated directly in front of a poppy-red wall.

After talking to someone on the phone, too quickly

for him to follow what she was saying, the attendant gestured to the left-hand side of the desk.

"Espere ahí por favor," she said, summarily dismissing Richard and looking past his shoulder at the man behind him.

Richard loped off and stood to the left of the front desk, wondering how long Isabel would keep him waiting there. As it turned out he didn't have to stand there for long.

A striking, tall woman with her long black curly hair restrained by a red bandana and dressed in a bright red suit with black wedges, walked through the entrance on the far side of the room. Isabel was wearing stylish black-rimmed glasses and she peered myopically at the various groups standing around the entrance as she searched for him.

As Richard began to walk towards her she clocked him, a huge smile breaking across her face and as soon as he was close enough, she reached up and gave him an enthusiastic double kiss on his cheeks.

"Richard! I'm so pleased to see you! How long has it been? Three, four years? Too long, my friend."

"I know, I know. It's been a while certainly, although it hasn't felt like it."

Isabel wagged a finger, admonishing him.

"You've been too busy. I can see that. That's not the kind of news someone like me likes to hear. We're the custodians of art and we're always terrified when we hear about art theft. Thankfully," she said, making the sign of the cross, "we've been spared that disaster here. As far as I know, that is."

Isabel grinned at him and shrugged.

"It's always impossible to say with a hundred per

cent certainty, of course, that no theft has occurred. Come, my friend, let's head to my office and drink some coffee or a glass of wine. Have you had lunch?"

Richard shook his head.

Isabel looked at her watch.

"One o'clock. It's too early for lunch. I'll get Marisa, my secretary, to bring us some tapas from the canteen."

She turned and made her way to the X-ray machines, waiting patiently while Richard had his briefcase scanned and checked. Richard approved of this and wasn't in the least bit offended that as an officer of the law he was getting subjected to security checks. He only wished other museums would be as scrupulous about their security.

He followed Isabel across several galleries and eventually they went through a thick metal door with a keypad that was marked *"Privado,'* leading downwards into the subterranean bowels of the building.

Ten minutes later, after walking down three different corridors, he was ensconced in Isabel's spacious office.

When entering Isabel's office, it always amused him to see that she had prints from the Reina Sofia Museum hanging up on her wall, because despite Isabel's preference for modern art, at the Prado she was surrounded by artworks of Spanish classicism.

In her room Dalí, Miró, Picasso, and Wifredo Lam prints were all vying for attention on the wall in their cheerful red, white, blue and yellow frames.

The office also had a massive, square desk dominating the center of the room. Richard knew this workspace was regularly used to check and study works of art, so the table had to be of this magnitude to fit a painting comfortably on the top of it.

Richard sat himself down on one of the cozy armchairs that were grouped together around a glass coffee table at one side of the room.

Isabel nipped out quickly to speak to her secretary and then came back in, a fiery whirlwind of activity. She sat down on a chair opposite Richard, crossed her arms and looked at him for a moment with a quizzical expression on her face.

"For your employers to have sent you all the way here, this must be serious."

Richard nodded.

"Yes, it's serious, but isn't art crime always so?" Richard asked whimsically, happy for once to be working with someone who venerated art in the way he did.

Isabel chewed her lip with obvious impatience.

"Of course it is. But some thefts are more tragic than others. Are we talking about a painting stolen from one of your galleries? I've had no notification of any major art theft the last few weeks."

"This painting was stolen from a private collector, Igor Babikov."

"Madre mía! Not *The Spanish Princess?"*

"Yes, I'm afraid so. Greco's portrait of Princess Catalina Micaela, verified by your team only last year."

Devastated, Isabel didn't seem able to speak.

She stared blindly at Richard, her face filled with overwhelming sadness and loss.

In the pervasive silence someone knocked on her office door and then knocked again impatiently when no one answered.

At the third knock on her door, Isabel stood up and went to open it.

There followed a heated, muted exchange at the half-open door, during which Isabel managed to vanquish her visitor because shortly afterwards she closed the door with a vigorous bang.

She turned to look at Richard, her face perplexed and unhappy.

"It's an absolute tragedy that portrait has gone missing, Richard. You always seem to be the bearer of bad news."

Richard nodded sympathetically, understanding and empathizing with her feelings.

"It's the nature of my job I'm afraid."

"I did a fair amount of research on that painting. I think you'll find it very interesting although it's doubtful it'll be of any help to you."

Isabel went over to where her laptop was perched on the corner of the square desk and brought it back to her seat, clasping it by the edge of its open screen.

Sitting down, she tapped on several keys and nodded with satisfaction when she saw the information she was looking for.

"El Greco was an artist so unusual he's never fitted into any one category in art history," she stated, as though lecturing a student.

Rather than getting offended by her manner Richard was intrigued to hear what she had to say. He had enormous respect for Isabel's intellect and he was also hoping to save up any nuggets of information that might help him with the case.

"Igor's portrait of Catalina Micaela was incredibly unique, Richard. For a start El Greco painted mostly male portraits so a female portrait is a rarity from this artist," Isabel continued. "And then there's the coloring in the portrait of *The Spanish Princess*. If you look at all of Domenico Greco's portraits you'll find they're mostly in somber, neutral and dark colors. He always reserved his bright colors for his surreal work on heavenly saints or for religious figures like the *Cardinal Fernando Niño de Guevara*."

Isabel turned her screen around and showed him El Greco's portrait of his son, *Jorge Manuel Theotocópuli*, and another portrait called *The Nobleman with his Hand on his Chest*. Both were dark portraits that seemed to have been composed mainly out of a white, brown and black palette.

Lastly she brought up on her laptop an image of the colorful but rather intimidating portrait of the *Cardinal Fernando Niño de Guevara* and showed it to Richard as an example of a portrait where colour and religion were linked together, with the yellow background and the red clerical garments of the Cardinal set in juxtaposition to each other.

"What amazed me was how in his painting of *The Spanish Princess* the colors were so vibrant. It was astonishing to see. Take the bright orange of her dress, for example, or the turquoise blue of the chair. No other non-religious El Greco portrait has this much colour. This adds to the painting's importance and uniqueness in my view. It's the one portrait where he deviated from his normal rules."

"Which begs the question, I suppose, is it really painted by El Greco?" asked Richard calmly, voicing his inner fear that all of this was leading the way to a well-conceived fake.

Glancing up from her laptop, Isabel smiled at him with amusement. Richard understood what was implied in her smile. El Prado had staked its reputation on claiming this picture as an original El Greco and they wouldn't have done that without good cause.

"We sent it to Orion Analytical," remarked Isabel, unmoved by Richard's doubts. "The wood the canvas was attached to was radiocarbon dated to the correct era. During their testing it became clear that salient features of El Greco's work were showing up... For example the X-ray and IR reflectography scan showed that there was a substantial amount of reworking done in making this portrait, there were many complex layers in the paintwork developing gradually to the final outcome. In a similar fashion to other El Greco paintings."

Isabel looked across to Richard to make sure he was following her. Seeing that Richard was listening to her with intense interest, she returned to studying her laptop screen.

"As I said, numerous layers of paintwork were discovered in the painting. It's a key signature of his work. The fact that many different types and sizes of brushes were used in *The Spanish Princess* is also a trademark of his. The general radiopacity of the painting when scanned was characteristic of El Greco. The insistent and firm strokes used for the flesh tones of the face, the way in which the painter mixed and developed the colors in the painting, were all indicating this was an El Greco original..."

Isabel paused for a moment, thinking back to the analysis of the painting.

"He had his own unique way of mixing and using

expensive pigments like lapis lazuli... Lastly and crucially, the way in which El Greco did the lacquer work on his paintings was very complex and sophisticated. His pupils and his copyists would always find this extremely difficult to imitate which makes the identification of El Greco's work all the easier."

She looked up at Richard and shrugged.

"So we verified it as an El Greco masterpiece on the basis of the evidence provided by the laboratory and our own research. Between ourselves we named the painting *The Spanish Princess* but I don't know if Igor Babikov uses another name or title for it. It was a beautiful portrait. More accomplished, I think, than the one in Glasgow's Pollok House. Having said that, if you compare the two heads, the one of Catalina Micaela in *Lady in a Fur Wrap* with the head in *The Spanish Princess* painting, they're similarly executed."

"The only caveat I have," remarked Richard, thinking back to what he had learnt about the artist, "is that El Greco fell out with the Spanish king over some petty disagreements and he subsequently removed himself to Toledo. Why on earth would he be painting the king's daughter, Princess Catalina Micaela? Nothing in your research explains the overtly provocative portrait of her that we're assuming El Greco did."

Isabel's intelligent, brown eyes peered at him from the top of her laptop screen.

"I have my own theory about that, my friend."

There was a loud knock at the door, making them both jump in their seats, so absorbed had they been in their discussion.

Isabel lowered her laptop onto the floor and went to answer her door again.

This time she fully opened the door so that a young girl could wheel in a trolley that contained a bottle of red wine, two wine glasses and several plates of intriguing-looking tapas.

After dismissing the girl with a friendly nod, Isabel pushed the trolley along to where they were sitting, poured them a couple of glasses of wine and passed one to Richard.

"Please, help yourself. This must be well past your lunch hour."

"Yes, it is rather," admitted Richard, feeling hungry.

He leaned forward to look at the food and picked up a long piece of toast with a slice of Manchego cheese on the top of it. He chewed away contentedly while Isabel took a lingering sip of her wine.

After they had consumed an adequate amount of food Isabel wiped her hands on a napkin, reached down to the side of her chair and hauled up her laptop again. Richard admired her single-mindedness and her thoroughness. She was selflessly handing over to him all her knowledge of the painting in the hope that something would aid him when it came to locating the missing masterpiece even when both of them knew it was a forlorn hope.

Isabel stared at her laptop screen for a few moments as if pondering how to present her ideas to him.

"Domenico Greco had a mistress called Jerónima de las Cuevas and had a beloved son, Jorge Manuel, with her. He never married her and yet he loved his son so much he painted the boy into one of his most famous paintings, *The Burial of the Count of Orgaz*. As you probably already know he's the boy on the left-hand side with a pocket handkerchief inscribed with the artist's signature and the date 1578."

She looked up at Richard with an infectious smile that caused dimples to appear in each cheek.

"Most scholars generally agree with the theory that El Greco was unable to marry Jerónima because he'd left a wife back in Crete or Italy and so could not legally marry his mistress. In spite of this he mentions his mistress in various documents, including his last testament."

Isabel reached over to the trolley and poured herself another glass of wine, her dangling silver earrings tinkling and spinning gently as she did so.

She picked up the glass and cradled it in both her hands as she turned to face Richard again.

"I think El Greco's religion might have been a problem for the couple too," she declared. "Back in those days, people of different religions lived together more harmoniously than they do today. Jews, Christians, Muslims were willing to share their ideas and knowledge, but even with this open-mindedness there were limits to what their communities would accept. El Greco probably belonged to the Greek-Orthodox religion and it would have been unacceptable back in those days for a man who was Greek-Orthodox to marry a Catholic."

"I'm aware of his mistress but you still haven't explained to me how Princess Catalina Micaela comes into his life," said Richard, wondering when she was going to get to the point.

"Patience, Richard, patience," said Isabel, swallowing a mouthful of wine and putting the half-empty glass on the coffee table. "I'm getting there, don't worry!

OK, so the inscription on the back of Igor's painting says *"For Catalina Micaela, my soulmate, Doménikos Theotokópoulos"*. That suggests a close friendship at the very least: a passionate love affair at the very most. The expression on her face is that of a seductress. A normal woman with that expression on her face might appeal to many men, but for a princess? It would be considered unappetizing and singularly inappropriate for a princess to be portrayed in such a way. And yet there she is, leering out at the viewer in all her pomp."

"Exactly. It isn't credible that El Greco would've been given permission to paint the King's favorite daughter not once, but twice. Let alone with that expression on her face too."

"Well, I think you make an interesting point there, Richard, because I think it was credible. Princess Catalina Micaela was the youngest daughter of King Philip II and his favorite, too. She had her father wrapped around her little finger."

Isabel started to turn a pretty silver bracelet on her wrist, looking down at the glittering stones intertwined on its fine silver threads. Observing it, Richard thought the bracelet itself was a work of art.

"Infanta Catalina Micaela was a very strong-minded woman, as proven by her future career as the Duchess of Savoy," she said quietly, almost as though talking to herself as she continued to play with her bracelet. "She did many extraordinary things in that role and gained widespread respect for her diplomatic and political skill. As the Duchess of Savoy she protected Savoy from becoming a satellite of Spain, refusing her father's underhanded offer to send a garrison into Savoy to supposedly "protect her"."

Isabel picked up her glass of wine again and drank some more.

Taking advantage of the break, Richard turned and looked at the remains of their tapas on the trolley. Spotting an enticing slice of Spanish tortilla, sitting by itself in the middle of a plate, he picked it up and proceeded to munch it.

"Most people said Catalina influenced her husband for the better and she ruled very successfully as his regent when he was away at war," continued Isabel. As he listened to her, Richard thought that like many other academics he had come across she seemed to be very much a perfectionist in her reasoning. At this rate they could be here all day. "Catalina greatly improved the cultural life in Savoy by inviting artists to reside in Turin and by commissioning the building of an art gallery."

"Are you suggesting Catalina Micaela was the one interested in El Greco?" asked Richard, trying to speed her on.

"I think they were both interested in each other. Catalina Micaela was a very intelligent, strong and beautiful woman who had an interest in art and artists. Later on, in Turin, she hosted many acclaimed artists such as Torquato Tasso, Chiabrera, Marini, Tassoni, and Botero. And as I said she built an art gallery, so this was a woman who was interested in art. As a princess in Madrid she probably led a very cloistered life and meeting El Greco would have interested her and allowed her to access a different world. He was from Crete and had the experience of living and working in Italy, the hub of Renaissance art."

"Isabel, I'm not sure where you're leading with all

of this. Are you suggesting that she was the one who requested her portrait to be done by El Greco?"

"No, no, of course not. I think it was a request from the King. I'm sure that before King Philip II suddenly (and strangely in my view) lost interest in El Greco's work, El Greco had been commissioned by the King to paint a portrait of his favorite daughter, Infanta Catalina Micaela. That's the one you now have in Glasgow, *Lady in a Fur Wrap*. I suspect that out of the sittings for the one portrait the artist managed to work on another painting that the King was never supposed to see."

The room was silent as Isabel watched Richard, trying to see how he would respond to this theory. They eyed each other up tentatively.

"It still seems a little far-fetched to me," remarked Richard, feeling guilty for refuting her convictions.

"I knew you'd say that! I've uncovered more evidence to support my theory. After seeing Igor Babikov's painting I started doing some research in my own time. I knew I had to dig deeper into that era and I requested permission to go to the AGS to immerse myself in their records. I spent a substantial amount of time trawling through the royal archives there."

"The AGS? What on earth is that?"

"The General Archive of Simancas. In the town of Simancas. It's where all the official, royal archives of that period were kept. Anyway, I found buried beneath a long inventory of staff working at the palace and their expenses two very interesting documents. A birth certificate dated 1582 for a child called Eleni Catalina Trastámara signed by a priest and by King Philip II, stating her mother as "Infanta Catalina

Micaela". There's no father mentioned on the certificate."

"Incredible. You're suggesting El Greco fathered a daughter with La Infanta Catalina Micaela?"

Isabel laughed at Richard's surprise and nodded.

"I am. The birth occurred close to the end of El Greco's commissions with the King. The child was given a Greek name, Eleni. The Spanish version would be Elena. Trastámara is a name that comes from a dynasty of Spanish kings."

"Have you told anyone about this?"

"I shared it with two of my colleagues who verified the painting with me. Other than that I've not told anyone. Igor Babikov, despite our pleas, wanted his painting to remain hidden in obscurity."

"What you're saying puts El Greco in a new light. I hadn't pictured him as a Lothario brave enough to mess with the King's daughter."

"El Greco wanted to be employed by King Philip, don't forget that. That's the reason why he went to Madrid in the first place. I think what happened between him and *La Infanta* was totally unpremeditated. I believe it was a case of sexual attraction and mutual chemistry breaking through the social norms of the time. It does also in part explain why El Greco spent the rest of his life out of Madrid, in Toledo. I don't think the King would have tolerated his presence in Madrid."

"Do you think El Greco knew about the child?"

"I doubt it. He was a loving and fond parent to his illegitimate son. I can't see him ignoring his own daughter. No, I think the royal family kept this secret. There was another document next to the birth certificate, dated 1582 and signed by the Mother Superior of the Convent of La Virgin de la Paz in Sevilla. This document formally accepts a baby girl called Eleni Catalina Trastámara into the convent."

Isabel put her laptop on the floor again much to Richard's relief. Fascinating as this was, his meeting had gone on for far longer than he had anticipated and he still had to go and visit his contact at the Heritage Team, based in the Central Operational Unit of the Guardia Civil, before heading back to London.

He had already decided he wasn't going to have enough time to revisit his favorite paintings in the Prado.

"Intrigued, I went to this convent in Sevilla," commented Isabel, oblivious to Richard's time-keeping anxiety. "The convent still functions as a convent to this very day and I asked the nuns if they could find out for me what happened to Eleni Catalina. After a month and a half I heard back from them. It turns out the girl was adopted, barely six months old, by a wealthy nobleman and his wife from Sevilla: Enrique and Francesca Arrazola."

11

Richard

Having arrived back at Heathrow again, Richard took the Piccadilly line to the South Kensington Tube stop and got off the train, exiting the crowded station with some relief. He stopped at Tesco Express for some pasta and sliced chicken, then walked along Sumner Place until he reached Fulham Road, tracing the familiar route home without even thinking about it.

Making his way across Fulham Road in the chilly dusk, he turned right into Drayton Gardens and strolled onwards, through the handsome and prosperous street, until he came to a stop in front of Grove Court, a tall, red-brick building with its windows edged with white paint.

At the top of the steps, he put his key into the front door lock and turned it. Pushing open the heavy door with his shoulder, he then walked over to the lift and ascended up to his small, two-bedroom flat on the top floor.

Many of his work colleagues thought of him as posh and he knew they were right.

There was no way that he could have afforded this flat on his police salary but he happened to be the lucky beneficiary of his parents" generosity and he was very grateful for their munificence because it enabled him to live in a part of London that he loved.

To live within easy distance of the Victoria and Albert Museum was something that he would never take for granted. He often by-passed the huge queues and tour groups outside both the Science Museum and the Natural History Museum on his way to the relative peace and quiet of the Victoria and Albert Museum.

Richard revered the place. He spent hours of his free time exploring the vast art and design collections in the museum and he never grew tired of it. In his opinion the Victoria and Albert Museum was underappreciated. There were plenty of gimmicks that appealed to both kids and adults in the Science Museum and the Natural History Museum but for the sheer quality and beauty of its contents he felt the Victoria and Albert Museum deserved to have the same crowds as the other two.

Having reached the top floor of his building, he walked along the corridor and opened the door to his flat, relishing hearing the habitual groan of the old hinges as he did so. A creature of habit, he dumped his briefcase next to the front door and went straight through to the sitting room where he then switched on the gas fire, wanting to chase away the autumnal cold that had penetrated through his thin jacket on the way home.

He left the room to heat up and went to the kitchen to make himself a cup of tea, enjoying the tranquility after having been stuck on the underground train for forty-five minutes, with its noisy tannoy system blaring out instructions at frequent intervals.

All he could hear within the confines of his flat was his large kitchen wall clock, ticking away contentedly. After swallowing a mouthful of the hot, soothing brew he went back to the sitting room and sat down as close as possible to the fire.

He took his phone out of his trouser pocket and switched it on.

Straightaway it started buzzing with messages.

He had two voicemails. The first one was from his mother, asking him if he was free to drop by for Sunday lunch in "the next month"; her tone was clipped and sharper than usual which suggested she was annoyed about the amount of time that had elapsed since he last saw them. The second voicemail was from Abdul, his normally reasoned and calm voice sounding strangely agitated, telling him there was a meeting arranged in Room 402 for ten o'clock the next morning.

There were three text messages, two of them from university friends who wanted to meet up for a drink. The third was from Eilidh Simmons and it said enigmatically, *"the men in blue have officially lost it"*.

Intrigued, Richard had a quick look at his work emails to see if any light could be shed on Eilidh's brief text and Abdul's voice message. Sure enough there was a short email from Lionel Grieves:

> *Dick, I need you to be at the meeting arranged for tomorrow. Room 402, 10 o'clock. Please prepare to report back on any information you have gleaned from Madrid.*

Richard took another thoughtful sip of his tea and then turned to watch the flames dancing away energetically in the fireplace. The flames pirouetted and waved with careless abandon and Richard found it strangely therapeutic, similar to watching fish in a tank of water turning around, cruising for a little while and then darting here and there as they floated about their watery kingdom.

Yet however much he tried to relax he still couldn't help thinking about the meeting arranged for the next day. What information did he really have to report back on?

A tenuous theory from Isabel regarding *The Spanish Princess* that probably had no relevance to the case at all.

A meeting with a senior police officer called Gonzalo Madraso, from the Heritage Team in Madrid, that had yielded a modest amount of information about Victoria Bretanzos Forentin, the lady Irina had sent a poster tube to the day before the painting went missing.

Finding it hard to believe that such a valuable painting would have been sent in a poster tube to Spain, the Heritage Team in Madrid were reluctant to approach Victoria Bretanzos Forentin with any query relating to the case, unless more evidence came to light.

Richard had been informed that Victoria was the hereditary owner of a well-known glassware company called Forentin Cristalería. Apparently Forentin Cristalería had existed for several generations in Spain, increasingly building up a worldwide reputation based on the quality of its glassware.

Victoria was 54 years old, divorced with two children. She had a reputation as a tough businesswoman, gradually constructing a monopoly for her company by buying up her competitors, and she circulated socially with the top tier of *Madrileño* society.

The result of all of this being that without more proof the Spanish police were not going to get involved and question Victoria about any packages she may or may not have received from Irina Kapitsa.

Richard knew without a doubt he was going to have to dress things up a bit tomorrow to make it seem like he hadn't been wasting his time in Madrid. Judging by his curt email, Lionel Grieves didn't sound like he was in a particularly forgiving or accommodating mood.

With a sigh, Richard reached for his music control and switched on *Everybody Digs Bill Evans*. As the jazzy notes melodiously echoed around the small room, Richard pulled another chair across and lifted both feet up onto it.

It was his opinion that every police officer had to find some haven or escape from the job if they wanted to survive its rigors mentally intact, and as far as he was concerned, his home was the one place that provided him with the much-needed solace and comfort from the disappointments of his work life.

He leaned back contentedly on his armchair, enjoying the lyrics, and began to gaze at the wall opposite him which shelved his meager but much treasured collection of Art Nouveau artifacts: an original bronze Tiffany lamp with a leaded wisteria glass shade in delicate lilac, milk-white and pastel green colors, a goblet designed by Otto Prutscher and a Palime König iridescent vase with its swirling metal tones ranging from green-blue to pale yellow to blushing pink at the top.

He derived so much pleasure from looking at and

studying his tiny collection that he couldn't help but feel a great deal of empathy for Igor.

Thinking back to the photos of Igor Babikov's lost painting, he really felt he couldn't blame the man for wanting to keep a stunning work of art within easy reach. Risky and unsafe as it was to have such a picture hanging up on his bedroom wall, Richard could understand Igor's wish to view the cherished artwork on a daily basis, within the privacy of his own home.

Beautiful artworks were made for viewing but even within this remit there was a moral code. Richard detested those criminals who considered it acceptable to steal public artworks in order to enjoy their aesthetic value in the privacy of their home.

This way of thinking led him to do some soul-searching and consider if he felt any less distressed by the theft of *The Spanish Princess* because it was a privately owned artwork. In the end he had decided he was equally upset by its loss because while the portrait had been in Igor's possession there was always a chance that El Greco's wonderful picture could one day be loaned for public viewing, whereas now it was stolen it was unlikely to voluntarily surface again. Whoever had nicked the painting from Igor would take good care it wasn't seen by anyone who could call its ownership into question.

He often wondered if Igor's painting was now hanging on someone's wall but even when he began to try to tentatively work out what kind of a person was most likely to have wanted Igor's painting and what role Irina could have taken in its disappearance, he came to realise it was impossible to come to any conclusions about the location of the painting.

The truth was, it could be anywhere by now.

However, he didn't feel all was lost... Even at this late stage they still had so many leads to follow through on; all it required was patience and tenacity.

Richard had heard before he left for Madrid that Igor had apparently uncovered new information on the case from the police in Russia.

They also had to do thorough interviews with the staff at Oliver's restoration firm and find out what Max was hiding from them. Richard was certain he knew something relevant to the case but getting him to talk wasn't going to be easy. Richard was pretty sure he would not have conspired to do anything detrimental to the painting itself, given his obvious appreciation and respect for the paintings he worked on.

But the man knew something...

He also needed to chase up Mike Telford and give him a firm nudge or reminder about the case. It was quite possible Mike had succeeded in tracking down further information on the stolen painting but he was a busy man, a man who was held in esteem and wanted by art collectors from around the world, so he didn't tend to check in with Richard very often.

He decided he would try and speak to Mike Telford before his ten o'clock meeting the next day, gambling on the chance that Mike might be able to give him something worthwhile to present to Lionel Grieves.

Looking at the clock on his mantelpiece he saw it was eight o'clock. It was still early for someone like Mike, who tended to work during the twilight hours and was never contactable before midday.

He picked up his mobile and dialed Mike's number. As usual, the phone rang out for a long time and at any second Richard expected to hear Mike's voicemail message.

There was a loud click on the other side.

"Bloody hell!" said Mike's voice before a resounding crash sounded in the background.

"Mike?"

There was no answer.

"Mike? Are you there?"

There was the sound of scraping and heavy panting which ended with a groan.

"Mike, are you OK?" asked Richard, starting to feel concerned.

"Yeah, I'm fine. Not sure this cellar is though. I seem to have toppled several crates of hundred-year-old wine onto the floor. Collateral damage..."

"You're in a cellar?"

"Sure am. I'm in Füssen, a town in Bavaria. What can I do for you, Richard?"

Richard knew better than to ask what he was up to.

"I was calling to see if you'd had any leads on the Greco painting. We've a meeting tomorrow, and so far I haven't come up with anything remotely useful."

"Richard, I'm sorry but nothing has come up at all. Not a crumb. I would've contacted you if it had."

There was a companionable silence for a moment between the two of them, spanning the many miles of sea and land.

Richard sighed.

"OK, thanks anyway. Thought it was worth a try."

"Lionel squeezing you hard?" asked Mike sympathetically.

"Well, patience was never one of his virtues, Mike. You know what it's like with art theft and Lionel lives in a world of targets and completions. It doesn't matter, we'll just have to brave the storm tomorrow. Even if he takes us off the case, I'm determined to continue working on it. I'm not prepared to let that painting vanish into thin air."

"I do wonder what they were thinking when they put Lionel in charge of the Art and Antiquities Unit. I mean, it isn't as though he's someone who has an appreciation or understanding of fine art."

Richard smiled to himself.

"No, he doesn't like art but he's willing to bend the rules at times and that can be very useful."

Mike grunted, obviously not convinced by this argument.

"OK, mate. I should be back in London in the next week or so. I'll send out feelers again for you but it's not looking good at the moment, I'm afraid to say."

"Thanks, Mike. I appreciate it. Enjoy the rest of your Bavarian stay."

"I certainly will! I've discovered Bavarian beer is in a class of its own. They're true connoisseurs here. See you back in town, my friend."

They hung up and Richard sat very rigidly on his chair, gazing at the fire in front of him as though hoping he could find the answers to the conundrum of *The Spanish Princess* within its flickering flames.

12

Eilidh

Eilidh woke up with a feeling of dread constricting her heart. It took a minute or two after opening her eyes to realise why it was there.

Today was going to be a matter of gearing up, as best one could, for what was probably going to be a tense bust-up in Room 402. Given the amount of time spent on this case they had come up with very little, and what little had come to light seemed to indicate the answers were going to be found across the continent in Russia.

Lionel was going to be livid.

She reached across and touched her bedside light gently.

It switched on with a familiar, faint orange glow. She lifted up her wrist and squinted blearily at her watch dial. It was half five in the morning, early enough at this time of year for it still to be dark outside.

She sighed, knowing full well she wasn't going to get back to sleep any time soon. She sat up and pushed the duvet away from her with a vigorous shove, doing so before her resolve weakened and she was tempted to stay inside her warm cocoon.

Swinging her legs across to the side of her bed she slipped on her sheepskin slippers and walked across the creaky old floorboards to the bedroom door.

Hanging on the back of the door was a thick, faux-fur dressing gown with leopard spots on it and a furry hood. She slipped it on and, because it was cold and she was feeling fragile, she lifted the hood up over her head, tucking it in tightly around her face.

She opened the old wooden door as quietly as she could and tiptoed down the narrow winding staircase, down two floors to the kitchen in the basement. The ancient stone floor seemed to radiate the early morning chill and Eilidh was thankful she had put on her sheep-skin slippers.

She ran the tap and filled the bright red kettle up until it was nearly full, knowing that she was going to need more than one mug of tea this morning.

Switching the kettle on, she then reached up to the shelf above the sink and brought down a large vintage teapot with a cracked royal-blue glaze on it.

Taking off its lid, she carelessly tossed in two Tetley teabags.

She stared into space while the kettle boiled, and once it had clicked off noisily she lifted it and poured the steaming water over the teabags. She stirred the teabags with a fork from the draining board, replaced the teapot lid and then poured herself a large mug of tea.

"Eilidh, are you OK?" asked a croaky voice at the doorway.

"Oh Gran, I'm sorry for waking you up," said Eilidh

contritely as she turned around to look at her grandmother.

Audrey Simmons walked into the kitchen wearing only her duffle pajamas and looking skeletally thin. Her cropped white hair and black eyes looked strangely youthful against a face that was sunken and lined with a multitude of little wrinkles.

She went up to Eilidh and patted her on the cheek.

"Don't be silly, my love, I was awake anyway," she said hoarsely.

"Is the immunotherapy bothering you again?"

Audrey nodded and touched the bag attached to her arm.

"This is my bad week. I suspect it's always going to be like this for as long as they treat me."

Eilidh smiled sadly.

"Can I get you some tea, Gran?"

"No, don't think I can stomach that just now. I'll have some Coca-Cola with a straw please," said Audrey, settling herself down on a kitchen chair.

Audrey's appetite had vanished with the immunotherapy treatment for her esophageal cancer. She had been told to have calorific drinks to help keep her weight steady but even then it was an uphill struggle because the stent the doctors had inserted to keep her esophagus open made it uncomfortable for Audrey to speak or eat, and the drugs given to her every three weeks made her feel sick, upsetting her stomach.

Eilidh always had her eye on her phone these days, waiting for the one day when she'd have to rush back home to help Audrey get to the hospital. For now Eilidh and her brother had arranged for carers to come in and help Audrey while they were at work. She wasn't sure, though, how much longer this arrangement would hold up.

"What's bothering you, Eilidh?" asked Audrey, sensing her granddaughter's anxiety and watching her with a concerned face.

Eilidh didn't answer.

Instead she brought a glass to the pine table and poured out some flat Coca-Cola from a half-empty bottle on the kitchen worktop. Stretching out, she grabbed a pink plastic straw from the multi-coloured batch lying on the center of the table and put it into the glass. She placed the glass in front of her grandmother and then went to the fridge, pulling out a milk carton and pouring the milk into her cup of tea.

Walking back to the table she left the carton out on the worktop. It was cold in the kitchen at this time in the morning so the milk would stay fresh for a while yet.

Audrey Simmons took a long drink through the straw, swallowing uncomfortably as she did so.

"There's not going to be many of my teeth left at the end of this," Audrey remarked philosophically once she'd stopped to take a breath.

Eilidh nodded.

Audrey reached across and laid her hand on top of Eilidh's.

Eilidh looked down at her grandmother's hand, noting the bulbous weaving of blue and red veins on it and thinking that despite being physically frailer, her grandmother was a much stronger woman than her. She had after all brought up her grandchildren single-handed after their mentally ill mother had taken her own life.

"We've a tough meeting at work today," commented

Eilidh, warming her other hand on her mug of tea. "I kind of wish I could stay out of it. I've been on the receiving end of Lionel's temper before and it's very unpleasant. It's guaranteed to be a nightmare because Abdul's absolutely determined to try and persuade Lionel to agree to send some of us to speak to the police in St Petersburg."

Eilidh gulped down her tea and, like a small child looking for comfort, kept her other hand under her grandmother's.

"Of course all of this is happening because Igor Babikov has requested that we go to Russia but even that isn't going to make it happen. It's absolutely pointless asking for it and it's just going to wind Lionel up. He's already totally fed up with our lack of progress in this case."

"If he's so fed up with your lack of progress, he might well agree to it."

"He never will. We're on the worst possible terms with Russia these days. He just can't authorize it."

Eilidh looked down into her mug of tea as if in there she'd find the answers to the day's problems.

She heard her grandmother sipping up the dregs of her Coca-Cola and got up to pour some more into her glass.

She gave herself a stern mental shake as she did so and when she came back to her chair she started to talk to her grandmother about her friend's plans for the Easter holidays.

Four hours later, back at New Scotland Yard, she still hadn't seen any sign of Abdul so she made her way down to Richard Langley's office and poked her head in through the half-open door.

Richard was crouched over a plastic box on the floor, looking at something with the avid attention of a naturalist.

"Richard, are you heading up to the meeting at 402?"

"Yep. In just a minute."

Eilidh walked into Richard's office and peered into the box. It seemed to contain a huge quantity of delicately carved ivory pieces: miniature elephants, people, dogs, birds and lions. All jumbled up on top of each other.

"Confiscated from a shop in Hampstead. An undercover journalist posing as a Chinese businessman walked in and was shown them. Unfortunately these don't appear to be antiques... They're recently made."

"What's going to happen to them?"

"They'll be stored with all the other confiscated ivory at Border Force's headquarters near Heathrow."

Eilidh glanced impatiently at her watch.

"Richard, we're going to be late for the meeting."

Richard looked at her with an eyebrow raised.

"Needing some Dutch courage are we?"

"Touché. I deserved that."

Richard smiled at her.

"No, you didn't," he said, replacing the lid on the box and carrying it across to a shelf on the other side of the room.

"Now I understand why there's a keypad on the door and no windows to this room," remarked Eilidh as she watched him.

"Yes, it's secure but also very claustrophobic. I get fed up opening the door to people so occasionally when I'm in here I keep the door slightly open."

Eilidh looked disapprovingly at Richard.

"Anyone could walk in here, clout you over the head and make off with the valuables," she scolded.

Richard laughed.

"If they can get through security on the floor above and then find their way to this room, in this veritable rabbit warren of a basement, they deserve a reward. Although they wouldn't get far if they did manage to take something," he added hastily, seeing Eilidh's expression. "My friends in surveillance watch this room too."

Richard pointed to the two corners of the room where a CCTV camera was positioned.

Eilidh didn't say anything. She was a perfectionist by nature and she wasn't sure she approved of Richard's lackadaisical approach to his work.

She waited outside while Richard cleared up the room and made sure the door was shut properly.

As they made their way to the glass lift, each of them lost in their own thoughts, Eilidh felt like they were two downtrodden peasants heading towards a sorry fate at the gallows as they headed to Room 402, but Richard was in a very different mood to hers; he was humming tunelessly to himself and he seemed surprisingly cheerful.

She began to wonder if he'd ever been confronted with Lionel's infamous temper.

13

Richard

Lionel was waiting for them in Room 402.

Abdul had at last materialized and was sitting at one end of the conference table.

Richard and Eilidh walked in and sat down without bothering to give the others any superfluous greeting.

Richard noticed Eilidh was sitting as far away as possible from Lionel, further along the table on his right-hand side whereas Lionel was seated on his left.

"Good of you two to make it on time," said Lionel, sarcastic.

Neither of them bothered to reply.

"Right, who's going to report to me first?" asked Lionel, sounding disappointed that Richard and Eilidh hadn't been baited into responding to his sarcasm.

It was obvious to everyone in the room that if they had made up some lame excuses for their lateness, it would have enabled Lionel to release some of the pent-up frustration that was bubbling under the surface of his outwardly professional demeanour.

"Happy to go first, sir," said Richard, determined to get what was likely to be an unproductive meeting over and done with, so they could get on with their other work.

Eilidh's face showed that she thought Richard's bravado verged on complete foolhardiness. Abdul, on the other hand, seemed mildly impressed by Richard's valor.

"This should be interesting," remarked Lionel. "I hope you haven't been wasting police time and taxpayers'" money over in Madrid? You appreciate that I had to put myself on the line for you to be allowed to go there?"

"Of course, sir. I understand that."

Lionel looked up from his notebook and turned his gimlet-sharp eyes onto Richard.

"Amusing yourself at my expense, Dick?"

"No, sir."

"Good. Carry on."

"I met with Isabel Perón who is the deputy director for the Prado Museum. After talking to her I think we can say the painting's validity and authenticity still stand intact. They've studied it fairly extensively."

There was silence in the room as the others waited to hear what else Richard discovered during his time in Madrid.

"As far as the background to the painting goes, after doing some research she came to the conclusion that El Greco had an affair with the painting's subject, Princess Catalina Micaela. Historically, this is breaking new ground. She thinks she's found evidence that they had a love child called Eleni Catalina. According to the records she's unearthed, this love child was accepted at the age of six months into the Convent of La Virgin de la Paz in Seville and later an aristocratic couple adopted the child."

There was another long pause.

"Is that bloody well it? Some crazy nonsense about a love child?" exploded Lionel. "Is that all we have?"

"Er, not entirely, sir. I also went to the Heritage Unit in Madrid to ask about Victoria Bretanzos Forentin. If you remember, this was the lady Rosamie mailed the poster tube to the day before the murder happened. She's the owner of a prosperous glassware company called Forentin Cristalería. The police aren't keen to ask her any questions until we've more evidence proving the poster tube could be relevant to this case."

"So you've damn well come back with nothing. Bloody nothing. Three damn weeks... Three weeks gone by and we've absolutely no idea what's going on with either the painting or the murdered victim."

Lionel put his head down, his elbows on the table, and started to pull at his ears in an unnervingly manic manner.

Richard wanted to contradict him and say that it was thanks to Eilidh they had discovered the victim was not Igor's girlfriend, but in fact her sister. Everyone agreed this put an entirely different complexion on the case.

Although Lionel must know about this new development regarding the murder victim, Richard thought it was unlikely that Lionel would be aware it had all been Eilidh's brainchild, but catching sight of Eilidh's apprehensive face next to him he decided to stay silent.

He didn't think she would appreciate him bringing her into the conversation.

"What's happened to Mike Telford? He's usually the one who sorts these cases out for you, Dick, isn't he?" asked Lionel in a petulant voice.

Richard wished for a moment that Lionel would go outside and get his nicotine fix before they continued with this conversation.

"Mike Telford has had nothing back on this painting as yet. I spoke to him last night," replied Richard.

"You're bloody useless, you know that, Dick? You might as well have handed over to some criminal a multi-million-pound masterpiece with your good wishes. It's a fucking disaster."

Richard began to feel his temper rising. Lionel was starting to get under his skin, but before he was tempted to say something he would regret later, Abdul stepped in.

"Sir, Igor Babikov's requesting that we go to St Petersburg and speak to the police there. It seems they've been digging up some interesting information on Igor's behalf. They're keen to meet with us and see how we can work together on this case."

Lionel snorted like a raging bull.

"This is the icing on the cake... After what they did in Salisbury they expect us to go to St Petersburg and speak to them? What planet is Igor Babikov on? Over my dead body, and I'm telling you now, Abdul, with next to no progress on this case I'm not paying out any more money or authorizing any more overseas travel."

"Igor Babikov says he'll arrange and pay for our visit himself and we don't have to go in an official capacity."

"Of course, why not take a leaf out of their book and go undercover as tourists, just like those idiots at the GRU did when they came to Salisbury? Let's just do this the Russian way, why don't we?" asked Lionel, his voice raised.

"We won't get any further on this case unless we communicate with the Russian police," replied Abdul, stubborn and persistent. "Irina took a flight to Moscow in her sister's name the evening of the murder and at the moment she's our main suspect."

There was quiet in the room while Lionel continued to tug restlessly at his long-suffering ears. Finally he straightened up and placed the palms of his hands on the table.

"We're not dedicating any more man hours to this case. It would be a complete waste of time," he said in a tone of voice that brooked no argument.

He caught Abdul's eye and pre-empted him.

"If you and Richard want to go to bloody St Petersburg, you can both bloody well take a holiday. I warn you, though, if anybody asks me about it I shall deny all knowledge of this. That's all I've to say in the matter."

Lionel then turned and stared at Eilidh.

"What have you got to say for yourself?"

"Nothing, sir," said Eilidh hastily.

"Why did you attend if you have nothing to say?" complained Lionel. "Don't bother coming to a meeting next time unless you have something to say."

"Yes, sir."

Lionel grunted.

He got up stiffly from his chair and gathered up his papers.

"From today, as far as I'm concerned, this case is

closed. I've got fourteen other homicide cases sitting on my desk. Let's just hope that this time someone with a modicum of intelligence will be able to solve some of them. Clearly it won't be you three."

With that he left the room but not before slamming the door behind him.

Richard looked at his watch. The meeting had barely lasted twenty minutes.

Lionel wasn't one to keep flogging a dead horse and it was blindingly obvious that this was what the case appeared to be as far as he was concerned. Lionel had given up on the case and the team working on it, but who could blame him when there were so many other incidents piling up on his desk?

"What's got into him?" asked Abdul, surprised. "I've not seen him as bad as that before."

"I have," chimed in Eilidh.

"He was obviously itching for a fag," remarked Richard, pulling at his jacket sleeves to straighten them.

"Or maybe it's a bad case of arthritis," added Abdul somewhat cattily. "Did you see how slowly he moved when he got up from his chair?"

Eilidh crossed her arms, feeling angry.

"Did you see how he never even noticed me until the end? It was as if I wasn't even here."

"I'm not surprised he didn't notice you. You were sitting there like a stuffed rabbit," said Abdul, not mincing his words.

He chuckled to himself and Richard grinned at Abdul's rare attempt at humor.

Eilidh, however, was not amused.

"Hey! That's enough, Abdul. A little bit more

respect, please. Let me remind you that I'm the only one of us three who's discovered anything remotely useful in this case."

"Yes, but if we can't go to Russia it's not going be of any help," Abdul said gloomily, sobering up as soon as he started to think about the case again.

Richard rubbed his chin as he pondered Abdul's comment.

"I don't mind taking some holiday and heading to St Petersburg. I've nothing needing urgent attention at the moment," he remarked at last.

The other two stared at him.

Eilidh burst out laughing, placing both her hands on her stomach as she tried to draw a breath.

"You're so funny, Richard. I mean you really crack me up. Haven't you got better things to do with your holidays?" she gasped.

Each time she looked at him it seemed to bring on a fresh paroxysm of laughter.

Embarrassed, Richard persevered.

"No, not really. I never use up all my holiday entitlement anyway and I've always had a notion to go and see the artwork at the Hermitage Museum in St Petersburg."

He glanced across the table to see if Abdul was showing any interest in joining him.

Richard knew that any visit to Russia would have to include both of them, as they would need to cover for each other and have another trustworthy witness to any relevant information given on the case.

"All right, Richard," said Abdul heavily, as Eilidh gazed at him in astonishment. "I'll go with you. I can try and take some time off in three weeks" time, around the middle of November."

Richard nodded, happy with this outcome.

"Excellent," he said. "Won't it be wonderful not to have to account for police time while we're there?"

14

Richard

As soon as Richard and Abdul came out of the arrivals gate at Pulkovo Airport, St Petersburg, they were approached by two men smartly dressed in suits, their long, black coats held under their arms and with brown fur-lined hats on their heads.

The taller of the two had large blue eyes and his pale face was clean-shaven. He looked to be in his mid-fifties and had a rather severe and puritanical face, in fact he could have easily passed muster as a hermitic monk from another age.

His colleague, meanwhile, was a swarthy, stockier man and his expression seemed very benign, possibly in part due to the white, bushy beard that covered a large portion of his face.

"Chief Inspectors Richard Langley and Abdul Hazim?" enquired the taller man, looking from one to the other of them.

Richard and Abdul nodded, although they suspected their small welcome party knew full well what they looked like. This little charade was no doubt enacted for the benefit of keeping their visit on a courteous footing.

"Yes, I'm Richard Langley," said Richard. He turned and gestured towards Abdul. "And this is my colleague, Abdul Hazim."

They shook hands with each other politely, finding they were all eyeing each other up with a great deal of interest. It was a rare occurrence for Richard and Abdul to negotiate with any police authorities outside of Europe, and equally the Russians wouldn't have had a lot of experience working with the British police.

"I'm Colonel Grigory Koikov," said the taller man, with barely a trace of an accent to his voice. Hearing the plummy notes in his speech Richard speculated the Colonel had been educated for a time at a British independent school. "And my colleague here is Lieutenant Colonel Andrei Mirskey. We're very happy you've decided to come here to St Petersburg because we believe we can help you. We believe we've information on Irina that might enable you to solve this case."

Half-distracted by the deafening noise levels in the arrivals hall, Richard and Abdul nodded and smiled their appreciation.

Unused to the din in the airport, the pair of them were standing like bewildered tourists next to the rowdy crowd waiting for the newly arrived passengers. Listening to the frenzied yells of "Taxi, taxi!" echoing all around them, Richard felt very relieved they had been met by the Russian police, especially when he saw the aggressive taxi drivers pouncing on the unwitting people who were streaming out of the double doors.

"Any word on the missing painting?" asked Richard, raising his voice above the background noise, eager as ever for some good news, although even he had to admit the noisy airport terminal was not the best place to be discussing police business.

"I'm very sorry to say this, Richard, but we've not been able to recover Igor Babikov's painting," replied Colonel Koikov, appearing to be genuinely upset by this.

Looking at him, Richard sensed he was telling the truth and tried to think what would have happened if the Russian police *had* found the masterpiece. Whether the Russian government would want such a valuable and historic painting to leave their country was a loaded question that he didn't, as yet, have the courage to ask. It would be interesting to hear what Igor Babikov's thoughts were on this.

Still, Richard would have been happier to have known the painting was in the safe hands of the Russian government rather than discover the painting had been secreted away to some unknown and inexperienced criminal destination where it might be damaged or lost forever.

The Colonel didn't seem keen to say any more so they walked away in silence from the crowded gathering of relatives, friends, taxi drivers and, in all probability, bogus taxi drivers at arrivals.

They went through the double doors at the entrance to the airport and into the frosty air outside.

A thin blanket of snow covered the sidewalk and the surrounding buildings but the roads were clear. The white icing effect of the snow brightened up what was otherwise an overcast day.

They waited while Colonel Koikov paid for the parking and then made their way along the lanes of parked cars to a smart black Mercedes car and left the airport.

Lieutenant Colonel Andrei Mirskey turned around to face them as they began to drive down the dual carriageway.

"This time of year the nights become very long," he said conversationally. "We've a big problem with people throwing themselves into the River Neva. The darkness isn't good for the head... It's very, very bad for the mind."

In the rear-view mirror Richard could see Colonel Koikov frowning, apparently not liking any aspersion to be cast on the city that many people believed was the true "Venice of the North".

The throwaway title "Venice of the North" seemed to be handed out to a large number of cities that had waterways running through them but many argued, with good reason, that none had the architectural magnificence of St Petersburg.

"I'm looking forward to seeing St Petersburg," remarked Richard in a quiet voice. "There are so many wonderful works of art in the Hermitage. I wish I'd time to see them all."

Glancing across at the rear-view mirror Richard could see Colonel Koikov's frigid expression ease up a little, the broad shoulders in front of him lowering noticeably as the Russian relaxed in his seat.

"I'm sure Igor Babikov will arrange for you to visit the Hermitage. I hope he also takes you to see the Cathedral of the Saviour on Spilled Blood. Most tourists wish to see it," said Colonel Koikov in an affable tone of voice.

"Yes, it's very popular," added Andrei irrepressibly.

He seemed to be the more talkative of the two men. "It was built on the very spot where Alexander II was assassinated... At first they only had a small wooden chapel marking the stones where he died but then later they rebuilt it into the cathedral that stands there today. The building is very like St Basil's Cathedral in Moscow. Do you know the one I mean?"

"Yes, of course. I'm sure everybody does," replied Richard politely.

"Tsar Alexander II did many good things for this country," commented Colonel Koikov as he weaved his way in and out of the traffic. "He was a very enlightened man. In 1861 he emancipated the serfs, which meant the end of slavery for them, and he did this five years before the emancipation of slaves in the USA happened."

Abdul and Richard exchanged glances and then looked away again. Politics was never going to be a comfortable subject between them all.

Richard turned to stare out of his window, straining to see the buildings on the side of the road because there was now a thick curtain of snowflakes falling; the multiple white splodges were dancing steadily downwards, undisturbed by any wind.

They were now passing many Soviet-era buildings, ugly and functional in their architecture. Coloured a dirty vanilla, rose-pink and pale grey, the multi-story blocks stretched away into the distance, unable to hide their ugliness behind the leafless trees that lined the road.

They drove on in silence, the water from the melted snow snaking down the car's windows and making Richard feel as dull as the grey day outside.

It wasn't long, fortunately, before the buildings began to show an impressive grandeur, shaking off the utilitarian starkness of the previous ones. Richard felt his spirits rise as he began to realise they were soon going to be approaching the beautiful neoclassical buildings constructed during the lifetimes of Tsar Peter the Great and Empress Catherine the Great.

Richard had done his research. He'd learnt that, inspired by the French architecture of the time (as well as the other palaces and buildings the Tsar had visited on his one incognito trip to Europe), Peter the Great had built an imposing city on a hostile swamp retaken from the Swedes. The city was soon to be nicknamed the "Window into Europe" because of its European-style architecture.

"This is the Neva River and the Palace Bridge," said Andrei cheerfully as they went over the bridge. "And you can see the Winter Palace on your left, which is now part of the State Hermitage Museum. You must also go to see the Marble Palace, it's worth the visit."

Richard and Abdul craned their necks to look at the magnificent, green-blue building gazing out over the water, with its classical white columns and manifold arched windows stretching along the Neva.

Seeing how close the river was to the palace Richard asked himself if, like Venice, St Petersburg had problems keeping the water at bay. Were floods a problem here too?

"Quickly! If you look back now you'll see the *Admiralteystvo*. That's the headquarters of the Russian Navy. Tsar Peter the Great was the one who modernized and enlarged the Russian navy," explained Andrei, twisting round to look at them and pointing behind them.

Richard and Abdul turned and stared at the tangerine-coloured building whose gold pinnacle was shining like a flame even on such a dank and grey day.

Richard's impression was that the *Admiralteystvo* had been built in such a way as to command attention and respect.

Situated behind a large fountain and numerous trees, its facade would always attract interest even when it was surrounded by more frivolous and regal buildings. Peter the Great's passion for the navy was evident in the Admiralty Building's position in the city's landscape with its tall, glowing pinnacle breaking up the skyline.

As the car drove slowly down Nevsky Avenue, Richard and Abdul were mute as they took in the city's amazing architecture.

"They're such stunning buildings. I feel very honoured to have had the opportunity to see them," remarked Abdul at last, turning to face the front of the car again.

"I've lived in St Petersburg for 53 years now and I still never tire of looking at its buildings. We're very fortunate," said Colonel Koikov, in a matter-of-fact voice.

"This smaller river is the Moyka River and that building there is the Stroganov Palace. It houses some of the fine art collection from the Russian Museum," chimed Andrei, like a clockwork tour guide, pointing to a sumptuous pale pink and white palace overlooking the water.

"What happened to its owners?" asked Abdul as he stared up at the palace towering above them.

"The Stroganov Palace was built for Baron Sergei Stroganov," replied the Colonel, who, like his colleague, seemed to be remarkably well informed.

Richard estimated how much information he knew about notable buildings in London and tried to compare it to the encyclopedic knowledge their police escort seemed to possess about buildings in St Petersburg. Was he as patriotic and proud of his city as Grigory and Andrei seemed to be of theirs? He doubted it.

"The Stroganovs were one of the richest families in Russia at the time, if not the richest," continued the Colonel. "A renowned Italian architect called Bartolomeo Rastrelli designed their palace. The Stroganov family left Russia after the October Revolution and the family line is said to be extinct now."

With such disparity between the wealthy and the poor that seemed evident in the grandeur and cost of the palaces and buildings in St Petersburg it was unsurprising that the worst-off sector of society decided to rebel in the Communist Revolution, thought Richard.

As though reading his mind the Colonel added: "St Petersburg's residents have a pretty egalitarian view on things... There are, of course, districts that are exclusively for the rich but many very wealthy inhabitants live in huge apartments in the same building as residents that can only afford a small studio flat."

"That sounds good," said Abdul, nodding in approval.

Richard didn't say anything. He was too busy absorbing the architecture around him to speak.

Looking up at the buildings they were driving past,

Richard thought he was looking forward to seeing what kind of a home Igor Babikov was living in. Would Igor be living in a similar building to the grandiose palaces they had just driven past? They were both due to meet with him early the next day but for now they were securely in the custody of their police escort.

They drove across the Griboyedov Canal and then passed Kazan Cathedral, whose appearance reminded Richard irresistibly of St Peter's Basilica in Rome. He decided the similarity between them had something to do with the impression made by the Kazan Cathedral's colonnaded arms extending out in a semi-circle from the main building, just as they did in the much bigger St Peter's Basilica.

They turned left a little further along Nevsky Prospekt and then the car came to a stop in a small police car park at the back of a multi-story building.

Richard and Abdul got out of the car and stared up at the vanilla-coloured, nondescript building in front of them. After being dazzled by some truly astounding buildings on the way there, the ugly exterior of the police station seemed a bit of an anti-climax.

"Please come along and we'll get some coffee," said Colonel Koikov. "Do leave your bags in the car. We'll get one of our men to drop you off at your hotel later on."

Richard and Abdul smiled their thanks and followed their two minders into the building.

The interior of the building looked rather tired but there was plenty of activity going on, with harassed-looking officers scurrying up and down the ground floor corridor.

They were taken up to the third floor in the lift and

then the Colonel ushered them into his office. Lieutenant Colonel Andrei Mirskey had given them a
wistful goodbye on the ground floor, looking disappointed that he was now returning to normal duties
again.

The Colonel's office was very neat.

Bundles of files tied up with elastic bands were
stacked on the right-hand side of his desk; on the left
there was a tray with a few unopened letters. A lavish
bunch of white roses and lilies reposed in a tall, lilac
glass vase on the filing cabinet and there was a large
pine-framed print taking up most of the space on one
wall.

Glancing at it, Richard saw the picture had a monument of Catherine the Great in the center and what he
guessed was the Alexandrinsky Theatre in the background. A suitably patriotic picture for a policeman's
wall. He was reminded of his own office in London
with his poster of Canaletto's painting *The River
Thames with St. Paul's Cathedral on Lord Mayor's Day*.
Maybe Colonel Koikov and himself had more in
common than he'd previously thought.

The walls of the room were coloured a restful shade
of pastel blue and had all the appearance of being
freshly painted as there wasn't a mark to be seen.
Richard kind of wished the same could be said of the
rooms in New Scotland Yard, which despite the building's relatively new decor were already showing plenty
of signs of wear and tear.

There was such a strong smell of vanilla in the room
that Richard guessed it must have come from an air
freshener. It seemed as though someone was trying very
hard to make a good impression and he couldn't think

why this would be the case because they had nothing to offer the Russians. Quite the reverse, in fact. They were hoping Colonel Koikov could provide them with some much-needed information on the case.

Abdul, oblivious to Richard's observations, was looking impatient. Having sacrificed some of his leave for this trip, Richard could tell he just wanted to get on with things.

"Please, take a seat," said the Colonel, sitting down on his desk chair.

Obediently Richard and Abdul took a seat each at the front of the desk.

Both of them were trying their hardest to look relaxed but Richard thought it must be pretty obvious to Grigory that they were consumed with curiosity and desperate to find out what was going to be discussed next.

The Colonel called out to his secretary, who appeared in the doorway with a beaming smile.

She was a matronly woman with dyed-red hair and had the circular appearance of someone who valued her food. The Colonel spoke to her quickly in Russian, and after nodding in agreement she left the room. Richard presumed an order for refreshments had been given, even though neither he nor Abdul had been asked what they wanted to drink.

Colonel Koikov was looking very pensive. He leaned forward and put his elbows on the desk, then he placed the tips of his long fingers against each other in a steeple effect, leaning them for a moment against his mouth.

Watching the Colonel, Richard felt himself becoming slightly mesmerized. He resisted the urge to yawn and decided he must be tired from his early start that morning. He shook his head, hoping his stupor would dissipate soon. His lethargy was only going to be a hindrance in such an important meeting.

Glancing across to Abdul he was relieved to see that his colleague was, as ever, on the ball and alert.

"Well, gentlemen, I want to thank you for coming to meet with us," said the Colonel with a dour smile.

"We appreciate you meeting with us, Colonel," responded Abdul, eager to begin official business. "The trail for this case leads here to Russia. So we won't be able to get any further on in solving this crime without your assistance."

"Please call me Grigory. Yes, Irina Kapitsa... That young lady is quite a conundrum. I think I'd better start from the beginning with the Kapitsa sisters."

Somewhat to Richard's irritation they were interrupted by a curt knock at the door and the Colonel's secretary walked in carrying a tray with three mugs of what looked to be instant coffee, a jug of milk and a plate of chocolate biscuits.

She left the tray on the desk, giving the visitors a broad smile at the same time, and then retreated out of the connecting door.

"Is coffee alright for you?" asked Grigory, looking across the table at them. "I'm afraid that here in St Petersburg we are called "coffee pots" unlike our friends in Moscow who much prefer tea and are affectionately named "tea pots"."

"Fantastic, thank you," said Richard, quickly helping himself to a dollop of milk and lifting a mug off the tray.

He didn't want to delay any talk of substance with

polite chit-chat over coffee. They hadn't travelled all the way to St Petersburg to exchange pleasantries with the Russian police.

He swallowed a generous mouthful of coffee and then felt the hot liquid burning the top layer of his tongue. Angry with himself, he resisted the impulse to swear out loud.

He couldn't believe how dopey he was. The caffeine had better start to kick in soon because his mental processes were not functioning at all well. In the end he decided his best option was to keep his mouth firmly shut, and holding his coffee in one hand he rested the mug nonchalantly on his thigh while he waited for it to cool down.

Like Abdul he was keen for Grigory to start telling them what he knew about Irina Kapitsa but a burnt tongue was an unnecessary price to pay for his impatience.

Unaware of Richard's discomfort, Abdul and Grigory helped themselves to milk and sugar and soon all three of them were sitting back, watching each other over their steaming mugs.

"The Kapitsa sisters have an interesting family history. Their father was the captain of a ship in the seaport of Vladivostok," began Grigory, sliding a hand around his coffee mug and leaning over the desk conspiratorially. "By all accounts he was an alcoholic. Someone who, according to his wife's hospital records, used to regularly beat up his wife... He died at the relatively young age of 51, leaving his wife with many debts. As a result both girls ended up working at a local brothel to make ends meet. Irina's sister, Tatiana Kapitsa, unfortunately picked up a heroin habit while working there and this eventually took her on to the streets of Vladivostok where she could earn more, though of course with added risk."

There was a momentary hush in the room as Grigory swallowed some of his coffee.

Outside, in the far distance, they could hear the siren of an ambulance or police car, reminding them that tragic occurrences were happening in every corner of the world. This awareness seemed to draw them closer together in the quietness of Grigory's office, the background siren somehow reinforcing their common humanity.

"Irina Kapitsa then seems to have been talent-spotted for better things according to the brothel where she worked," continued Grigory. "Apparently she was offered a position as part of a network of high-class escort girls in Moscow. Which is how I suspect she crossed paths with Igor Babikov."

Richard thought back to what Igor had said about meeting Irina for the first time in a hotel in Moscow. It seemed to fit in with what Grigory was telling them although Irina's English must have been superb to pass muster as a translator. Igor Babikov was no fool, although he was probably feeling like one now that Irina had absconded.

Gratified by the earnest, fixed attention of the two men in front of him, Grigory smiled.

"A few weeks ago, we were notified by Igor Babikov that Irina might be travelling back to Russia with a valuable painting in tow, under the name of her sister Tatiana Kapitsa. We checked this out and sure enough Tatiana Kapitsa, or should I say Irina Kapitsa, arrived at Moscow airport on the 24th of September, at around seven o'clock in the evening. Her trail after she goes through passport control in Moscow goes completely cold which suggests to us that she must have been carrying a substantial amount of ready cash on her. Either that or someone was helping her cover her tracks."

Shrugging his shoulders, Grigory lifted the palms of his hands.

"Because we couldn't trace her, there was nothing we could do at the time to find her. We checked all the bank accounts that were in Irina's name. There was nothing of interest, no movement on the accounts what-soever. Nothing at all. So then we decided to access Irina's email records..."

Grigory paused dramatically for a moment, his light blue eyes boring into theirs. In true Russian tradition he was turning out to be an adept storyteller.

"Her emails were very, very interesting. At the start of January this year she was contacted by someone we assume was an old client of hers, a man by the name of Luka Petrov. He says he wants to meet up with her. She demurs several times but Luka is extremely persistent and his emails start to become more threatening. By this point it's near the end of January and things start to turn nasty; Luka Petrov threatens to tell Igor Babikov all about her past life as a prostitute unless she meets up with him. He says he needs her to do an important favour for his boss and that she'll be compensated for it. She agrees to meet up with him in London on the 5th of February at the Serpentine Gallery in Hyde Park..."

Richard and Abdul carried on sitting as still as two effigies after Grigory finished speaking.

After a minute Richard stirred on his chair.

"And? What happened then?" he asked impatiently.

"There were no further emails between Luka Petrov and Irina Kapitsa after that last email. There was no clue whatsoever as to what Luka Petrov wanted her to do. So knowing very little about her whereabouts we put out an alert on her disappearance and we left things for a short while. We let things "brew" as you British like to say."

"Your information is very revealing. It does at least in part explain why Irina might have decided to disappear," remarked Abdul thoughtfully.

"It explains nothing about why the painting was taken though," contradicted Richard, his single-minded focus solely on the valuable picture.

"It depends, my friend, on what Luka Petrov's "boss" wanted from Irina. We're assuming she was dealing with a demand for sexual favours or monetary blackmail but it could have been more complicated than that," said Grigory with the wisdom of someone who knew a lot more about the case then they did.

Looking as though the conversation was tiring him out, Grigory stretched out his arms and yawned. He then rubbed his eyes before placing his hands around his mug again.

After a little pause he lifted the mug and swallowed some coffee, his eyes twinkling mischievously at them over its rim. Despite seeing their riveted faces in front of him, it was clear Grigory was going to do the briefing in his own good time.

What a tease, thought Richard, feeling fed up with the humdrum pace of their conversation.

He couldn't help but feel that Grigory was amusing

himself at their expense, but soon afterwards he felt ashamed of his accusation because without Grigory's help they'd be no further forward in discovering what had happened to the painting or Irina.

It was the Colonel's legitimate right to lay things out at his own pace and maybe the tempo was simply a cultural difference; after all, things might well move at a slower, more considered speed in Russia. And of course, Abdul and himself were used to Lionel's hasty briefings that were always kept as short and scant as possible...

"Anyway, for a while we heard nothing," said the Colonel at last. "Then on the 31st of October we were notified of a homicide in Derbent, an ancient city that lies on the edge of the Caspian Sea. The local police in Derbent were called out by the Hotel Golden Beach to a murder scene in one of their rooms. The dead body of Irina was found in the hotel room with a passport in the name of Tatiana Kapitsa, false identity papers and bankcards."

"Does Igor know that Irina's body was found?" asked Richard, surprised. "He certainly hasn't mentioned any of this on the phone to me."

"Of course he knows. I don't know why he hasn't informed you but he'll no doubt have his reasons. This happened just over three weeks ago. He had her body transferred to St Petersburg once the police work in Derbent was finished and her funeral was only two days ago. Igor has the means to pull strings and can make things happen very quickly..."

Lifting his mug, Grigory took another drink of coffee, as though the mere thought of all the administration involved in Irina's death and funeral was making him thirsty.

"I feel very bad for him," he commented. "The poor man has buried both sisters within a short space of time. After what they did to him it's astonishing that he's been willing to take on that responsibility. I imagine that what he's learnt about their traumatic childhood may have made him more understanding..." He shrugged. "That man has a heart and a forgiving soul. After Tatiana's body was repatriated he made sure the two sisters were buried side by side in the cemetery. To his credit, Irina's funeral in the Church of the Nativity of John the Baptist was both dignified and moving. I was there for the service..."

Grigory reached across to take a chocolate biscuit from the plate on his desk.

Sensing that his stomach was about to growl angrily with hunger, Richard decided to take one too. They munched their biscuits in unison as Abdul leaned back on his chair and crossed his legs.

Richard was pleased to see Abdul relaxing a little more. Bending the rules was something he was used to doing within the ambiguous remit of his department but Abdul liked to follow protocol. This trip was definitely out of Abdul's comfort zone and so, for his sake, Richard was relieved it hadn't been a wasted a trip for them both.

"Was Irina's mother there for the funeral?" wondered Richard.

"I don't know. You'll have to ask Igor that. There were very few people there, to be honest with you. I didn't know who they were."

"Have you informed Igor Babikov about everything you've found out regarding Irina?" asked Abdul curiously.

Grigory smiled to himself, looking impressed at Abdul's foresight.

"We've informed Igor of some things. We've been selective. There are still many loose ends that we need to tie up and this is where we might need to work together."

He paused for a moment as though choosing his words with care.

"We haven't as yet told Igor some of the pertinent details about the way in which Irina was killed, nor have we told him about the vast sums of money she had squirrelled away in a bank account under the name of Nadia Jelena Vasilek," Grigory said at last with surprising candor. "We wanted to have a clearer picture of what's going on before we reported back to Igor with our conclusions. Igor Babikov happens to be friends with some very influential people both in Moscow and here in St Petersburg... As investigators in this case we have to be very careful how we handle things."

Richard tried to work out what Grigory was implying when he said they had to be careful. Was he suggesting Igor Babikov could possibly be in some way implicated in the case? Or were the police simply wanting to keep quiet about the money so they could have it appropriated as soon as it was feasible?

"How much money was there exactly in that bank account and where did it come from?" asked Richard, intrigued. Any money was bound to give them clues as to what had happened to the missing painting.

Grigory shot him a penetrating look.

"There were two separate payments into the account of Nadia Jelena Vasilek," he said. "One payment came into the account on the 16th of October.

It was transferred from an account in Tatiana Kapitsa's name with Nomos Bank. Approximately 78 million rubles... This sum originally came to Nomos Bank on the 27th of September from a Swiss bank account. So as you can see it was fairly recent. Untraceable of course..."

Grigory sniffed and started to toy restlessly with a large piece of paper on his desk.

Eventually he picked it up and started to fold it into what looked like the beginning of an intricate origami shape.

Watching in surprise as Grigory carefully bent and turned the paper, Richard realized that as far as he was aware he had never met with a police officer familiar with the art of origami. There was a first for everything.

"The second payment went directly to the account of Nadia Vasilek on the 30th of September from a small bank in Uruguay, Carasa Bank," continued Grigory, still focused on shaping and molding his piece of paper. "It was for approximately 126 million rubles. The name of the sender was an off-shore shell company called *Pelicano Azul*. Interesting, isn't it?"

Richard and Abdul nodded simultaneously.

"What we also haven't mentioned to Igor is that Irina's murder had all the signs of a revenge killing by a Russian mafia group called *Volch'ya staya*. They're called "Wolf Pack" in English. They mainly operate on the East Coast of Russia but they've a hold in parts of Siberia as well."

Putting down his half-finished origami, Grigory opened a drawer in his desk and started searching for something.

While he waited, Richard studied Grigory's origami

work and tried to guess what it was supposed to be. It looked a little like a squat dragon but it wasn't easy at this stage to decipher what it was meant to look like.

Meanwhile Grigory took out a file from his desk drawer and opened it, removing several photographs which he then laid out in front of them.

They were all photographs of torn skin and flesh that had been sliced open. Congealed blood edged the wounds in a thick crust. Each photo showed a different angle of what was clearly a macabre cross, cut across the woman's breasts and straight down between them.

"Irina wasn't killed by a knife. She was killed at close range with a bullet from a Maxim 9, which is a 9mm semi-automatic silencer handgun."

"Sorry, you probably knew that already," added Grigory apologetically. "It's easy to forget I'm talking to two policemen."

Abdul nodded but Richard didn't express any opinion on the matter, too embarrassed to admit he hadn't a clue about guns other than those portrayed in artworks such as Andy Warhol's *Bang!* or, memorably, Renee Stout's *Baby's First Gun* and Mel Chin's sculpture *Cross for the Unforgiven*.

"The bullet went straight through the frontal lobe. It was an execution really. The cross they slashed across her skin, that's what this gang uses to ward off others who might betray them. It's their signature mark for traitors."

Richard picked up a photo and studied it.

Abdul leaned forward and stared at the wall opposite, his eyes abstracted as he processed all the information they'd been given.

Grigory meanwhile picked up his origami again and

began to bend and turn the paper with renewed intensity as he gave the others time to think.

"So do you think this gang has its hands on the painting?" enquired Richard, glancing across to Grigory.

"No. I don't. I think if they had it she wouldn't be dead right now. Something went wrong, that's what I think happened. I reckon they paid her for it but something occurred that infuriated them and meant she lost her life as a result."

"This sounds very vague to me. A lot of conjecture," complained Abdul, frowning. "Two strange payments into a fake account and a dead body... That's all there is. There's nothing to indicate the painting's mixed up in all of this."

Richard cleared his throat.

"I beg to differ, Abdul. I think with a sum of money that large there's a very good chance the painting is behind it all. We're talking millions of pounds here... After all, what else did Irina have that would've justified them paying her such large sums of money? The only thing of value she could've put her hands on was the painting. However, two payments from such different sources is very confusing. Maybe she was playing two people off against each other and it didn't end well."

"Maybe," said Grigory, non-committal. "But this is all speculation. I've told you everything that we know about the case."

Abdul looked sharply at Grigory.

"Yes, you've been very frank with us. More than I expected, to be honest with you. Would you like to tell us why?" he asked in his usual blunt manner.

"Surely it's obvious?"

Richard smiled.

"The painting?" he asked.

"Yes, of course," replied Grigory, not bothering to look up from his origami work. "We're very interested in this masterpiece by El Greco. If we had the painting you wouldn't have heard anything from us, but we want it back in Russia and we're making overtures to Igor and to yourselves in the hope that if this painting does appear again, it'll find a home back here in Russia once more."

"I'm afraid we're still very far from figuring out where the painting is. I've got an expert at tracking stolen or lost paintings looking into things and as yet he's turned up diddly squat," said Richard pessimistically.

"I'm sorry, what do you mean by "diddly squat"?" asked Grigory, puzzled.

He straightened up and looked at Richard with interest.

Abdul laughed out loud.

"It's slang, Grigory," he said with amusement. "It means this expert of Richard's has discovered nothing at all."

Leaning forward, Abdul smiled at Grigory.

"In other words, the man he uses to track down stolen paintings hasn't heard any news of it whatsoever," he explained helpfully. "Mike Telford's a private investigator. He has many contacts in the art world and he usually figures out what's happening when paintings like this one go missing. He helped recover Edvard Munch's *The Scream* when it was stolen. I don't know if you remember that robbery?"

"Yes, of course," said Grigory. "I remember it well. Nobody was told how that painting was recovered."

"Exactly," affirmed Richard. "That's how Mike Telford works. No one ever finds out how he recovers these paintings. It's reassuring for the huge network of dodgy minions he's got working for him and for anyone else who's willing to grass up. At the end of the day all anyone is ever interested in is getting the paintings back."

Seeming to understand Richard's slang this time, Grigory nodded, his austere face softening. Watching him Richard could see he totally understood the grey areas in police work. Unfortunately nowadays you often didn't get very far unless you were willing to make overtures in the shady arena of the criminal underworld.

For some reason, Mike Telford had managed to build up trust in some very dubious characters, leaving them undisturbed in their illicit activities, and often in return they were willing to cooperate when he needed them to. There was nearly always money involved as an incentive, of course. Richard had yet to find a criminal who didn't need some form of financial lubrication to provide help to someone, even if that someone was as genial and likeable as Mike Telford.

"OK. I've put all my cards on the table for you," said Grigory, fiddling with his finished origami as he looked at Richard and Abdul. "I hope that you two will keep in touch with me and let our side know if any further discoveries are made in this case."

"Of course. By the way, could you give us the bank account details for Irina's fake accounts? We might be able to trace things a bit further."

"I doubt that very much," said Grigory with certainty. "We've had our own experts look into them. But of course it isn't a problem to give you that information. I'll get my secretary to print out the details for you. I should also mention that at the moment those assets have been frozen, at our request, until things are resolved further."

"We'll also be in touch with Igor Babikov," said Abdul.

"Good. Excellent, in fact. Whatever happens in the future it would be good for us all to have a part in it, don't you think? It's good for our Anglo-Russian relationship."

Richard thought about the expelled diplomats from both countries as he nodded respectfully.

The Skripal affair...

He had an incongruous newspaper image pop into his head of a Russian child, the child of an expelled Russian diplomat, climbing up the stairs of a plane, holding onto a huge furry teddy bear.

"As I said, we're very keen to have this painting stay in Russia," repeated Grigory, now beginning to sound like a broken record. "We hope that after it's been stolen with such ease in London, Igor will think seriously about keeping it safe in a museum here. If it's ever recovered, that is."

"Of course," said Richard, thinking that poor Igor was really going to be put into an awkward corner if this priceless painting was ever located.

He had no idea what nebulous pressure the Russian government was prepared to put on Igor in their desire to have this artwork kept as their national treasure and not someone else's. But he agreed with Grigory that the painting, if it were ever found, would need to have the protection of a national museum, whether that was here in Russia or back home in London or anywhere else for that matter. Personally, he didn't care where the painting ended up as long as it was safe.

"Have you any other questions before we escort you to your hotel?" asked Grigory, with an expression on his face that suggested he hoped they were done for the day.

"Yes, I do," answered Abdul much to Richard's surprise. "What were you making with that paper?"

He pointed at the origami on the desk, lying on its side with its little delicate edges sticking out.

Grigory laughed with genuine amusement and delight.

He picked up the origami and sat it upright, so it was facing Richard and Abdul.

They bent their heads and looked at it in astonishment.

It was an origami version of Yoda, the Jedi Master.

Very apt, thought Richard. They were all needing Yoda to tell them what to do now…

15

Richard

Igor, holding a half-empty gin and tonic in his hand, sighed as he looked out of the window of his apartment.

"This road, the Kamennoostrovsky Prospekt, linking the center of the city with the north western boroughs, is often labeled "northern modern." If you're an Art Nouveau fan, Richard, you should take the time to look at some of the buildings along this road, especially the Chubakov Apartment Building..."

He stared out of the window and narrowed his eyes, his brow creasing with concentration.

"I can see your friends are keeping a close eye on you."

Richard and Abdul got up and looked out of the large sitting room window to where Igor was pointing. All they could see was a stream of people marching purposefully up and down the pavement.

"Over there, the man in the black coat standing with a briefcase at the bus stop," said Igor, continuing to point with his finger.

There was a man at the bus stop but he wasn't

looking at their building. Indeed he seemed to be intensely engrossed in his phone. He lifted his head and did a cursory scan of his surroundings before bending his head to his phone again.

"He's been there for last hour and a quarter. I'm guessing someone else is concealed on our side of the street. Not unexpected given there's two British police officers here."

Igor walked across to a sumptuous cream sofa and sat down.

"Well, my friends, what do you think of St Petersburg?" he asked with ill- concealed pride.

"It's stunning," said Richard enthusiastically, returning to the sofa with him.

"I'd like to come back here one day and have enough time to look at all the sights," added Abdul, craning his neck to see if he could spot a watcher beneath the window.

When he couldn't see past the balustrade he gave up and joined Richard on the sofa opposite Igor.

"Excellent," said Igor looking pleased. "I know I'm biased but I've never stayed in a city as beautiful as St Petersburg. I'll live and die here."

"Really?" asked Richard in surprise. "Rumor had it you were going to move to London in the future."

Igor smiled sardonically.

"There's always rumours, Richard, you should know that by now. Your papers are full of them. I admit Irina had a soft spot for London. She might've swayed me but I doubt it," ruminated Igor, gazing into the distance. He put his glass down and placed his hands behind his head. "My ancestors lived and died here and so will I. I love it here. I'm no communist but I love the egalitarian culture of this city. There are a few very exclusive areas in the city, like the homes on Primorsky Prospekt, for example, or Krestovsky Island, but I can live here very comfortably and safely beside my compatriots. Besides, both Primorsky Prospekt and Krestovsky Ostrov are too close to the Baltic Sea and the snow is very heavy when you live close to the sea."

Richard glanced at Abdul. It was strange to find Igor so calm and composed. Surely the tragedy of losing the Kapitsa sisters should have had an impact on the iron nerve of the man, quite aside from the devastating loss of an immensely valuable painting.

"What's on your mind, Richard?" asked Igor suddenly, with uncanny prescience.

"Oh, many things," said Richard dismissively. "There's been a lot to take in since we arrived yesterday."

"There has, hasn't there," agreed Igor with sarcastic understatement. "No doubt you are wondering why I'm not crumbling before your very eyes..." He smiled as he caught the look of surprise on Richard's face. "The truth is that I'm tough. I didn't build up my business to what it is today by being weak. As I've told you before, here in Russia the sharks are always circling. A large portion of the business world in Russia is criminal and corrupt and you've to keep your wits about you to survive. Every time you're knocked down you've to come back up fighting if you want to survive. That's how I survive."

Igor leaned forward and reached for his glass, taking a big swig from it.

"I was taken for a sucker by Irina," he admitted. "That'll never happen again. I've been wise in business but exceptionally foolish with my heart. I've rebuilt my armor and I'll carry on. It doesn't mean I've given up on relationships completely or that I can't trust anyone again, but I'll be more careful in future."

Richard wondered what he meant by "more careful". Was he going to pay for some private investigator to run background checks on future girlfriends? Or was he simply going to stick to girls he could vouch for? Either option seemed sensible given what he had been through with Irina.

"Did the police give you any information that was of interest in this case?" asked Igor, watching them both closely.

Taken by surprise, Richard had the fleeting impression that Abdul and himself were two mice being toyed with by a large, malevolent cat.

"Yes, they said some things that were interesting," said Abdul, coolly prevaricating when confronted with Igor's steely blue eyes. "Colonel Koikov told us you've been apprised of the pertinent facts in Irina's death."

"Murder," corrected Igor.

"Murder," agreed Abdul.

"Why do I have the impression you now know more about the case than I do?" asked Igor, crossing his arms and staring at them.

"Igor, we might or might not know more than you but until we make any inroads into this case it's pointless for us to be making speculations," said Richard soothingly, hoping to assuage Igor's suspicions. "You know that both the Russian police and my department are searching for your painting and that means exploring multiple possibilities. We're not going to waste your time with every single line of enquiry we have, but rest assured you'll be among the first to be informed if anything of interest turns up. For now both sides have to start shaking the tree and see what falls out."

Igor stuck out his lower lip but seemed to accept the sense in this.

Both Abdul and Richard felt themselves relax at the temporary reprieve. Igor would be a bad man to cross. It was important that they had him on their side if they were going to have any success in tracing the painting. The last thing they needed was for Igor to lose trust in them and decide to take matters into his own hands.

Richard leaned back on the sofa and accepted the offer of another Coca-Cola from Igor's butler as he came into the room and picked up their empty glasses.

"Come on, guys, you're not technically on duty now. You need to relax. At least have a glass of wine," pleaded Igor.

"All right then. A glass of wine would be nice, thank you," said Richard, giving in and smiling at the butler.

"Red or white, sir?" asked Dmitry in his heavily accented English.

"Red, thank you," replied Richard.

He caught an accusatory look from Abdul and shrugged it off. He was technically on his holiday after all.

"Just a Coca-Cola for me please," insisted Abdul primly.

The rules had clearly been bent enough for Abdul and he wasn't prepared to push the limits any further. Especially not when he was in the presence of a charismatic and powerful oligarch who also seemed to be something of a dark horse.

"Some food too please, Dmitry," said Igor handing his gin and tonic glass to him.

As they waited for Dmitry to return, there was an uncomfortable silence through which they could hear the noise of the traffic on the road outside.

Richard found it quite easy to distract himself; all he had to do was to look around the room they were in. He was in the presence of so much art he soon found himself daydreaming as he studied the fascinating ornaments on the bookcases and assessed the artwork on the walls.

Igor had already taken them on a tour of the room, pointing out objects of interest like the ornate hilt of a Viking sword discovered in Belarus in 1905 and a silver and bronze inlaid Buddha from twelfth-century Tibet.

The walls of the vast room had on them a number of paintings by contemporary Russian artists. There was a vivid painting by Alexey Chernigin, capturing a couple kissing at a train station as the train moved away, and an amusing portrait by Konstantin Lupanov of his cat Philip, sleeping soundly across his feet. Unfamiliar with Russian art, Richard had no idea as to their value but he hoped Igor had chosen these pictures because he liked them and not solely as a financial investment.

On the floor and leaning carelessly against a wall was a portrait of Irina Kapitsa by the renowned artist Nikolai Blokhin.

In the picture Irina was wearing a red dress that showed up her pale skin and black hair to best effect. She was staring out of the painting and whenever Richard happened to look at the picture he felt as though her large, black eyes were following him, pleading with him to find her murderers. Gazing down at it, Richard speculated for a moment as to what Igor planned to do with the painting. Sell it maybe?

He felt himself instinctively shudder.

He turned away from Irina's portrait and searched for Igor's watercolor by Kandinsky instead.

In the far corner of the room, hanging above an antique chest made of wood and inlaid mother-of-pearl, was a gorgeous, small watercolor by Kandinsky. Its vibrant red, yellow and blue colors glowed like a prism despite being in the most dimly lit part of the room. Admiring it, Richard couldn't understand why Igor had chosen such an understated location for the lovely painting, as he would have hung it up in a prominent place where its beauty could be fully appreciated.

Dmitry came in with the drinks on a tray and in the prolonged silence calmly proceeded to set out the glasses alongside heaped plates of food.

"Help yourselves. You have here Ukrainian sausage," said Igor in a crisp voice, as though subtly trying to remind them of Russia's historical ties to the Ukraine. "As well as some caviar, pickled herring, rye bread, and these," he said pointing to a lavishly filled plate," are some mini-pies filled with cabbage, potato, egg and cheese."

"Thank you," said Richard, leaning forward and looking appreciatively at the feast before him.

Taking a serviette, he grabbed a neat oval of toast and caviar and took a large bite, munching it happily.

"That caviar is from the Caspian Sea," commented Igor, helping himself to some of the same.

For a few minutes silence reigned once more as the

three of them ate and drank, but this time it was a companionable interlude.

Eventually their host sat back and smiled at them.

Richard felt himself tensing up because it looked as though Igor was going to try to milk them for some more information again.

"My friends, I'm very grateful to you for coming. You don't need to tell me it wasn't easy for you. I'm guessing your superiors thought this trip was most irregular."

"Actually, yes they did," said Abdul. "We ended up using some of our vacation to come here."

"Well, then I'm even more impressed you came. I hope this visit will be of use to you, if nothing else because you'll have a better understanding of what happened to poor Irina."

Igor glanced across at her portrait and his face seemed to spasm.

"Do you have anything else regarding my painting?" he pleaded, his face for the first time showing an almost childish vulnerability as his eyes filled with unshed tears. He stared across at them beseechingly.

Richard sighed.

"Irina seems to have received a large amount of money from two sources. We don't know if this is connected to your missing painting," said Richard, deciding there was nothing to lose by telling Igor this. Igor's face showed no surprise, only weary resignation. "We can only presume it was for the painting but I'm sure the Russian police will be doing all they can to trace the people who were in contact with her."

"Of course they will," said Igor with a sharp note of

bitterness in his voice. "They'll be sniffing out anything that has money behind it."

"What are you going to do with the masterpiece if they or we recover it for you?" asked Richard, interested.

Igor didn't reply.

He stood up abruptly and walked over to the window again, staring across at the bus stop.

Worried he'd offended him, Richard watched Igor as he stood there, silent and alone in a self-contained bubble.

Abdul turned and gave Richard a cheeky grin and wink, secure in the knowledge he would never have asked the oligarch so presumptuous and tactless a question. Richard had audaciously lobbed into the conversation a sensitive topic and that wasn't Abdul's style at all. Unlike Richard, he wasn't impetuous and in these kinds of situations he preferred to act sensitively and wait for the answers, rather than risk causing offence.

"Have you ever heard of a composer called Dmitri Shostakovich?" asked Igor after a while, still gazing out of the window.

"No, I haven't," answered Richard, relieved that Igor was communicating once more. "What about you, Abdul?"

"No, I'm sorry but I don't know an awful lot about Russian culture," said Abdul, looking a little bemused.

From the confused expression on Abdul's face Richard could tell he was wondering why they were now having a conversation about a Russian composer, and Richard didn't blame him because he was struggling to keep up with the workings of Igor's mercurial mind himself.

"He was a talented Russian composer. In my opinion Dmitri Shostakovich was a wonderful, creative man but he was curtailed by the Soviet government. They interfered too much..." commented Igor. "At first he received accolades and awards from the state but later, just like that..." Igor snapped his fingers, "it all turned nasty. The party denounced him in 1948 for not writing music accessible enough for the masses. Nobody wanted to go to the Gulag in those days so the composer surrendered his artistic integrity, even though he hated doing so..."

Igor turned around to face them.

"Apparently, his son would ask him, "Papa, what if they hang you for this?" It wasn't worth taking any risks so after he was dismissed from the Leningrad and Moscow Conservatories, he accepted film commissions glorifying Stalin and won even more prizes for doing so. His heart wasn't in it though."

Igor walked back to the sofa and sat down again. He looked across at Abdul and Richard, his face very somber.

"I can't blame Dmitri Shostakovich for capitulating. And I say this because there might come the day when I too might have to capitulate to the Russian government over *The Spanish Princess*. But that day hasn't happened yet..."

Igor's words hung about the room and haunted Richard for the rest of the afternoon.

And he remembered them later on that evening when Igor took them to see an opera performance of *Boris Godunov*. As Richard listened spellbound to the chorus of praise rising to a dramatic climax and watched the crowd on the stage kneeling to reveal the newly anointed tsar, Boris Godunov, he was reminded once again that Russia had lived with an autocracy for longer than most European countries.

The set and the costumes on stage were truly magnificent but not as impressive as the combined voices of the opera singers which ebbed and flowed with all the power of a restless ocean.

It was hard to believe they were watching *Boris Godunov* in the same theatre in which the opera had made its premiere. The Mariinsky Theatre with its beautifully preserved interior brought back echoes of Imperial Russia at the height of its power.

Richard loved the theatre's neo-Byzantine circular ceiling which had painted Grecian figures holding hands with cherubs. The theatre still had the original gilt and blue chairs in the stalls and its four tiers wrapped themselves around the theatre in a horseshoe shape. The refined gilt, white and blue decor took Richard back to a golden age in Russia's history.

Strangely, though, the performance on stage seemed to contradict all the imperial grandeur of the theatre, because in real life Tsar Godunov's death heralded many years of chaos and disorder in the Russian monarchy, right up until the Romanov dynasty ascended the throne.

Reading his English program, Richard learnt that the opera had been performed for the first time in 1874 to great acclaim, although several witnesses at the time had noted that some members of the imperial family hadn't been at all keen on it and had disparaged the opera as much as they could.

The opera program also pointed out that modern-day scholars believe Tsarevich Dmitry's death was in fact accidental, but unfortunately while Tsar Boris Godunov was in power there were many rumours accusing him of having murdered the true heir to the throne and these rumours had stuck.

Richard thought this was probably the reason why the latter-day imperial family took such a dislike to the opera when it was first performed, but as plenty of notoriety of the murderous kind had dogged the British royal family over the ages, Richard failed to see why the Russian imperial family had an issue with Mussorgsky's work. Scandal seemed to follow all royal families to some degree. It was part of the job description.

Maybe the Tsar's family were insecure about their position in Russian society which, given the events of the Russian Revolution forty-three years later, made sense...

As they had arrived at the theatre very early Richard had plenty of time to learn about the opera while leaving Abdul and Igor to chat eagerly to each other about Chelsea Football Club, a conversation he was unable to take part in as he had no interest in anything to do with football, including penalties, transfers or red cards.

After reading about Mussorgsky's work Richard decided the ambitious opera seemed to contain in its plot a mix of *Hamlet*, *King Lear*, and *Macbeth*; all rolled into one dramatic performance.

In the production Boris Godunov had visions of his murdered heir and this had echoes of *Hamlet*, his guilt and remorse at the boy's murder had similarities with *Macbeth*, and the deranged questions he was going to ask Prince Shuysky in Act 3 brought to mind the madness of King Lear.

Mussorgsky, who must have been quite a character, seemed to be channeling all the pathos and tragedy of Shakespeare and Russian literature in general into his masterpiece.

Igor had secured them seats in the box where they had a view of both audience and stage. This was a bonus for Abdul, who wasn't a big fan of opera and seemed to enjoy watching the audience just as much as the performers on the stage.

During a mournful aria Richard glanced across to Abdul and saw that he was chewing a piece of gum and staring up at the ceiling, a glazed expression on his face. Looking at his evident boredom, Richard couldn't help but feel a sense of overwhelming gratitude towards Abdul for agreeing to join him on this short trip to Russia. Richard had enjoyed visiting the sights and had been able to thoroughly indulge himself inside the Hermitage, but none of their cultural visits had been of any interest at all to Abdul.

Abdul had stoically listened to long explanations on the Hermitage's paintings by Igor's secretary, Anna, who had appointed herself a tour guide for the after-noon, pretending to be interested when no doubt he would rather have been at home getting a takeout in time for the Tottenham game.

While Richard had spent several minutes exam-ining the Matisse paintings in Hall 440, Abdul had sat himself down on a sofa and studied his phone. Later on, while Richard had gazed in ecstasy at *Apostles Peter and Paul* by El Greco, Abdul had taken an extended toilet break.

After an hour of viewing paintings, Abdul offered to meet Richard and Anna in the gallery café, an offer to which they both thankfully agreed. Abdul's boredom radiated out of him and seemed to suck the enjoyment out of a visit to the Hermitage. From then on Anna and Richard made excellent progress through the gallery, viewing works by Raphael, Rembrandt, Gainsborough, Michelangelo, Gainsborough, Titian, Picasso and Van Gogh.

But funnily enough, out of all the artworks they saw, the one that remained in Richard's mind long after he had left the Hermitage was Henri Rousseau's *In a Tropical Forest. Struggle between Tiger and Bull.*

He felt it was a jewel of a picture, painted in Rousseau's recognizably naive style. The luscious green plants of the tropical forest in the painting were broken up by the bright orange, yellow and red colors which drew the eye to the dramatic hunting scene in the center. Henri Rousseau had many detractors but there was the undeniable fact that Pablo Picasso had recognized and admired the artist's work.

After seeing Rousseau's painting in the Hermitage, Richard decided the artist was undervalued and to make a point he bought a postcard of his painting in the Hermitage gift shop.

He would pin it up in his office when he got back.

From the Hermitage they had then gone on to meet Igor at a Russian restaurant and, after a delicious meal, made their way in heavy traffic to the Mariinsky Theatre.

Finally, after two hours of impassioned singing, the heavy blue curtain fell and the Mariinsky Theatre burst into applause, bringing Richard's focus back to the opera. By which time Richard was feeling thoroughly exhausted and was thinking fondly of his hotel bed with its soft, fluffy pillows.

"Well, did you enjoy it?" asked Igor, looking at them proudly, almost as though he had himself composed the opera.

"Yes, absolutely. It was incredible. I can't remember the last time I saw an opera like this one," Richard replied, as they all stood clapping their hands.

"What about you, Abdul?" asked Igor, turning to him with a half-smile.

"It'll be a show I'll never forget, Igor. I can promise you that. I've never seen or heard anything like it," said Abdul, looking sincere, much to Richard's surprise.

"This cast is very famous. The best opera singers in Russia are in it."

Richard and Abdul nodded and looked down at the singers who now had huge smiles on their faces after an evening of conveying pain and suffering in every note and gesture.

After the curtain fell for the last time, Igor sat back on his chair and stretched out his legs. He was wearing a shirt and tie with a jumper whereas Richard and Abdul were more formally attired in their work suits.

"Tomorrow my driver will take you to the airport. What time did you have to be there?"

"We need to be there at ten in the morning," said Abdul.

"Perfect. I'll send him along at a quarter to nine. The morning traffic can be very slow. Please give my regards to Detective Inspector Simmons."

"We will do," promised Richard. "Are you planning to come back to London in the near future, sir?"

"I'm planning to make a business trip to London in

January. I'm toying with the notion of investing in a large printing firm based in Reading. Before that, though, I'll be occupied. The run up to the Christmas vacation is a very busy time for my business... Christmas," added Igor heavily, "is not going to be easy this year, but as you Brits say, "the show must go on"."

Igor shrugged off his melancholy.

"I can't complain," he said. "I've plenty of support from my family, thankfully. Anyway, I hope you both enjoy the vacation."

"Christmas means nothing to me," remarked Abdul, forthright as ever. "We celebrate the Eid in my family, which isn't until May. I'm the black sheep in the family because I don't follow Ramadan, but I do join them for the Eid al-Fitr."

"Of course. At least you'll be getting some peace and quiet during this time then. What about you, Richard? Will you be celebrating Christmas?"

"Yes, probably with my family. If my mother is still talking to me, that is. She's very miffed she hasn't seen me recently. Life's just been too busy."

"Well, you can thank her from me for the time you've spent on my case. I hope, by the way, you'll keep me posted as to any developments regarding my painting. No matter how small, I want to hear about them."

"Of course," said Richard, feeling a little guilty as he said this because he believed it was going to be a remote possibility.

He didn't know how long Igor was going to keep his hopes up with the expectation that Scotland Yard could somehow manage to find his missing painting.

He would keep working on the case, with or without Lionel's blessing, but unfortunately after talking to Colonel Grigory Koikov he had little faith they would manage to find *The Spanish Princess*.

In all honesty, he didn't think the picture was in the UK any more.

The money that had come to Irina had stemmed from foreign bank accounts and, as was often the case with priceless works of art that attracted international interest, he thought the painting was probably abroad somewhere. Unless they somehow managed to decipher the money trail they were unlikely ever to know where the painting was.

16

Richard

It was the 22nd of January and in London the trees were barren. What had been a blanket of pristine white snow had now turned into brown slush and the festive lights had been taken down all over the city.

Tempers were frayed as the New Year seemed to stretch endlessly into the distance. Gyms were full to bursting with people who had overindulged over the Christmas break and the uncertain conundrum of Brexit lingered on in everyone's minds as they walked into their workplaces.

Richard had more or less relegated *The Spanish Princess* to the back of his mind when Mike Telford suddenly popped into his life and, like the ghost of Jacob Marley appearing before Scrooge, reminded him once again of his obligations regarding Igor's stolen painting.

Richard was in his South Kensington flat, dressed in stripy pajamas and brushing his teeth, when Mike had called.

As soon as he saw his phone vibrating, Richard

hastily spat out his toothpaste and reached for it thinking it was a friend who had arrived in London and was looking to meet up during his stay.

His felt a sudden rush of adrenalin hit him when he saw Mike's number on the screen, knowing that the call could herald progress or a new discovery in any one of the five significant art robbery cases pending on his desk.

"Richard?"

"Hi Mike. How are you doing?"

"Good, mate, good. Listen, I've been contacted by one of my pilot fish. It's about that El Greco painting *The Spanish Princess*. They want to meet with us in two days" time at five o'clock in the morning inside the Russian Cathedral of the Nativity of the Most Holy Mother of God and the Royal Martyrs. It's in Chiswick."

"Sorry, say that again?" asked Richard, befuddled by one of the longest names he had ever heard for a religious building.

"The Cathedral of the Nativity of the Most Holy Mother of God and the Royal Martyrs," repeated Mike. "It's in Chiswick. Please don't ask me to say the name again. It seems likely that Chiswick will now be given the status of a city by dint of having this cathedral in it and it sounds like the members of the congregation aren't big fans of the Communist Party either, given the building's dedicated to the Royal Martyrs, aka the Romanov family. Anyway, sorry, I'm digressing. He says they can restore the painting to us, but of course they want money for it. They were asking for twenty grand straight up. I managed to negotiate them down to ten grand because they're not letting us bring in any experts to check the painting, so it's just the two of us. It's a risk we'll have to take."

"Don't they know about Igor's offer for a million?"

"No, they don't actually. If I'd put it about that there was a million up for grabs I wouldn't have had a minute's peace. I'd have had calls every single day from anyone and everyone offering to return that painting. They know if they work with me there's a reward to be had but it would've been madness to tell them a million pounds was on offer. Absolute madness, my friend."

Richard thought for a moment.

Ten thousand pounds didn't seem a credible amount for such a risky robbery and a painting deemed to be unique masterpiece. Could it be that someone else had managed to get hold of the painting and was now wanting to sell it off cheap?

Mike cleared his throat on the other end of the line.

"I'm not saying that I don't hand over a big amount, because in most of my cases the price does end up reaching the million-pound mark," he said. "But you never start off negotiating with a million. You have to sound each other out or you get stung. This isn't dealing with children in a playground, for Christ's sake. These guys play hardball and there aren't any rules in their game."

Richard smiled to himself because he knew for a fact Mike had agreed with Igor to let it be known that a reward of a million pounds was being offered for the return of his painting. But Mike had his own idio-syncratic ways of working and he wasn't about to ques-tion Mike's reasons for not following through on Igor's request. Mike had restored many precious works of art to their rightful owners and in Richard's opinion he was one of London's best private investigators. That was all that mattered.

"So, ten grand straight up. I'll have to ask Igor and see if he can arrange for that sum of money to be made available so quickly. The whole thing seems risky."

"It is and it isn't. Not many people knew of the painting or had access to it. They could have had a fake made up but it would cost them a pretty penny and a very skilled artist to make a decent copy. It wouldn't be worth their while. Not for ten grand. And, anyway, let's hope if it isn't the original painting that we'll spot the fake before we hand over the dosh to them."

"Yes, absolutely. Interesting there's still that Russian connection. It fits in with what Colonel Koikov told us."

"Mmm. I don't think it's particularly significant. Lots of them around in London."

"I'll have to keep Lionel Grieves in the loop."

"Of course. It's all fine as long as he doesn't bring in the big guns and scare my people off. The usual rules apply here: Scotland Yard are to keep out their prying noses out of this or you lot will get nothing."

"Yes, he knows the score, Mike. Are you sure this isn't going to be a wild goose chase?"

"I don't think so. I know this chap. He's pretty well connected. I have to say, though, times are changing when they request to see us at bloody five in the morning. What's happening to them? I mean, in the past most of these guys wouldn't have been seen before lunchtime."

Richard decided he had better stay on topic before Mike started a rant about a criminal's business hours.

"OK, Mike. So just to be clear, I'll meet you outside

the church at 4.45 that morning. I'll call Igor to let him
know what's happening and see if he can arrange to
drop off the money with you. I can't be involved in the
financial aspect of this arrangement so you'd better not
tell me any more about it."

"Sure. No problemo, amigo. I'll see you there then.
I've never been in a Russian cathedral before so this
should be interesting. There's a first time for
everything."

"I don't know if this cathedral's Russian Orthodox
but most Russian Orthodox churches are absolutely
stunning inside. Usually very plain on the outside but
rich in decorative detail on the inside. Representative of
one's inner spiritual life, I suppose. Anyway, see you in
two days unless something else comes up."

"Indeed. Goodbye for now."

Richard put down the phone and, feeling the dry
crust of toothpaste in his mouth, went over to the sink to
rinse his mouth out one more time.

Later that night, as he lay in bed, he wondered
about the Russian cathedral and the part they were
playing in retrieving the stolen painting. Had they
agreed to help out in order to right a wrong? It would be
hard to tell. Like the Italian mafia, the Russia mafia
probably had plenty of connections within the Church
as well...

Lionel was going to be his next biggest challenge.
Richard couldn't predict what his response would be
towards the arranged meeting at the Russian Orthodox
cathedral.

If Lionel had a weak spot, it was that he cared about
results, and so if they came back with the original
painting there was no doubting he would be extremely

pleased to add the success story to the list of his department's achievements.

However, despite Mike's optimism Richard still distrusted that *The Spanish Princess* would appear. For a start the monetary price put on the painting was far too low and there were still questions about where the two large payments Irina had received into her fake bank account had come from. Two different sources suggested two sets of criminals, not one. Had one been duped? They would soon be finding out.

Either way, he knew he had to let Lionel know about the arranged meeting because the secretive exchange at the cathedral could lead to further consequences down the line that would be difficult to explain if he didn't keep Lionel informed.

Lionel hadn't rapped their knuckles for heading to St Petersburg and had seemed quite pleased with the amount of information they had been given by the Russian police, so "unofficially" the case was still open.

Reaching for his mobile, Richard sent Lionel a text message requesting a brief chat regarding *The Spanish Princess* and then dropped off to sleep.

In the morning, when he switched his phone back on, he discovered Lionel had stayed up later than him, for he had texted him back close on midnight suggesting a meeting outside the office at a quarter to twelve the following day.

By the time Richard made it out of New Scotland Yard to meet Lionel, Lionel was already there, waiting for him on the other side of the road with a cigarette in his hand.

"So, you think we might get this painting of Igor's back?" asked Lionel, when Richard reached him.

He took a deep drag from his cigarette and watched the plume of smoke meander upwards as he exhaled.

Richard leaned forward and gazed down at the sluggish grey water of the Thames meandering past them.

A white plastic bottle was bobbing up and down, swept up by the current and adding to the daily rubbish that found itself in the river's waters.

"It's a remote possibility, I guess," said Richard at last, not willing to commit himself. "Wouldn't surprise me if no one turned up at this Russian cathedral to be honest with you. I simply can't understand why they would be willing to sell a valuable painting for just ten thousand pounds. It doesn't make sense. Irina had enormous sums of money paid to her from two very different sources and I'm beginning to wonder how she managed to play them both. We shall see. Igor seems to think it's worth paying the money in any case. It's his risk."

"Do you need any undercover support?" asked Lionel bluntly, looking at Richard in the eye.

"No. Mike only wants the two of us there. He's arranged all of this with a contact and he knows what he's doing. He's done this sort of thing many times before. A cathedral doesn't strike me as a particularly dangerous venue. And in any case, I can't help feeling it's all a big ruse."

"OK. We'll find out soon enough, no doubt. Have you had a go at getting the money from those accounts traced?"

Feeling sheepish due to his lack of progress, Richard turned around and faced New Scotland Yard.

He looked up at the windows stretching up over several floors of the Art Deco building and tried to guess which one belonged to Room 402. The room where all the hullabaloo about *The Spanish Princess* had begun...

"I took it to the DCPCU and they haven't been able to dig up anything on those accounts," he said despondently. "But I've been giving it some thought since Mike got in touch with me and I'm wondering whether to tap Sheila."

"Your friend who works in PwC?"

"Yes, on the tech side of things. She's sometimes willing to do me a favour."

"Go for it. If we can crack those accounts we'll know for sure who's behind all of this."

"And yet even then it might be impossible to bring them to justice."

"Yes, things are becoming harder and harder when these guys reach across international borders. Don't even get me started on Brexit. Without the help and cooperation of our allies in Europe we're going to be in a very tight corner in future. I don't want to even think about it."

Lionel threw his cigarette end to the ground, stubbed it out with the toe of his shoe and then picked it up.

Tossing it into the Thames, he buttoned up his coat and prepared to make his way to his favorite lunchtime venue, Greggs.

"Keep me posted with any developments. I've had the Minister for the Arts on my back regarding this case, as well as representatives from the National Gallery, who are panicking about the repercussions for them if Igor decides to remove his paintings. I've placated them by suggesting we've a few leads on this case so that should keep them happy for a while. As if we didn't have enough on our hands..."

Nodding to Richard in dismissal, he sauntered off.

Richard watched his boss leave, then picked up his briefcase and, enjoying the bright sunshine which was causing the remaining clumps of snow to melt into rivulets of water, he started to walk towards Great Peter Street.

He was pleased he had secured Lionel's blessing in requesting help from Sheila because he had already arranged to meet her that very day, at his favorite restaurant, The Saffron House, situated in the Borough of Westminster.

It hadn't taken him long to contact Sheila after receiving Mike's call.

His interest in *The Spanish Princess* had resurfaced with Mike's encouraging news and he now couldn't shake the painting from his mind.

After walking for fifteen minutes he came to a stop in front of the Indian restaurant, which had a cheerful red billboard outside it announcing the lunchtime menu as a bargain at £25.00 for three courses.

Richard had a weakness for spicy food and had been visiting this restaurant, on and off, for the better part of ten years.

He popped in through the beaded doorway and was instantly accosted by Dasya, a huge man wearing neat navy trousers and a spotless white Kurta tunic.

"Richard, my friend! Back already. You just can't keep away from this place. I don't know how you're so skinny!" joked Dasya, patting Richard on the back and laughing at his blushing face.

Embarrassed because he had been here only the

week before with a copy of *The Spectator* for company, Richard looked around to see if his favorite table by the window was available.

"We're very quiet today, Richard, and as you can see your table awaits you," said Dasya. "However, you'd better reserve a table in future if you like that spot. Yesterday we had a lot of MPs eating here."

Dasya bunched his fingers together and waved a hand expressively, his thick black eyebrows waggling in emphasis.

"Yes, you're right but I'm afraid I'm not that organized, Dasya."

"Don't be so silly! How would you do your job if you weren't organized?" remonstrated Dasya. "Would you like a non-alcoholic beer?"

Richard nodded and, encouraged by the delicious smells emanating from the kitchen, walked to his table while Dasya bustled off to the bar area to fetch his beer.

The Saffron House was like a second home to Richard. Whenever he stepped inside its welcoming portal he felt the exotic Moroccan decor in the restaurant soothe his troubled workday mind. The restaurant had symmetrical, coloured tiles on its walls, metallic lanterns dangling from the ceiling, embroidered wall hangings tied up between the tables and intricately carved wooden chairs and tables. There was also a bright tufted rug at the entrance. All it needed was a calming pool of water in the center of the restaurant and Richard could have been transported to the Marrakesh.

The restaurant's owner, Arjun Vaid, had travelled around Morocco as a young man, had straightaway fallen in love with its culture, and didn't seem to feel there was anything incompatible with having Moroccan decor inside an Indian restaurant or, for that matter, in a restaurant located in Westminster of all places.

However, the unusual decor didn't seem to have done his business any harm or put off any of the customers. Then again, thought Richard, maybe that had something to do with the quality of the food rather than the furnishings.

The restaurant door opened, letting in a blast of cold air, and the hanging beads at the door rustled gently as a young woman walked in.

Richard smiled when he saw her and waved to her from the other side of the room.

Sheila Mackenzie was a long-time school friend of Richard's. After both of them were initially shunned and categorized as nerds at their private school, they had ended up bonding with each other and in the process had somehow managed to withstand all the darker temptations involved in becoming a teenager.

During their time at school they had avoided the excesses of their peers, refusing to be pressurized into anything they weren't comfortable with, and generally did their own thing. They had chummed each other on visits to restaurants, cinemas, galleries and theatres, while managing at the same time to ignore the fact that everyone else assumed they were a loved-up couple.

Watching her, Richard thought she hadn't changed much over the years.

As always she sported a mullet haircut that seemed to be in fashion in the 1980s, she was evidently still refusing to wear make-up, and her round, gold-rimmed glasses seemed to have stayed with her since her mother purchased them on the NHS.

Her face hadn't aged either so she looked young for her years, her intelligent blue eyes viewing the world around her with a quaint cynicism.

Her overall appearance might not have changed much from her school days but her clothing had. Sheila's wine-coloured handbag was a Mulberry, her knee-high black boots, as far as he could tell, seemed to be Louboutins, but even that wasn't what declared her stature as the whizz kid of PricewaterhouseCoopers" IT department.

Once she had removed her gloves, scarf and coat he saw that she was ostentatiously wearing a huge rock of a diamond on her engagement finger. A pretty ruby bracelet encircled her wrist and a large diamond and platinum cross pendant hung from her neck.

Sheila was highly paid enough to indulge her penchant for expensive and unique pieces of jewelry. The magnificent engagement ring, though, had been given to her by her fiancé.

She had found love at last with a City fund manager, initially meeting him over their shared love of rescue dogs. They first met at a dog rescue center, where they soon discovered they lived within easy reach of each other; from then on they had met at Regent's Park for walks every weekend and the rest was history...

"Richard, it's good to see you," said Sheila, kissing him on both cheeks. "It's been a while."

"Yes, it has, though it isn't my fault we haven't met more often," replied Richard with a grin.

Sheila looked a little stricken.

"I know. You're so right. I haven't had much time for my friends since I got engaged."

"A glass of wine for you?" asked Richard as he saw Dasya approaching.

"Yes, perfect. A house white."

"Did you hear that, Dasya?"

"Yes, indeed I did. Very nice to meet you…"

"Sheila. Sheila Mackenzie."

"Delighted, Sheila. I'm Dasya," said Dasya, beaming from ear to ear.

He looked over to Richard and winked at him slyly.

Inured by many years of the same from his schoolmates, Richard lifted his eyes up to heaven and a disappointed Dasya then went off to fetch the glass of wine.

"As I was saying, I'm sorry I've been so uncommunicative," said Sheila. "I'd no idea what getting engaged was going to unleash. My parents expected me to die a spinster and now they've all but killed the fatted calf. I've told David a hundred times I wish we'd taken the first flight to Las Vegas after he proposed. Anyway, enough about me, how are things with you?"

"Good thanks. Same old at work. Too many unresolved cases and beautiful pieces of art disappearing into thin air." He shrugged. "Hopefully when austerity ends we'll get to persuade the powers that be that our department deserves more funding."

"Ha! Good luck with that one… Thanks, Dasya," said Sheila receiving her glass of wine from him.

Richard and Sheila placed their order with the ease of two people who had shared many an Indian meal over the years and whose tastes and habits hadn't changed much from when they'd tucked into their first takeout.

"Sheila, I've a favour to ask you," mumbled Richard towards the end of the meal as they sponged up the remaining traces of sauce in their dishes with bits of garlic naan bread.

"So it wasn't because you missed me, you humbug," said Sheila, grinning at him.

Richard had the grace to look contrite.

"OK. I've been pretty busy too," he admitted. "But it's always good to see you. Anyway, stop trying to distract me, Sheila! This case is important because we're trying to find a painting that's potentially worth millions."

"Fine. You've caught my interest. Out with it. What is it you want me to do?"

"The Russian police came across two large sums of money in a suspect's account and we're trying to trace both sources but as yet to no avail. Could you have a go at cracking it?"

"Yes, of course I can. But you do know that if I'm going to find that out for you it'll almost certainly mean me doing something illegal."

Richard put his chin on his hand and looked at her.

"Yes, I guessed as much. How much exposure will you have?"

"Not much. I'm good at covering my tracks. Hasn't failed me yet."

"Are you in the habit of doing this often?" asked Richard, fascinated.

"Can't tell you that I'm afraid, Richard. Don't tell me you policemen don't have to turn a blind eye to things at times," replied Sheila in a coy tone of voice.

"Yes, quite often actually, but please don't quote me on that."

Richard bent down, opened his briefcase and pulled out a folder with Colonel Koikov's emails in it.

"All the information on the transfers are in these emails. Good luck with it."

Sheila picked up file and without another look, shoved it into her capacious handbag.

"No problem, Richard. I'll do what I can. Now I've a favour to ask you."

"Anything."

Sheila looked at him with a playful sparkle in her eye.

"You might regret saying that. I want you to be my bridesmaid."

Richard choked on the last dregs of his beer. Putting the glass down, he coughed into his serviette.

"What? Sheila, you can't be serious," he said at last.

Sheila placed a hand on his, her eyes pleading with him.

"I'm deadly serious, Richard. Come on, you know me better than anyone. You didn't expect me to be conventional, did you?"

Richard forced a smile.

"I guess not."

Looking anxiously at him, Sheila said nothing.

Against his better judgement, Richard felt himself weakening. This was a big deal to her.

"I refuse to wear a dress though."

Sheila burst into a peal of laughter.

"I totally agree with you. I don't want you to steal the show. Don't worry, you'll have a posh suit to wear."

"And I'm not carrying the veil or a bouquet of flowers."

"Of course not."

"Well, what can I say except that I'm honoured, Sheila."

They grinned at each other until Richard had another thought come to him.

"Hold on a minute. I don't have to organise a hen night, do I?" asked Richard, with dawning horror.

"Now that I'll expect you to do."

"Sheila, I'm pretty clueless as far as women go, and from what I've heard hen nights are far too risqué for me. I wouldn't even know where to start."

"My friend, I know you'll do just fine. We've both got the same taste. I'm looking for something classy, nothing tacky or crude. Whatever you come up with I'll have an absolute ball and that's all that matters. I'll send you details of the budget and the date as soon as I've got it organized."

Looking at her, Richard could see she was set on this. His mood sank a little lower. He wasn't someone who liked to be conventional but this venture seemed to him to be a step too far in eccentricity.

Later on, as he walked back to the office, he continued to mull over his new responsibility. Sheila was easy-going and laidback, but she would have expectations that he would do his best for her as far as her hen night went.

He groaned to himself when he thought about the amount of time it was going to take him to find a suitable venue.

Nearing the entrance of New Scotland Yard, he was distracted by a Bentley with tinted windows that was parked next to the pavement, right on the double yellow lines.

He was surprised no traffic warden had appeared to move the car on. Before he could investigate further, the driver got out of the car and opened the Bentley's rear door.

A pair of long, slim legs appeared, encased in black tights and high heels.

Shortly afterwards Eilidh Simmons pushed herself out of the Bentley, dressed in a smart black suit and looking very pleased with herself.

"Hi Richard!" she called out cheerily, when she spotted him standing rooted to the spot in front of her.

Richard turned and watched as the Bentley drove off.

"Out for lunch were you?" asked Richard, intrigued.

She looked at him with a wary expression in her eyes and became a little aloof.

"Yes, I was actually. With Igor Babikov," she replied, sounding defensive.

"Oh right. Good," said Richard, not knowing what else to say.

They both started to walk into New Scotland Yard as the lunchtime crowd emerged from the building.

Neither of them said another word to each other as they parted in the foyer and went their separate ways.

17

Richard

Richard had been standing next to the Cathedral of the Nativity of the Most Holy Mother of God and the Royal Martyrs in Chiswick for half an hour and he was beginning to lose the feeling in his toes.

As the early morning chill began to creep up his legs, Richard bent his head so that his thick woolen scarf covered his mouth and the bottom of his nose. He disliked the itchy texture of his scarf, which had been given to him as a gift at Christmas, but he felt honour bound to wear it because it was a Burberry scarf and must have cost his mother a pretty penny.

Knowing Mike as well as he did, he should have turned up later. The private investigator always arrived late to his meetings; it seemed to be an ingrained habit of his.

Richard liked to be punctual and so on this cold January morning he had shown up before time and was now bitterly regretting it. He could feel the icy air burning his face and fingers.

Proving that most people were creatures of custom

and routine, he had turned up early even when he knew he would probably end up standing alone like this, in an empty street and waiting in the freezing cold for Mike to turn up.

He started to stamp his feet and jog on the spot, watching his breath puff out in small white clouds as he did so.

The cathedral had been completely silent. There wasn't even the whisper of the wind to listen to and the naked branches of the tree next to him were standing as still and upright as sentinels.

The distinctive, royal-blue onion dome of the cathedral declared its presence above the tree line and the cathedral walls glowed a ghostly white behind the outline of the surrounding dark tree trunks.

There was a light on inside the building, which looked promising. Shimmering through one of the small arched windows it was a beacon of warmth in an otherwise uninviting landscape. The metal gate at the entrance was also slightly open.

Turning to face the road again, Richard saw the headlights of a car in the distance and watched as it slowly reached the bottom of the road. The red Land Rover was driving towards him, then stopped and started reversing into an empty parking space.

Soon afterwards the portly figure of Mike Telford emerged from the car, shutting the car door with a loud clang that echoed up and down the empty street, and then made his way towards him, briefcase in hand.

Mike believed himself to be the epitome of sartorial taste, meaning that he had on an eclectic outfit composed of a fitted brown tweed jacket and cap, with a bright yellow jumper and a red spotted tie underneath.

He was also wearing a pair of dark blue corduroy trousers and tan leather shoes.

Richard, who was wearing his navy suit and long, black coat, felt decidedly dull in comparison to his flamboyant colleague.

There was a lot to be said about the way a person walked and Mike's style of walking was a jaunty one, as though he hadn't a care in the world.

Watching Mike loping along the pavement towards him, Richard thought about the many times he had admired and envied Mike's insouciance, knowing he could never aspire to be as relaxed as him, working as he did for the police force. Mike Telford no doubt had his own tribulations to deal with in his line of work but he was self-employed, which meant he was the boss and therefore master of his own destiny.

"Richard, good to see you!" said Mike, reaching out to shake his hand.

Richard shook his hand, noticing Mike's cheeks were ruddy because of the cold morning air and that his cherubic blue eyes were watering a little. It was definitely time for them both to find somewhere warmer.

Mike turned and studied the cathedral for a moment.

"Good, looks like there's somebody in there. That can only be a good thing. Right, let's get going. I'm running a little late this morning and we don't want them to hedge off."

With that, Mike pushed the gate wide open and made his way around to the side of the cathedral.

Richard followed close behind him, looking around quickly for anything that seemed out of the ordinary or suspicious. He had no idea what to expect that morning.

What was evident was that it wasn't clear where the cathedral's main door was. After walking up and down aimlessly for a couple of minutes they finally discovered a sign that said the entrance was on the other side of the cathedral.

Making their way there, they found a set of stone steps leading downwards to the basement level.

At the bottom of the stairs they pushed open a large wooden door and walked through a long corridor, which thankfully was lit up and heated.

Both of them came to an abrupt standstill when they reached the entrance to the sanctuary, not out of fear or confusion, but because they were both awestruck by the outstanding beauty of the cathedral interior.

Numerous Russian Orthodox icons covered the front wall of the sanctuary, each painted icon surrounded by a gilt background that shimmered and shone in the light reflected from the candles on the altar.

Having studied a little Byzantine art, Richard knew iconography came into its own in Russian Orthodox art. Derived from the art of the Byzantine Empire and influenced by Ancient Egyptian and Greek traditions, Russian icons tried their best to convey the light and beauty of God's world, and what a world it was, thought Richard, gazing at the scene before him.

He looked up at the ceiling and admired the tasteful religious tableaux painted on it in predomi-nantly gold, white and blue colors. The other three walls also displayed Christian figures and events; there was almost too much to take in.

In the past, Russian icons were painted with natural pigments, derived from stones and mixed with egg or water, but even though Richard knew the icons in this present-day cathedral must have been formed with modern materials, each icon had been beautifully depicted by a skilled artist and they took the viewer back in time to another era.

Both Richard and Mike dealt with artworks year after year in their jobs, but this had not dulled their enthusiasm for or minimized their appreciation of beauty. They stood side by side absorbing the decorative art surrounding them and only stopped when a sharp cough from behind them made them jump and turn around quickly.

A priest, dressed in white vestments and with a long black beard, had appeared at an open side door and was watching them with interest.

"Welcome, gentlemen. I've been expecting you. I was told you were Mike Telford and Richard Langley?"

Both of them nodded.

"If you don't mind, I'd like to see some identification before we proceed with this matter. I hope I don't offend you. I'm here as a mediator and I want to ensure we get this painting restored to its rightful owner."

Without saying a word, Richard and Mike pulled out their identification and showed it to the priest. He studied their cards carefully and then handed them back.

"Good, good," he said, smiling at them. "My name is Archpriest Fedor Gushchin. You must be wondering how I'm involved in all of this. I was approached by one of my parishioners who confessed to me that he knew where a valuable stolen painting was. He's a relative of one of the thieves and he told me they were interested in selling it back to its owner. I offered to mediate and so here we are. Gentlemen, if you'll come through to the vestry you can have a look for yourselves..."

The priest turned and led the way to the vestry. As Richard and Mike followed him down another corridor, Richard felt his hands begin to shake with adrenalin and excitement as he realized they were finally coming face to face with the masterpiece that had eluded them for so long.

They entered a small room and Richard saw there were candles lit in the vestry too, giving out a deceptively peaceful ambience given they were about to carry out a transaction with a criminal.

A large Bible with gilt-edged pages was open on a lectern, and on the wall in front of them there was an enameled portrait of the Virgin Mary.

Richard glanced across at a wooden table placed against the far wall and his heart jumped when he saw what looked to be a large canvas stretched out on the top of it.

There were several chairs in the room and sitting on the one nearest the table was a boy with a shaved head, looking no older than thirteen years of age and with an apathetic face. His eyes when he looked up at them showed no emotion whatsoever. He had on jeans that hung loosely on his scrawny hips, a black T-shirt with *"Thug Life"* written across it in large letters and a pair of bleach-white trainers.

"Eh, this is Robbie. He's acting as their representative and he'll be responsible for collecting the money," said Archpriest Fedor Gushchin, as if it was the most normal thing in the world to have a thirteen year old collecting ten thousand pounds.

Richard knew that young boys were used in a number of ways by experienced criminals; sometimes they were sent to rob houses or used as drug and money couriers, as the sentences were lower for underage kids, but to entrust a multi-million-pound masterpiece to a teenage boy seemed to him to be the height of lunacy.

He caught a malevolent glare from Robbie's cold blue eyes and thought maybe the criminals in charge weren't so crazy after all.

"Can we look at the painting, Robbie?" asked Mike in a jovial tone of voice.

"Sure, but don't take too long. I've been told to get the deal done in fifteen minutes max."

Richard and Mike exchanged glances, signalling they were going to ignore this stipulation. If Robbie's bosses wanted the money they would have to be patient.

"I'm sorry, mate, but if I'm going to hand over ten grand we need to have a good look at the painting," explained Mike calmly.

Robbie shrugged his shoulders but didn't protest.

They went up to the painting and stared down at it.

Richard felt a thrill as sudden as an electric shock go through him when he looked down and saw Princess Catalina Micaela staring up at him from the table.

He opened up his briefcase and took out some of Igor's photos.

"Excuse me, but do you mind putting the main light on, please?" asked Mike, turning around and looking at the priest, who nodded and switched it on.

Both men began to examine the painting closely, Mike with a large magnifying glass and Richard with his photos as reference. They studied the surface of the canvas and all the tiny cracks in the varnish. The colors seemed almost too bright and vibrant for such an old painting but this was understandable given it had been restored less than a year previously.

After twenty minutes Richard decided every detail in the picture was identical to those in Igor's photos.

The only issue was the canvas itself.

Mike lifted the picture gingerly with gloved hands and looked underneath it. El Greco's Greek inscription was on the back and the canvas looked oxidized, tinged a mushroom brown and stained in certain places. This was what they expected to see in such an old canvas. The weave was loose, too, at the edges, and there were minute holes in the woven fabric, as there would be in a canvas from the sixteenth century.

However, something didn't look right to Richard.

He had looked closely at the remains of the canvas in Igor Babikov's bedroom and had noticed that the painting had been cut out by what seemed to be a very sharp Stanley knife. In Igor's flat the leftover edges of the canvas were cut shear and straight as opposed to the painting they were now viewing with its irregular, jagged sides.

"What do you think?" whispered Mike into Richard's ear.

"I've got my doubts. The edging isn't right. It was sliced cleanly out of its frame."

They heard Robbie moving restlessly on his chair. He wasn't going to let them take much longer, especially not if he thought they were having doubts about the painting's authenticity.

With a pensive face, Mike bent down and studied the edge of the canvas, running a gloved finger along it as he did so.

After a minute he stood up again.

"I think we should take it, Richard. It's too risky to let it go. Depending on how they kept this, the edges might have been roughened up while it was in their possession."

Deciding he wasn't going to argue the point with Mike, Richard shrugged. They would find out soon enough if they had been duped.

"It's your call, Mike. Igor left the money to you."

Mike grinned, gave him a wink and then bent down to pick up the thick briefcase that had been sitting between his legs while he inspected the painting. He held it out to Robbie.

"OK, Robbie. Here's the dosh."

Without saying a word, Robbie picked up the brief-case, took it to the other side of the room and unzipped it. He laid out the wads of fifty-pound notes on the ground and then took a pen out of his back pocket. Quickly and randomly he ran the counterfeit note detector pen over the wads, before chucking them into an empty grey rucksack.

Richard watched him in some amusement, thinking it was a bizarre situation in which they were worried about the authenticity of the painting and Robbie in turn was concerned with the validity of their bank notes. There was little trust on either side...

Once Robbie had left, Mike Telford went to his car and fetched a large plastic case into which he slid the canvas, ready for transportation to Orion Analytical. He had advised Igor that it would be sensible to have the painting authenticated again for insurance purposes because neither Richard nor himself were in a position to vouch for its validity and their scrutiny of the picture wasn't infallible. Luckily for them, Igor was good-natured and had deep enough pockets to approve of this expensive precaution.

In the end it took Orion Analytical only a week to declare Robbie's version of *The Spanish Princess* a fake.

There were very few people who had been given access to the original painting and even fewer who might have possessed the skill to produce an identical copy of it.

Before long Richard and Abdul turned their attention towards Max Hofmann, the talented restorer who had worked on the painting less than a year ago.

He was invited in to speak to the police at New Scotland Yard and it was no surprise to them when he turned up with his lawyer.

Both were now seated side by side in the interview room and both Richard and Abdul watched them for a moment through the CCTV before entering the room.

Dressed all in black and still wearing his thick puffer jacket, Max Hofmann's body posture was nervous; he was leaning forward and one of his legs was jigging up and down. The lawyer accompanying him was a very young man who looked like he had only just finished his legal training.

They were talking to each other in a desultory manner, only occasionally looking up at the camera on the ceiling as though they were aware they were being spied on.

"Time to go in," said Abdul.

Richard nodded his agreement and followed Abdul as he traversed the long corridor and walked into the interview room. They took a seat each in front of Max and his lawyer.

Richard turned towards the lawyer in polite enquiry.

"Your name is?"

"Stephen. Stephen Fallow."

"Could we see your ID please?"

"Certainly," replied Stephen obligingly, bending down and retrieving it from his briefcase. He passed it over to Richard.

Richard and Abdul glanced at it and nodded, handing it back to him.

"Well, Max. Thank you for coming in today," said Abdul in a cheerful voice.

Max didn't say anything, glowering at them as though he were being subjected to the most inhumane and degrading treatment.

His hair color was still the same luminous blue, noted Richard, thinking he must have attracted a fair amount of interest walking into New Scotland Yard that afternoon. Maybe that was the point.

Abdul reeled off the standard caution, telling him that he had the right to silence and that the content of the interview could be used against him as evidence. Max refused to look at anyone during this, instead choosing to stare at the door as though wishing he could leave.

"OK, Max. We can see you want to get on your way but I'm afraid we do need to ask you a few questions," said Richard softly.

Max remained silent, turning his large dark eyes towards him. All Richard could see in the depths of them was contempt and possibly even fear.

"We were sold a fake copy of Igor Babikov's painting a week ago. It was a very skilled copy and given there have been so few people that had access to the original, let alone with the skill to make up a convincing copy, we are looking to ask you if you've painted a copy of *The Spanish Princess*, and if so why?"

Watching Richard's face, Max said nothing.

"With Oliver Newton's permission we've spoken to the security guards. They say you stayed late at work several weeknights when you were working on restoration of *The Spanish Princess*."

"So? What's the crime in that? I was doing some overtime. That's all it was."

"They also say you came in for two consecutive weekends, which was very uncharacteristic behaviour for you," stated Richard in a long-suffering voice.

"As I said, I was just putting in some overtime. I was skint after Christmas and I still needed to pay off several bills in February."

"Fair enough. The CCTV footage shows that you weren't working on Igor's painting during that time. In fact it shows you spending an inordinate amount of time going in and out of the stockroom. You are seen on camera looking closely at the original *The Spanish Princess* on several occasions and then walking back into the stockroom."

A thin sheen of sweat was developing on Max's upper lip and forehead. His already pale skin seemed a shade lighter.

"I can only say, Max, that it could work in your

favour to come clean about this. Sooner or later we'll find out what's been happening with that painting. We've links to the men who sold the fake painting to us and we can pursue things that way but I suspect you'd prefer we didn't do that."

Running a tongue over his dry lips, Max nodded. He didn't seem to have conceded defeat but he was at least engaging for the first time with what Richard was saying to him.

"OK. Is there anything you'd like to say to us about the fake?" asked Abdul, with an impatient edge to his voice.

Max lowered his head and looked down at the table for a moment.

"Irina asked me to paint a duplicate," he said at last. "She said she'd pay good money for it and I needed the dosh. That's all I know."

He lifted his eyes from the table and glanced at Richard and Abdul for a brief moment, before shifting his gaze again.

Richard didn't believe him. There was no explanation for his nervousness if that was all he knew. Something or someone was putting the fear of God into him.

For a minute he wondered if the fake had replaced the original painting in Igor's flat. It was plausible given Irina's duplicity but it didn't really wash. One thing was for sure, it certainly hadn't happened during the time *The Spanish Princess* was getting restored. Oliver Newton's security was so tight around the artworks he cared for in his firm it would have been near impossible to exchange the two paintings. They might not have been able to observe what Max was up to in the storeroom but the original *The Spanish Princess* would have been under the watch of a camera or a guard pretty much from the time it left Igor's flat to when it returned.

Could Irina have had the paintings swapped once they were both at the flat? It was feasible but then Richard thought about the two monstrous payments Irina had received and how both were transferred within a few weeks of each other. This tended to suggest she had disposed of both paintings at a similar time.

"Did she tell you why she wanted a duplicate?" asked Richard.

Max shook his head, silent again.

"Max, I don't think you're telling us the whole story here. How well did you know Irina?" questioned Abdul, looking more and more impatient as the interview continued.

This question startled Max into sitting upright. Stephen Fallow put a cautionary hand on his arm but didn't say anything.

"What do you mean?" Max asked, his bulging eyes making him look a little like an alarmed lemur.

"I mean if we dig around, will we find that you knew Irina better than you're letting on?" said Richard calmly.

Max thought about this.

"We did meet up a few times near her flat," he admitted reluctantly. "It wasn't anything to do with a romantic relationship, if that's what you're suggesting. We connected, that's all."

"It's difficult for us to comprehend why Irina would be interested in meeting up clandestinely with you."

"Clandestinely? With my hair? Seriously, are you having a laugh?" asked Max, full of scorn.

"OK. So you and Irina met up a few times," continued Richard undeterred. "Did Igor know about your meetings?"

Max shrugged.

"I don't think so."

"What did you both talk about?" interjected Abdul.

Max took a deep breath.

"I told you. She wanted me to paint a realistic copy of *The Spanish Princess*. We met up a few times to discuss progress on the painting."

"It was certainly a very convincing fake. I imagine only a restorer like you could have produced such an authentic copy," agreed Richard. "How much did you get paid?"

"She paid me fifteen grand for it. It wasn't an easy painting to copy and I had the added problem of having to age the duplicate, so that it would look like a convincing sixteenth-century painting to any layman. It worked because they fell for it."

"Who fell for it?" asked Abdul.

The ever-ready fear crept back into Max's eyes.

"I'm sorry, I can't tell you that."

"Has this person, or these people, threatened you, Max? It sure sounds like it," commented Richard, attempting to be persuasive but knowing he wasn't fooling anyone, least of all the two men on the other side of the table.

Max's lawyer cleared his throat.

"I wouldn't say anything, Max," said Stephen Fallow hurriedly.

But his warning was needless. Both Richard and

Abdul had read many people's faces in their time at New Scotland Yard and they could see the terror written all over Max's face was going to override any temptation he might have had to spill the beans.

"OK. Did Igor not wonder what Irina was spending fifteen grand on?" asked Abdul after a pregnant pause.

A smile surfaced on Max's face, the first one since he had entered the interview room, as Max began to look amused.

"You've got to be kidding! Irina regularly bought five grand designer dresses at Harrods. Fifteen grand was a drop in the ocean of her spending. I mean, that girl liked to shop... All she had to do was make three separate payments to my sister's clothing store in Richmond and it was done. No questions asked."

"What happened after you finished working on the paintings? Did you still meet up with Irina or did you simply lose contact?" asked Richard.

"I didn't see Irina after both paintings were handed over to her."

"Do you know that Irina was discovered murdered in a hotel room in Russia?"

Max's face showed no emotion as he stared at the two detectives. He was clearly thinking through his reply to this question.

After a couple of minutes he sighed despondently and nodded, his blue hair flopping up and down.

"How did you find out, Max?" asked Abdul, leaning forward as though to hear him better.

"I heard through Oliver Newton."

"Interesting. We've not informed anyone about Irina's death so I'm very curious to know how Oliver Newton heard about it," lied Abdul pensively, knowing it was unlikely Oliver Newton would be telling his staff about the murder. "Maybe we should ask him."

Stephen Fallow cleared his throat as Max sat stricken and mute.

"That's enough, gentlemen. You've no reason to keep badgering my client in this way."

"I'm afraid I beg to differ. We have two murders unresolved and a masterpiece, potentially worth millions, missing. That gives us every right," said Richard in an astringent voice.

Max and Stephen registered the note of anger in Richard's speech and visibly quailed before it, but they still said nothing.

Richard sighed as he looked at his colleague.

He caught Abdul's eye and received a slight nod from him, indicating it was time to wrap things up.

They would summon Max back again and again if they had to, until he cracked like a hazelnut. His admission that he had in fact forged *The Spanish Princess* for Irina made him an important informant, if not suspect, in the case. But it was obvious they weren't going to get any more out of him today and it was best to leave him to stew a bit, to think over his choices and decide whether it was worth his while volunteering more information to the police.

"That'll be all for today, Max," said Abdul. "We'll be looking to speak to you again in the near future so please keep us informed of your movements. I hope you'll reconsider and tell us all that you know. We could turn out to be a safer bet than those people who are hovering over you."

Max's contemptuous, disbelieving expression denied this assertion. He did not think the police would be able to save him from the consequences of grassing up, which in itself spoke volumes about the control and reach of the people he was involved with.

Richard started to worry for a moment that Max might have forged other well-known paintings and sincerely hoped there wasn't a stately home or museum with a Max Hofmann painting hanging in the stead of a valuable masterpiece.

They would have to speak to Oliver Newton about the forgery but Max would already know his days at the restoration firm were finished now that he had confessed to creating a fake masterpiece. It was going to be an ignominious ending to the career of a talented conservator-restorer.

Getting up hastily, scraping his chair across the floor in the process, Max stood up and left the room without a backwards glance. His lawyer calmly picked up his briefcase and with an apologetic smile followed suit.

In a strange way Richard felt sorry for Max but he wasn't sure why. Despite Max's outward bravado, he sensed Max was already regretting taking on Irina's commission and suspected that the people they had flogged the fake painting to might well be keen to meet with its creator. Defiant, grumpy and awkward, Max was still not going to be a match for any ruthless criminal bent on getting revenge.

Just over a week later Richard's premonition proved to be correct.

On the 12th of February Abdul made his way down to Richard's office, a somber expression on his face.

"Abdul! Everything OK?"

As he held open the door, Richard worried that

something had happened to Eilidh and then dismissed the thought as ludicrous.

"It's Max... He was waiting at a bus stop in Camden at eleven o'clock last night when a man, in a grey balaclava and approximately 6 foot 1 according to witnesses, suddenly came up to Max and stabbed him in the back of his neck, right at the base of his skull, shoving him onto the road just as a taxi was driving down the bus lane."

"And?"

"And he didn't survive it..."

"For God's sake! Didn't anyone try to help him?"

"From what the witnesses say, it all happened so quickly no one had time to respond. They were all in shock, understandably. Two of the passers-by who saw it happen started running after the attacker but he outran them."

Richard leant back against the wall for support.

"Poor sod. A professional hit... It's not exactly an everyday occurrence, is it?" he asked.

"It was definitely the work of a professional judging by the knife wound; it severed the brain stem straight-away. As for pushing him onto the road... that stuff tends to happen more on railway or underground platforms."

Abdul sighed.

"I think we're hitting another blind alley with this case." In his irritation Abdul had started to chew a nail, continuing to speak through his gritted teeth. "It seems everywhere we turn we keep coming up against a brick wall. They're always one step ahead of us."

"I don't think so. Don't forget we still have Mike Telford. He'll be keeping an eye out for that painting and Sheila Mackenzie might well come up with something... She's very good at what she does. Let's not lose heart."

Having taken a covert look around Richard's workspace, Abdul turned to face him.

"Is it really worth it?" he asked.

"What do you mean?"

Abdul pointed to all the weighted shelves in the room.

"I mean all these deaths because of an oil painting. Think of the amount of resources we're putting into tracing one old picture."

Richard sighed. He had been here many times before.

"It depends on your point of view of course. These Old Masters are a reflection of our humanity; the form in which we revere our past, our culture and development. Our appreciation of art is unique in the animal world, it represents our higher calling if you like. But I can understand your frustration. At the end of the day they're only objects, not people."

Abdul looked Richard squarely in the eye.

"I feel gutted that we didn't crack Max during our interview. If we had, he might well be alive today."

"I doubt it. If Irina was double-crossing the Russian mafia there'll be a whole network existing in the shadows. If we'd arrested anyone, there would be plenty more to step up and take their place," said Richard, crossing his arms. "My priority is to find the damn painting so this toxic chain reaction can come to a stop. As long as that painting remains in private hands there'll be others looking for it. We've to get there first, in my view."

Abdul nodded, a resigned expression on his face.

"What I don't get is why Irina took such a big risk with the painting," he reflected. "She might have been plain greedy and played two buyers at the same time. But look what happened to her. Why would she take such a big risk? I can't think why she would have given the original to someone else and not to the nasty piece of work threatening her. What was her motivation? None of it makes sense. Forgive me for being despondent but I'm not sure we'll ever find out what really went on with that painting."

Richard grinned.

"Well I'm an optimist so I'll keep on hoping we find out more. A deluded optimist possibly, but there we are."

"Did you hear about Eilidh's grandmother?" Abdul asked, all of a sudden.

"No," said Richard, feeling surprised. It wasn't like Abdul to volunteer information in this confiding manner.

"She's been admitted into hospital. They've discovered she now has a brain tumor and it isn't looking good. She doesn't have many days left to live. Eilidh's been off since the end of last week."

"That's grim. Which hospital was she admitted into?"

"Kingston Hospital. We're arranging a collection for some flowers if you're interested in contributing."

Richard nodded and went to fetch his wallet.

He hoped they weren't going to buy roses. He still vividly remembered the drooping, dying blood-red roses in Igor's bedroom.

18

Eilidh

Eilidh stretched out a leg, feeling the pins and needles tingling along its length as the blood circulation returned to it.

The hospital armchair she was sitting on was uncomfortable to say the least; made of heavy-duty padding and plastic, the chair was easy to clean but it had not been designed with the sitter's pleasure in mind because it felt as hard as a rock.

Outside the small hospital room nurses were racing back and forth across the hallway.

She was grateful her grandmother had a single room to herself but even there it was hard to get any peace. Nurses came in constantly (at night switching on the lights as they did their checks), in the mornings the cleaners barged in, banging around with their bucket and mop, the tea lady popped in at regular intervals (to be fair, mostly for Eilidh's benefit), the mealtime staff and even the doctors made an appearance, even though there was little they could do now for Audrey Simmons.

Audrey was nearing the end of her time on earth

but she had lived a very positive and fruitful life, during which she had dedicated a good number of years to supporting her two motherless grandchildren. Eilidh knew her grandmother would have no regrets.

It was a small consolation.

Oblivious to what was going on in the room, Eilidh's grandmother floated in between two worlds, the morphine often taking her back to her childhood and leaving her to murmur and ramble to herself.

She looked skeletal and tousled, her frail body stretching down the length of the bed but barely covering half of its width. Eilidh itched to fix her hair and put some make-up on her pallid cheeks, anything to restore some pride and dignity to her last hours, but she did not want to disturb her uneasy slumber. Her grandmother was not at peace; her face looked tormented and anxious as she fought against an illness that was stronger than her indomitable will.

The room smelt strongly of flowers.

Sitting on the bedside table was a magnificent bouquet kindly sent by Igor, made up of mauve roses, pale pink veronica, and green thlaspi. A smaller bunch of flowers made of daffodils, yellow alstroemeria and purple-edged lisianthus, from Eilidh's colleagues at New Scotland Yard, had arrived the day before and was brightening up the window ledge.

The only thing that looked out of place in the room was a wet pool of water that had gathered by the door to the toilet. Eilidh had soon discovered the adjoining bathroom had a leakage problem when she showered in it for the first time and watched helplessly as the water began spreading outwards until even the bedroom began to flood. The cleaners, used to the shower's idiosyncrasies, cursed the building's poor design every time they cleaned the room and had to mop up the water-logged bathroom.

Refreshed by her shower earlier that morning but still feeling exhausted, Eilidh tried to get herself comfortable on the rigid armchair and looked at her watch.

It was eleven o'clock in the morning and Mark, her brother, was due to take over in only an hour but given how tired she was feeling that felt like a century away.

With her head tilted back against the headrest she tried to take a nap, letting the book she was holding in her hand slowly edge downwards towards the floor. *Where the Crawdads Sing* was an enthralling book but she was so tired she couldn't take in the words any more, finding that she was reading the same line once, twice, three times, before realizing her mind had wandered elsewhere.

A sharp knock at the door startled her.

It wasn't the usual apologetic tap of a visiting doctor; it seemed more like an authoritative demand to enter the room.

The book slid unnoticed to the floor as she sat up.

Looking across at the glass window separating their room from the corridor outside, she saw Richard stooping down and smiling at her through it, with his floppy hair looking badly in need of a cut and his fringe covering the top of his glasses.

Pleased to see him, she smiled and got up to open the door.

"Richard! What are you doing here?"

"Providing some HR support," said Richard humorously.

Eilidh giggled, realizing as she did so that she was getting a little hysterical with tiredness.

Richard's comments often made her want to laugh and although his latest gag wasn't very funny, his attempt at comedy in such a ghastly location tickled her. Only Richard could seem to be so utterly impervious to the horror of being in a hospital ward and already she was feeling all the better for his visit.

"Are you able to take a break for coffee?" asked Richard, looking over at Eilidh's grandmother as she murmured to herself, her hands twitching restlessly on the bed sheet.

Eilidh shook her head.

"No, I'm afraid not. I don't think she has much longer to go. We want to be by her side when it happens."

Richard nodded, a compassionate look in his eyes as he smiled at her.

"Then it's just as well I brought you some coffee and muffins."

He lifted the plastic bag he was carrying and showed her the contents before handing it over. Two Starbucks drinks were inside it, rammed into a cardboard holder, and a large paper bag filled with chocolate muffins.

Abdul had told her all about Richard's coffee shop addiction and his frequent trips to the Starbucks near their work. Abdul (who was a bit tight, it had to be said) frowned upon wasting money on hot drinks and brought in his own thermos flask of hot coffee on the days he was at the office.

Eilidh, who was something of a coffee addict herself, saw nothing wrong in downing several shots of caffeine a day. In her opinion there were worse vices one could have, especially given the number of people in the force who seemed to be functioning alcoholics.

"Perfect," said Eilidh, walking back into the room and moving a plastic chair from the wall so Richard could sit down.

She lifted the cardboard container carefully out of the bag, presenting it to Richard first. Richard turned the cups around until he identified his drink by the scribble on the side, and then freed his cup from its base.

He leant back and drank a mouthful of coffee.

Eilidh picked up the remaining cup and took a tentative sip, pleasantly surprised to find it was a cappuccino, her favorite coffee. Richard had done his homework.

"So what's happening back at work?" she asked in a matter-of-fact voice, disguising her pleasure at this unexpected treat.

"You mean with *The Spanish Princess* case?"

"Of course, you eejit. It's the only case we've worked on together."

"Well, I think Abdul is about ready to throw the towel in. I don't know how much Abdul has told you about the latest events. Max, the restorer who worked on the painting, was knifed in the neck two nights ago in a professional hit. We don't think we'll ever get who did it."

Eilidh nodded impatiently. She had heard all this from Abdul.

"They must've been watching him," continued Richard. "It seems Max knew the people Irina was involved with a little too well. He was so afraid of them he didn't give us any information whatsoever during our interview but we had hoped to get him to open up eventually."

"Didn't these guys want to grill Max about the original painting? After all, that's what they must desperately want now they know they've been sold a dud."

"I've no idea if they did question him about the original painting but I suspect he knew nothing about where the authentic picture ended up. Irina was a canny woman. He was right to be scared in the end, poor git. So, we're back to square one, unless Mike turns up with something new. That's often the way it is with art crime, these types of cases always take their time to get resolved, if at all. That's not Abdul's style, though."

He crossed his legs and smiled to himself.

"Or Lionel's for that matter," he added, following this observation with another swig of his coffee.

Swirling her drink around in its cup, Eilidh thought about this.

From the moment she had begun dating Igor she had spent a fair amount of time talking to him about the painting, thinking about the details of the case and trying to figure a way out of the conundrum; all in her own time, of course, because officially she wasn't supposed to working on the case anymore.

She noticed Richard seemed a little taken aback by her interest in the stolen painting, especially when her grandmother was slowly dying in front of them, but she didn't care. She wasn't in the mood for polite chit-chat.

While she fidgeted with her coffee Richard had taken a large bite out of a chocolate muffin and was munching it contentedly, looking as much at home in the hospital room as he was at the office.

"Who's Sheila, by the way?" asked Eilidh, out of the blue.

Richard stopped chewing for a moment and looked at her. After they had stared each other down for a few seconds, he finished his mouthful.

"Who told you about Sheila?" he asked.

"Abdul. Who else?"

"I hope he doesn't spread the word around because he could be putting her at risk," said Richard, looking annoyed. "She's helping me in an unofficial capacity."

"So, who is she?"

"She works in the IT department at an accounting firm and is a real genius at it. I went to school with her."

"Wow! That's going back a long way. Are you romantically

involved?"

"Yes, well, that's what everyone else assumes," said Richard with some bitterness in his voice. "But no, we're not romantically involved. We're just very close friends."

"I didn't think that ever worked between men and women."

"Well it does for us," responded Richard with some heat. "And I don't understand why there always has to be an agenda when there's a close friendship between a man and woman. It's slightly prehistoric, if you don't mind me saying so."

"Sorry, I didn't mean to touch a nerve," said Eilidh in an apologetic voice.

But in reality she was not feeling in the least bit remorseful. If anything, she was finding their conversation amusing and a welcome distraction given the circumstances.

"What's the deal with you and Igor?" asked Richard in return.

She had indeed touched a nerve.

Richard's desire to exact revenge for her awkward, probing questions took her by surprise but she was not displeased to find that he had some claws on him after all.

Eilidh put her coffee down and started picking at a loose nail. She wasn't sure how to answer Richard's pertinent question.

"It's not going anywhere really... Just a bit of harmless fun, I guess. It's very nice to be spoilt now and again but you know Igor's way of life. He spends most of his time in Russia, so it isn't going to last," replied Eilidh eventually, glancing across at her grandmother to check how she was.

Richard smiled back at her.

He seemed to appreciate her bluntness, which was another surprising revelation for Eilidh. Pleased by this, Eilidh found herself suppressing a long-held, heartfelt wish that her closest friends would also prize her truthfulness. Her friends all too often complained about her brutal honesty, grumbling that she never flinched from an awkward question, had no delicacy whatsoever and wasn't afraid to make a fool of herself. Apparently, far too often for their liking, she ended up embarrassing them.

At times, she felt she couldn't do anything right in their eyes, other than give herself a lobotomy and become someone else.

"You never know, Igor might well be serious about his relationship with you. He didn't strike me as the type to mess around. He seemed a bit too intense, if anything," remarked Richard as she drank her coffee.

It seemed like he wanted to console her and this riled Eilidh as she didn't want him to feel sorry for her, quite the opposite in fact.

"Yes. He's a pretty decent man. But there's no spark there, if you know what I mean," she said, showing her indifference to Igor's charms.

Richard laughed.

The cynicism in his manner made her grit her teeth because she was starting to feel as though he was treating her like a two year old.

She glared back at him.

"Actually, no, I don't know what you mean. I've never had the "spark" myself in any relationship," Richard replied, defensive in the face of her obvious irritation.

"Never?"

"No."

Eilidh studied him while he finished his coffee.

He *was* cute in a kind of foppish way. His skin was very pale and his thick wavy hair was dark blonde, badly in need of a cut but shaped by a good hairdresser.

She didn't think he took very good care of himself.

His shoes looked expensive, yet badly needed a polish, his suit trousers were so worn they were shiny in places and his shirt hadn't been ironed very well. But there was definitely something about him that intrigued her.

Richard, looking a little self-conscious at her scrutiny of him, cleared his throat loudly.

"One downside of being good friends is that Sheila

now wants me to be her chief bridesmaid at her wedding."

"No!" exclaimed Eilidh in astonishment, noting at the same time how adept Richard was at changing the subject.

She couldn't help laughing at the thought of him acting as a bridesmaid, lifting up the sleeve of her jumper to cover her mouth, and it didn't take Richard long to follow suit, after he tried but failed to look offended and hurt by her laughter.

"She wants me to book the venue for a hen night and I've literally no idea what to do. I've never done anything like this before."

"It's kind of sweet. She must rate you very highly." Eilidh turned so she was facing Richard. "I'll put my thinking cap on."

"Thank you. I'd be grateful for any help you could give me."

"When is the wedding?"

"Oh, not for ages yet. March next year."

"It's crazy, isn't it, how people have to book wedding venues so far in advance these days. I reckon they got it right in the old days when they had very short engagements. I mean, anything could happen, people change their minds all the time."

"I suspect with mortality rates being higher and weddings being more in the nature of a financial contract, they had more incentive to get things done speedily in bygone days."

"You're a real romantic at heart," remarked Eilidh, sarcastic but regretting it straightaway.

This was a side of herself she didn't like, hard as granite.

What a pair Richard and she were turning out to be! But then again the police force tended to be like that, wiping away any intrinsic naivety or belief in the goodness of mankind.

The beginnings of an embarrassed flush started making its way up Richard's cheeks.

He bent down hurriedly to pick up the bag with the muffins, opening it up and offering her one.

She couldn't resist taking one; the moist sponge was glistening enticingly, except for where a few hard-edged lumps of chocolate poked out. A delicate eater, she began to break off small bits of chocolate sponge as she ate it.

"Anyway, back to work, " she said with single-minded focus, in between nibbling bits of muffin, hoping that talking about work would put Richard at ease and feed her insatiable curiosity about the case. "I was thinking about *The Spanish Princess* and was wondering why you haven't pursued the Spanish side of things? Like that lady who received the poster tube."

"You know we can't just go to Spain and interrogate the woman without the agreement and authority of the Spanish police."

"You could get Isabel Perón to persuade them. They might listen to her."

Eilidh watched as Richard, looking uncomfortable, shifted on his seat.

"To be honest I'm hoping Sheila can come up with something that gives us a lead or connection. We've really got very little else to go on. Isabel Perón even less."

"Did Isabel ever trace the family tree for Catalina Micaela's love child?" mused Eilidh. "It would be fascinating to see how many present-day relatives she might have."

"I know. Will they be in Spain or scattered across the world? It would be quite something to find out you were related to Spanish royalty," agreed Richard, reaching down for another muffin.

"Eilidh!" said a husky and breathless voice from the bed.

Still holding her muffin, Eilidh jumped up from her armchair and went to Audrey's bedside.

She looked down sadly at her grandmother's face as her grandmother in turn gazed up at her with watery black eyes.

"I'm going to leave you soon. I'm sorry..."

"There's nothing for you to be sorry about, Gran," she said firmly.

Eilidh heard and then saw Richard quickly picking up their empty coffee containers and the muffin bag. He emptied them into the bin in the bathroom.

"I'll head now but I'll be touch," said Richard quietly as he walked past the bed.

Eilidh nodded, her hand on her grandmother's frail wrist.

As Richard made his way to the door, she remembered something.

"Richard!"

He turned, looking at her enquiringly.

"Could you send me Isabel Perón's number?"

"Of course, no problem."

The door shut behind him and Eilidh turned back to her grandmother who was watching her with an appraising gleam in her teary eyes.

"Who was that?" she gasped out.

"A work colleague," said Eilidh.

"Oh."

Her grandmother reached up to grab Eilidh's arm.

"Eilidh, where's Mark?"

"He'll be here very soon," reassured Eilidh, pulling her mobile phone out of her shirt pocket and texting her brother, hoping he wouldn't take too long to arrive because these days it was a rare event for her grandmother to be lucid.

"The house is already in both your names," whispered Audrey, gazing at the opposite wall.

Resisting the urge to roll up her eyes, Eilidh nodded.

"Yes, we know. Don't worry about that stuff, Gran. We'll be fine."

It was a mystery to her how so many people in the midst of a crisis focused on the financial aspect of things. Only a few months ago she had spoken to a couple whose son had been beaten to death during a night out in Shepherd's Bush and their primary concern seemed to be that they had nobody else to leave their money to, as the deceased was their only child and they had no close relatives. Eilidh was tempted at the time to say to them "Spend it! Have a ball! Live your life to the full!" but she had wisely refrained from giving them any unsolicited advice. After all, who was she to judge? She only had a limited life experience and no family of her own to think of.

Restless, Audrey moved her head from side to side as she looked around the room.

"Where did the flowers come from?"

Every word seemed to consume precious oxygen

from her grandmother's lungs and Eilidh was finding it painful to watch her labored breathing.

"Those were given to you by my work colleagues and a friend," she replied with great patience, having already explained this to her grandmother five times.

"Oh, they are so pretty!"

Audrey continued to look at the flowers by the window for a few seconds before staring intently back up at her granddaughter.

"You need to do something you enjoy. You're not happy where you are."

"I know. I'll get it sorted," said Eilidh soothingly, stroking Audrey's hand and hoping she wasn't about to get a pep talk about her work.

But Audrey had relapsed again into the other world in her head, the one where she was a child asking her mother for her soft toy "Pati". She pawed Eilidh's hand, begging her to go fetch "Pati" from the washing line and to let her have it for bedtime.

The nurse came into the room just as Audrey began to sob, berating Eilidh for not fetching her cuddly toy.

Unfazed by this scene, the nurse went across to the bed and scolded Audrey in her cheerful Caribbean accent, "Come now, Mrs Simmons. No more tears, it is no good for you. You are going to get some rest now, OK? You need to calm down. We don't want to see no tears here."

The voice of authority had its effect, much to Eilidh's relief, and Audrey's moans and cries diminished to faint whimpers as the nurse took her blood pressure and temperature.

"I think the doctor should have a look at her and see

if the morphine needs to be increased," said the nurse to Eilidh. "It's not good for her to get upset."

"No," agreed Eilidh, feeling drained.

The nurse gave her a hearty, commiserating pat on the shoulder and went out to do her next round.

Eilidh's phone beeped loudly, twice.

Expecting to see a text from her brother, she saw the text was from Richard with Isabel Perón's number on it.

She smiled.

When Mark arrived to take over, she would be going home to take an extended nap and after that she would then be making an important call to Spain.

The others might be willing to stand back and wait but Eilidh preferred to be proactive. She had never lost interest in *The Spanish Princess*, nor had she forgotten about it when dealing with the other cases that were piling up on her desk at New Scotland Yard.

19

Richard

Someone was kicking the door vigorously as Richard held the phone to his ear. He swiveled around to have a look, which of course was pointless as he could only see the thick metal door.

The bangs on the door became even more frenetic.

"I'm sorry, could I call you back?" asked Richard.

"Certainly, I'll be in my office all of today," said the polite voice on the other end of the phone.

"Thank you," said Richard, feeling grateful for their acquiescence mixed in with huge irritation towards the person trying to kick his office door down.

He hung up the phone and went to open the door.

Standing on the other side, clutching a pile of folders, was Eilidh Simmons.

"Finally! What took you so long?" she asked as she brushed past him and released her load onto his desk.

"I was on the phone," explained Richard, watching her in some bemusement.

The last thing he needed on his desk was more paperwork.

Released from her heavy burden, Eilidh stood and turned to him, her excitement vibrating out of her like the taut strings plucked on a harp.

"I think we've got a breakthrough, Richard."

"We have?" asked Richard, wondering what on earth she was talking about.

"Yes. We've found a link to Victoria Bretanzos Forentin."

For a moment Richard stared blankly at Eilidh, who was standing with her hands on her hips, and then he suddenly remembered *The Spanish Princess*.

"Oh, yes, *The Spanish Princess*. You've evidence connecting the painting to Victoria Bretanzos Forentin?"

"Yes," said Eilidh impatiently, as though he was being very obtuse.

Richard slowly sat down on his seat, unwilling to let Eilidh's enthusiasm carry him away. It was a month since they had last discussed the painting and Eilidh was beginning to remind him of a tenacious terrier with the case, refusing to let it go no matter how long it lingered on.

He did wonder if she was using the case to distract herself from her grandmother's death. She had been back at her desk only two weeks after her grandmother's funeral and Richard felt it was far too early for someone who had just lost their closest relative.

"What are these for?" he asked Eilidh, pointing towards the folders she had just dumped on his desk.

Eilidh waved dismissively at them.

"Those are files I was taking to be processed at the Criminal Investigation Office. Half the staff in the office are off with the cold so we're all trying to help out. Well, actually, a lot of them are calling it the flu but I wouldn't want to bet on it."

"OK. So, what do you have?" asked Richard, interested to hear what she had to say.

Eilidh sat herself down on the chair facing him and leaned forward.

"I phoned Isabel Perón and she was happy to dig into the family tree of El Greco's love child for me," said Eilidh. "Eleni Catalina Trastámara, remember? Isabel told me the Spanish were incredibly good at keeping records in the past, and especially genealogical ones. They seem to have been quite anal about it, actually. You know the sunken Spanish treasure ships found off the Florida coast? A lot of information about them was sourced from the meticulous maritime records kept in Seville and Cádiz from the sixteenth to the eighteenth centuries."

Richard smiled at her enthusiasm. He had no idea how Eilidh had ended up working in the police force and in the Homicide Command of all things. She was definitely in the wrong vocation.

"What are you smiling at?" asked Eilidh, looking at him suspiciously.

"I was thinking you're in the wrong job. You should've been a historian."

"Ha, ha. Very funny. Anyway, Isabel Perón spent a while collating all the information, along with a contact of hers who works for one of those ancestry websites. It turns out Victoria Bretanzos Forentin is one out of five living descendants who are related to Eleni Catalina Trastámara. Isn't that incredible?"

"That's amazing!" exclaimed Richard.

"It really is. I couldn't help but think there was a

personal connection in this case. It doesn't make sense otherwise. Irina sold the dud painting to the Russian mafia and took a huge risk doing so. Why would she have done that if she didn't have some pull towards the other buyer? Irina was close to Max and you told me Max seemed to have an overdeveloped sense of responsibility towards the artists whose pictures he restored."

"Don't get carried away, Eilidh. I think you're reading far too much into it. It's certainly a remarkable find but I don't see how the connection is going to help us find the painting."

"What do you mean? We have to get in touch with the Heritage Team in Madrid and get them to issue a warrant so they can search Victoria's house for the painting!"

"Whoa! Hold on for a minute. You can't get a search warrant on the basis of a genealogical connection to the artist of a missing sixteenth-century painting. It's ludicrous."

"No, it's not, Richard. I can't believe this. How much more evidence do you need, for heaven's sake? The poster tube that was sent the day of the murder was posted to Victoria's home address."

"Yes, but if you remember, the Heritage Team still didn't think the poster tube was enough evidence to justify questioning her. I can't see how a family tree, fascinating as it is, is going to convince them that there's a case against her."

"Couldn't you at least try?"

"I could," said Richard reluctantly. "But I really think it would be a waste of time."

"You're chickening out of it, aren't you?" asked

Eilidh, aggressive. In Richard's opinion she was acting very like a wayward teenager.

Richard noticed that whenever he riled Eilidh, it seemed trigger a response in her that was distinctly infantile. It wouldn't be the first time he had had that effect on a woman either.

He sighed.

"Fine. I will send Gonzalo Madraso an email and tell him about your discovery. Don't get your hopes up, though," added Richard, thinking his credibility with the Spanish police was going to be shot to pieces after he sent the email.

"Brilliant. That would be wonderful, thank you. Sorry about getting cross," apologized Eilidh, sounding embarrassed after her outburst. "It's just that there are now two trails pointing towards Victoria. I'm positive it means something."

Richard wasn't going to argue against her again so he just nodded.

"No worries. I'll let you know as soon as I hear anything back from Gonzalo," he said.

"Great, thanks. Well, see you later then. I'd best get back," said Eilidh, sounding much happier.

She picked up the files she had dropped on Richard's desk and started heading towards the door.

Richard ran forward to open the heavy door for her and smiled at her as she left.

When he came back to his desk he questioned if Eilidh always managed to get what she wanted from her other work colleagues. She seemed to have the knack. There was something about her that made him want to please her, even when his rational mind was telling him it was a complete waste of time.

In the end he typed up an email to Gonzalo that seemed to him to reduce as much as possible his exposure to ridicule.

Dear Gonzalo,

I hope you are well and not knee-deep in art theft cases. I am writing to you regarding the El Greco painting The Spanish Princess that was stolen from a London flat at the end of September. I spoke to you about it back in October, when I was visiting Madrid to check on the painting's authentication with the Prado and to find out more information about it.

Recently, one of my colleagues, in partnership with Isabel Perón who is deputy director at the Prado, has discovered there is another link between Victoria Bretanzos Forentin and the artist El Greco.

As there was a poster tube sent to Victoria from the scene of the crime, on the day of the murder and at the same time as the painting vanished, we were wondering if you would be able to conduct discreet enquiries, possibly with some of the staff who work in Victoria's home, to see if there is any chance the Old Master could possibly be located there.

We would very much appreciate your cooperation in this matter,

Kind regards,
Richard

It left things a little vague but it was a start. If Gonzalo needed more information he could direct him to Isabel or Eilidh, but in the meantime he wanted to get in touch with Sheila Mackenzie and see if she had uncovered anything on the accounts he had given her.

Sheila had been away, working at the office in Stockholm as she sorted out teething problems with a new software package the company was using.

He felt guilty pestering her, but now that Eilidh had persuaded him to send an email to the Guardia Civil in Madrid he felt he should really make a push to see if they could uncover any more information on the two accounts that had sent money Irina's way.

He typed a quick text message to her:

Hi Sheila

Sorry to bug you – I know you are busy but was wondering if you have had any luck sniffing out any names with the accounts I gave you?

Deciding he had done as much as could be reasonably expected, he turned his attention to other matters for the rest of the morning but by lunchtime he had received a disappointing response to both of his messages.

Gonzalo had responded courteously but without any willingness to take matters further.

Richard thought his response was unsurprising. It was all down to priorities. Each art theft had to argue its case for resources, and in truth theirs was a pretty flimsy argument which he didn't think really justified the Spanish police expending a full-blown effort around Victoria.

Dear Richard

Thank you very much for your email. I have spoken to Isabel Perón about the link between Victoria Bretanzos Forentin and the artist El Greco.

She does seem to feel there is an interesting genealog-
ical connection there but I'm afraid my superiors do
not believe this is of sufficient significance to enable
us to deploy our detectives to converse with staff
working at Victoria's residence or indeed justify us
interviewing Victoria herself. I am very sorry.

Please do let us know if any other information
comes to light that might warrant us searching her
property but I'm afraid what we have, at the moment,
isn't sufficient.

Good luck with your investigation,
Kind Regards
Gonzalo

Meanwhile Sheila had responded with four words:

Not yet. Will do.

Then she had added, an hour and a half later:

It's tough. Not surprised Russian police couldn't
crack it. Patience. I'll get there.

Sighing to himself, he worried how Eilidh would
react to the news.

At lunchtime he went and seated himself next to
Eilidh, who informed him she had kept a seat free especially for him, straightaway making him feel he was
back at school again.

Without saying anything, he showed her the email
from Gonzalo on his mobile phone and she studied it
eagerly as he ate his lunch.

He had helped himself to some linguini but the

tomato sauce was far too watery and it had splashed over his tray and the table as he ate. To his annoyance it had also stained his shirt and tie which meant a battle with the Vanish bottle when he got back home, always assuming he remembered to deal with the stains before shoving his dirty clothes in the washing machine.

Eilidh was taking her time reading the email, so long, in fact, that even after he had gone up to the canteen for some more water and serviettes, she was still looking at his phone.

As he sat down Eilidh placed his mobile phone back on his tray.

"I'm sorry, Eilidh," he said, as he mopped up the tomato stains. "It was just too little to go on. They have to justify their resources as much as we do."

"I know, thanks for trying anyway, Richard."

"No problem. Do let me know if there is anything else I can do for you."

She turned to him in surprise, her intense, chocolate eyes boring into him as though testing his commitment and truthfulness.

"I might hold you to that," she said, suddenly smiling.

He couldn't take his eyes off her, noticing her nostrils were flared and that there was a curious upturn to the curve of her lips. For a few intense seconds, time seemed to stand still for him.

Then she looked away quickly to wave and smile at someone who happened to be passing their table and the spell broke.

Later on, as he made his way back down to his office, he realized he had spoken nothing less than the truth. He would indeed be happy to do anything for her.

A dangerous situation to be in with someone like Eilidh, who wasn't prepared to let things go with *The Spanish Princess*. Whether she was still working on the finding *The Spanish Princess* for Igor's sake or for her own fulfillment and distraction, he didn't know. But somehow he didn't think this was the end of Eilidh's interest in the case or the last time she would call on him for a favour.

20

Eilidh

"Do let me know if there's anything else I can do for you."

Richard's words echoed in Eilidh's mind as the plane sped down the runway and took off; the plane heaving itself up into the air, leaving behind the grey concrete buildings and heading upwards to the white canopy above them.

Once they were through the clouds, she turned and smiled at the passenger sitting next to her.

Reading a copy of *The Times* and dressed in a panama shirt, loose camel-coloured trousers and wearing a pair of Doc Martens was Mike Telford, with his briefcase neatly tucked under the seat in front of him.

In her frustration with the inaction of New Scotland Yard, Eilidh had contacted the private detective in the hope that he would be willing to lend a hand in investigating the connection between Victoria Bretanzos Forentin and *The Spanish Princess*.

While Richard had eaten his lunch and gone to

fetch serviettes, it had taken her barely a minute to look up and memorize Mike's number from the list of contacts on Richard's phone.

She didn't feel remotely guilty abusing Richard's goodwill by taking his colleague's phone number because it had become clear to her that neither the Spanish police nor New Scotland Yard were willing or able to investigate the Victoria link.

Eilidh was convinced that the woman had Igor's painting, even though her belief so far was mostly based on gut instinct and this did not qualify as a valid argument in any police force. Lionel Grieves, for example, was someone who refused to believe in intuition and dismissed any such thing as hocus pocus. Lionel only liked facts and reasoned arguments, not least because these covered his back if something were to go wrong with a case.

Mike had been eager to step up to the task because he was working on Igor's behalf and therefore wasn't concerned with any of the political games going on at New Scotland Yard or in the Guardia Civil.

He could hardly contain his anger when he heard that a poster tube had been sent from Igor's flat to Victoria's home address on the day of the murder. He struggled to understand why the Spanish police had decided not to investigate Victoria and wanted to know why Richard had not mentioned the poster tube to him, especially since Richard was well aware that Mike had his own unorthodox ways of working and that as a private investigator he could get things done outside of official protocol.

Eilidh knew Mike didn't think much of the genealogical connection between the artist and Victoria, coincidental and interesting as it was, but he had none-theless humored Eilidh and lent an ear to her convic-tion that Victoria had an emotional attachment to the painting due to the fact she was a present-day descen-dant of El Greco and Princess Catalina Micaela.

After his initial meeting with Eilidh, Mike Telford had then disappeared off Eilidh's radar for a while, leaving her to stew in the homicide cases on her desk, cases that were now only holding half of her attention.

She was ruefully aware that something had to change in her work situation and she had to dig herself out of the hole she was in but it was easy to put off facing reality when you barely had time to think, let alone time to take any introspective action to change jobs.

Then, little over a couple of weeks ago, Mike had called her mobile one evening and told her that he had made progress.

A Spanish employee of his had approached Victo-ria's gardener and over several meetings at the local tapas bar had managed to dig up a substantial amount of information about Victoria's schedule. The gardener worked in her garden every other day throughout the year, cleaning the pool and tending to the plants, and he knew the family intimately, as well as the other staff members working at the residence.

Thanks to the gardener and the reconnaissance work done by Mike's agent, Mike had established Victo-ria's workday routines and had also managed to get his hands on a detailed plan with the layout of her house on it.

And, according to him, it was at this point he decided to phone Eilidh and request she accompany him on a trip to Madrid on the 29th of March. He told her he believed he had reached a potential break-through in the case. Elusive as ever, he hadn't elabo-rated on what he had discovered but insisted it was important Eilidh came with him.

Now their EasyJet flight was bringing them ever closer to what they both hoped would be a successful mission in Madrid, Eilidh was starting to question more and more why Mike wanted her there. It was very irri-tating of him not to share what his plans with her were and she wanted to know if Richard too had accompa-nied Mike blindly on some of his secretive ventures.

Although Eilidh had no idea what Mike's strategy was once they arrived in Madrid, she still felt she could trust him because Mike had a sterling reputation as a top-tier specialist in returning missing or stolen artworks. Of course, she was hoping the journey wouldn't be a waste of time, but given Mike's mythical status in art crime circles she felt optimistic and genuinely believed there would be a positive outcome to their short trip to Spain.

"The weather in Madrid is meant to be a balmy 25 degrees centigrade," said Mike, looking up from his newspaper. "Sounds about perfect to me. Can't stand the cold or the heat."

Eilidh laughed and took a handful of cashew nuts from a tub Mike was offering her.

"Where are we staying, by the way?" she asked, before popping a nut into her mouth.

"It's all sorted, my dear. I've rented a flat in El Viso for the two nights we'll be there. All undeclared lease, of course. Victoria lives in an enormous villa in the area, in fact I believe it used to be an embassy before it was bought by her. More importantly, there's an excellent Basque restaurant called Jai Alai nearby, which we shall visit on Igor's expense account..."

Mike stopped talking when he saw the disapproving look on Eilidh's face.

"What?" he asked her, genuinely confused.

"Should we be paying for expensive restaurants on Igor's expense account? I mean, the poor guy has already lost ten thousand pounds after we messed up the exchange at the church."

Mike patted Eilidh's arm in a fatherly manner.

"Igor's fine with it, Eilidh. We're working solely on his behalf and if we find the painting it'll be returning straight back to him. I went over everything with Igor before we left. He knows what we're up to."

"He knows what you're planning to do in Madrid?" asked Eilidh, feeling miffed that Igor hadn't told her anything about it.

"Yes, of course he does. He's a hundred per cent for it. It should be pretty straightforward but, of course, things can always go wrong. I'm pretty confident we'll extract the painting without too much trouble."

Eilidh felt an adrenalin rush hit her at the thought of finding the valuable oil painting and returning it back to Igor, yet she also had to admit to herself that lurking at the back of her mind there was also the recognition that there would be great kudos for her in doing so.

"Mind telling me what arrangement the pair of you have concocted to retrieve the painting?" she asked, turning to look at Mike.

Mike eyed her doubtfully for a moment and then smiled.

"It's probably best if you don't know at this stage.

But I promise you, I'll explain everything before we set out to get it."

Eilidh felt her heart sink.

She had an uneasy notion that whatever scheme Mike and Igor had been working on between themselves, it was potentially outside the rule of the law and she was unconvinced, being a police officer, that she should be lending her support to it. She wondered for a moment if this was why Mike had insisted she join him in Madrid, because any dodgy or illicit venture would be given the seal of validity if there was an actual member of the British police force involved.

Her doubts were confirmed later on when the pair of them sat picking over the remains of their main course at Jai Alai that evening.

As Mike explained to her his detailed plans, Eilidh felt her appetite abandoning her and eventually dropped her knife and fork onto the plate in defeat, leaving the dregs of her meal untouched.

"Mike, I can't do it. I can't go along with this crazy plot you've hatched up with Igor. Don't you understand that? I'd lose my job if we got caught."

"But we won't get caught," contradicted Mike, calmly. "The plan's foolproof, and as I told you she's away to her house in Sotogrande."

Eilidh picked up her wine glass and took a mouthful, thinking hard as she felt the Merlot fill her taste buds with warm, cherry notes.

"There has to be another way," she said at last.

"There isn't," said Mike with authority. "This woman has, in the most unprincipled manner, stolen a priceless masterpiece, and in doing so enabled the murder of two victims. You think she'll just hand over the painting to us? And do you think the police are going to do anything about it, when they haven't lifted a finger so far? It doesn't matter if I give them the information we've received because they'll interview the staff and in the meantime put the fear of God into Victoria, who'll no doubt remove the painting as quickly as she can. It'll vanish into thin air and it will be our word against hers."

Putting her wine glass down, Eilidh stared across at Mike, who was munching happily on his last bit of Basque casserole.

"I don't have to join you in this, Mike."

Mike looked up from his plate.

"Of course not. You can stay put at the flat, if you like. I'm not dismissing your qualms. I won't deny it would be useful to have you there, in case anything does go pear-shaped, but it's your choice. I thought you'd like to be part of the action, given your interest in the case so far. Plus, who knows? You might be able to write a bestseller about it one of these days. It's become quite the vogue, you know. "Detective Inspector rescues unique and priceless portrait by El Greco." That kind of thing."

"You're such a bullshitter," remarked Eilidh, nodding at the waiter as he removed her plate.

Unperturbed by her language, Mike grinned at her.

"Anyway, while you decide if you're joining me, I'm going to have a quick scan of the pudding menu."

Mike turned his attention to deciding what to have for dessert and shortly afterwards put in an order for Goxua to the waiter.

Eilidh declined on dessert but accepted having her wine glass filled again.

She was going to need some Dutch courage if she

was going to participate in Mike's outlandish plans and sure enough, by the time she had drunk another half bottle of wine, she had decided she was going to accompany Mike on his housebreaking adventure.

"Do let me know if there's anything else I can do for you."

The words swirled around her head and gave her a renewed determination to see this thing through. If it all went wrong, she'd have to hope Richard would use his authority at the Art and Antiquities Unit to come to their rescue.

They left the restaurant shortly after seven and walked for twenty minutes alongside busy evening traffic, following the satnav on Mike's phone as they made their way towards Victoria's house in Charmartín.

Once they were outside Victoria's mansion, Eilidh stared up at the thick forest of bamboo planted right in front of the tall garden fence and then looked at the massive, solid metal, external door they were standing next to.

Mike, for a start, did not have the physique to climb over a high fence but she knew better than to say anything to him because it was obvious to her by now that this was not the first time he had broken into someone's house. This all seemed to be a run-of-the-mill activity to him.

Mike put down his briefcase and, wearing gloves, withdrew a set of keys from his trouser pocket. He carefully picked out a large key and then opened the metal door with ease, holding it open politely for Eilidh to enter.

She pointed up to the CCTV camera on the house roof.

"I'll get it disabled," said Mike shortly.

It soon became clear that the front door to the house was going to be more of a challenge to Mike. He had no idea which key, out of the many on his keyring, belonged to the front door and as he proceeded to try out various keys in the lock Eilidh wandered off and did a quick reconnaissance of the exterior of the property.

There was a neat garden stretching outwards on the right-hand side, with a swimming pool at the far end, built against a high wall and, alarmingly, also a couple of kennels.

On the left-hand side of the mansion there was a small, detached building which looked like a granny flat or a guest home.

"Mike, what's happened to the dogs?"

Wrestling with the front door lock, Mike grunted.

"The dogs were drugged. They'll be fine. The guard, Mateo, is currently with his girlfriend in Aravaca."

"What? "*Drugged*"? Who drugged them?"

"My Woman in Madrid," said Mike, humorously parodying Graham Greene's book *Our Man in Havana*.

His face now had a sheen of sweat on it which didn't reassure Eilidh at all.

He lifted up his thick bunch of keys and waved them in the air.

"She's the one who managed to get me a copy of the guard's keys."

Mike returned to wrangling with the door lock and left Eilidh to her inevitable reflections on the weakness of the male sex in the face of very attractive women. Had Mike's agent also met the guard at the local tapas bar? How on earth had she managed to get her hands on his set of keys?

She thought about the many women who had helped change the course of history with their enthralling beauty; there were the two famous spies, Betty Pack and Anna Chapman, all the way back in time to the likes of Cleopatra and Helen of Troy. And these were probably but a few of the many intrepid women who had used their wiles and good looks to get what they wanted.

She was certain that Mike's agent had to be a stunner.

With a click and a sigh of satisfaction from Mike, the front door opened and within a few seconds the alarm started to sound, screaming out into the relative quiet of the evening.

Eilidh watched in amazement as Mike disappeared indoors.

She wanted to run away. She could not understand what he thought he was doing entering a house when the alarm had gone off. Every instinct in her was calling out for her to make a fast exit but she stayed put, waiting to see what happened next.

The alarm stopped just as she was glancing nervously about her, expecting a nosy neighbor to turn up on the doorstep at any moment.

Encouraged by the silence, Eilidh stepped into the tiled hallway, closed the front door quietly behind her and looked around.

Mike had switched the hall light on and she wasn't sure this was a good idea. Even though it was dark outside, if the neighbors knew that Victoria's family were away on holiday, wouldn't they become suspicious when they saw the house lights switched on?

She bit her tongue because she did not want to slow Mike down with her inane questions, quite the reverse in fact. He seemed to know what he was doing and she was keen to get out of there as soon as possible.

She walked into a lit room at the end of the hallway and saw that Mike, with all the appearance of a proficient workman, was kneeling at an open cabinet with a pair of wire clippers in his hand. She left him to fiddle with the security system while she went back out and familiarized herself with the ground floor layout.

She soon discovered that the ground floor had an indoor cinema, a large kitchen, sitting room, dining room, conservatory and bathroom. What seemed to be a maid's bedroom was at the back of the kitchen with a small shower room adjoining it.

She was walking back through to the hallway when she heard Mike calling out her name.

"Ah, there you are!" he said irritably, catching sight of her. Mike had lost his laidback attitude within a very short space of time. "Listen, you'd better stay with me from now on. I don't want to have to search and wait for you once I've got my hands on the painting."

"You know where the painting is?" asked Eilidh in surprise, realizing how stupid the question was once she had said it. There was no way they had enough time to search the house from top to bottom.

She was starting to think that if Mike's Mata Hari spy was the one who had uncovered where the painting was located she needed to present her to GCHQ; after all, they were desperately trying to encourage more women to think about a career in espionage these days.

One female MI6 officer had once told Eilidh that women made "bloody good spies," and seeing how much information Mike's mysterious agent had dug up for him she was inclined to agree with her.

Lost in his own thoughts, Mike hadn't registered her question and was steadily climbing up the stairs, two steps at a time.

Eilidh began to climb the steps behind him, enjoying for a moment watching the investigator plying his craft and accepting she was there to tag along and not get in the way.

Like a bloodhound intent on following a scent, Mike turned sharply to the left at the top of the staircase and flicked on the lights.

Before Eilidh was given the opportunity to properly explore the top floor, Mike had disappeared into a room on the left-hand side of the stairwell.

With a sigh, she decided not to dawdle, as in so large a house it would not take much to lose him completely. She walked along the passageway and then poked her head in the doorway that Mike had sauntered through a minute ago.

She guessed the room they were in was the main bedroom.

All the furnishings were gleaming white except for a large oil painting hanging up on the opposite wall. A four-poster bed with thick hangings was placed next to the door and the left-hand wall had a floor-to-ceiling window, with its white shutters folded shut.

There was the musty smell of a recently used bedroom.

Bright-coloured clothes were piled messily onto a chaise longue in the middle of the room and the

dressing table was crowded with a woman's parapher-
nalia: perfume bottles, trinkets, make-up and numerous
department store boxes.

Eilidh wished she had the time to look at the attractive modern painting on the opposite wall but Mike was
now standing in front of a locked door adjoining the
bedroom and fiddling with his set of keys again. She
walked over and stood next to him, watching as he tried
out different keys in the two door locks.

"Sylvia reckoned if the painting was anywhere in
the house, it would be in this room. It's where Victoria
keeps her jewelry, too, apparently," muttered Mike, as
he flicked a key further round his keyring and then tried
to open the lock with another one.

Now feeling like a real housebreaker, she wondered
for a moment if Mike had ever done time in Her
Majesty's Prison. He was far too comfortable and
familiar with this kind of work, in her opinion, to not
have started out on his illustrious career as a common
thief.

A minute later Mike managed to open the door and
they both walked into an enormous dressing room with
fitted cupboards stretching along two walls.

There was another sofa, also covered in carelessly
tossed garments.

Eilidh picked up the clothing gingerly and saw that
Balenciaga, Prada, Versace and Chanel were all
designers on the labels. Several pairs of high-heeled
shoes were scattered like confetti across the floor.

"Get your hands off those!" warned Mike, when he
caught sight of her lifting up the garments.

He reached into his briefcase and tossed her a pair
of gloves.

He then turned to the open cupboard in front of him and began to rummage around inside it.

On one side of the cupboard there was a slate-grey safe bolted to the floor, reaching a third of the way up the wall. Mike ignored it, which made sense as the only way *The Spanish Princess* could have fitted inside of it was if the canvas had been folded over several times, and that would never have happened as the painting would then have been damaged.

Whatever else Victoria was, she was unlikely to be so foolish as to risk her investment in that way.

Before long Mike was opening all the other cupboard doors as well, thrusting clothing aside impatiently as he searched. The frenzied manner in which he was moving things around indicated his anxiety and impatience.

Watching him, Eilidh thought he was a remarkably active man for such a lethargic and plump person. This was a side of Mike she hadn't seen until now.

"Mike, do you really think Victoria would keep the painting in there, behind all her clothes?" asked Eilidh, utterly skeptical.

She had decided from the start to kowtow to Mike's superior experience in housebreaking but now she couldn't help intervening because it was obvious that Mike was assuming Victoria would keep the precious painting at the back of a clothes cupboard.

The mere idea of it was ridiculous. Victoria would want to gaze at the painting, Eilidh was sure of it, otherwise what was the point?

Mike didn't waste time replying to her question but continued to push aside coat hangers with increasing desperation.

Giving up on getting his attention, Eilidh turned around and had a good look at the enclosed room.

She tried to imagine where she would have kept a valuable painting. Mike had been directed to this room by his informer and so somewhere within it the painting must be hiding, cleverly concealed.

She stared across at the large mirror on the opposite wall.

It was an odd size for a dressing room mirror because it wasn't full length, so Eilidh couldn't view herself completely in it. She struggled to come up with a good reason why a woman with so many expensive designer dresses would have decided to have a half-length mirror in her dressing room and not a full-length one.

She walked over to it and studied the frame carefully.

Meanwhile, she could see in the mirror's reflection that Mike had decided to empty all the cupboards in the room and was beginning to throw clothes and shoe boxes out onto the carpet behind him.

Focusing on the mirror once more, she noted how, strangely, the mirror didn't seem to be hanging on a nail.

Examining the sides, Eilidh thought it looked as though the mirror had been somehow screwed into the wall behind it, so tightly that there were no visible gaps to be seen.

For no particular reason she began to yank at the edges of the frame, as though trying to detach it from the wall. Nothing moved until she pulled on the right-hand side of the mirror and then felt something give way a little.

Encouraged, she gave the frame another sharp tug and with a loud click one side of the mirror started moving away from the wall and began swinging towards her.

"Mike!" she whispered breathlessly, as she held on to the edge of the mirror.

Mike hadn't heard her.

Steady grunts and the metallic sound of clothes hangers hitting the floor continued to resound from the other end of the room.

Eilidh opened the mirror door to a ninety-degree angle and then stood there immobile, staring open-mouthed at Princess Catalina Micaela.

"Mike!" she yelled at last, finding her voice.

"Fuck me! You found it!" shouted Mike with great excitement, running across the room.

He stood next to Eilidh and the pair of them gazed for a moment at the old masterpiece that had eluded them for so long.

Serene and bold as ever, Catalina Micaela stared back at them from a rectangular alcove that had been cleverly built into the wall behind the mirror.

Mike came to his senses before Eilidh did. He went up close to the painting and inspected it for a moment, touching the canvas gently with his gloved hands.

He then went and fetched his briefcase. Bringing it over to the mirror, he pulled out a long, thin metal instrument, which looked to Eilidh like a knife but with a blunt edge to it, and slid the slender blade carefully into the back of the canvas, moving it slowly upwards.

With a ripping noise, the painting detached itself from the wall with very little persuasion, flopping forwards as he reached the top of it with his knife.

"What's holding it onto the wall?" asked Eilidh, intrigued.

"I think she must have used a water-based adhesive of some kind. It's coming loose quite easily," Mike replied, as he continued to work the knife around the edges of the canvas.

They heard the sirens in the far distance just at the point when Mike had freed the painting from the wall behind it.

They both stood still and tried to ascertain if the sirens were heading towards them or not.

Unfortunately, the noise was only getting louder and louder.

Mike swore and, no longer cautious, started rolling up the painting at breakneck speed.

Once the canvas was coiled up, he dropped it onto the floor and ran to the wall.

With the help of his blunt knife, he started lifting up the edge of the carpet.

Eilidh had no idea what he was up to but she raced over to join him and began pulling back the thick, cream carpet, along with the underlay. Before long they had exposed a big expanse of wooden floor beneath the carpet.

Without saying a word, Mike went into his brief-case again and pulled out a metal bar, which he then used to try to lever up a floorboard. With a protesting crack, the wooden board popped up and Mike yanked it off the floor.

Into the dusty, dark space underneath the floor-boards Mike dumped his keys, all the tools in his brief-case and the rolled-up painting. Both of them took off their gloves and dropped them into the cavity.

The sirens had stopped and the front doorbell was now ringing impatiently.

Mike speedily replaced the missing floorboard and then pulled the carpet and underlay down on top of it. Eilidh knelt and patted down the carpet while Mike proceeded to stamp on the edges, attempting to flatten the carpet still further.

Soon it was impossible to tell where the carpet had been pulled up from the floor. But Mike didn't stop there. Running across to the open mirror, he pushed it back towards the wall until it clicked shut again.

Downstairs they heard loud bangs at the front door, increasing in vigor until a resounding crash indicated the door had been smashed open.

Frenzied shouts started echoing up from the hallway.

Mike and Eilidh walked into the bedroom, switching off the lights in the dressing room and shutting the door before they left. Eilidh could feel her heart thumping in her chest and was sure she was going to pass out.

Mike grabbed hold of her hand and squeezed it reassuringly.

"Don't worry," he whispered. "It'll be fine, I promise you. It's not the first time this has happened to me."

Cross, Eilidh turned to glare at Mike and then nearly burst out laughing when she noticed he was still clutching his empty briefcase.

The funny side of things didn't last for long because four policemen burst into the room, with guns at the ready.

Mike and 'Eilidh slowly lifted their hands above their heads.

Questions in Spanish were yelled at them but they couldn't understand a word of what was being asked of them. They both stared back with confused expressions on their faces, hoping the police would understand they couldn't make out what was being said.

One of the policemen went up to them and roughly pulled their hands down, handcuffing them.

Mike let his briefcase drop onto the floor and it was quickly picked up by another policeman, who had a look inside it and then threw it away.

Feeling the cold metal of the handcuffs on her wrists, Eilidh realized she had reached an all-time low. If her grandmother could have seen her, she would have been horrified. There was a big difference between getting despondent about one's job, which her grandmother had sympathized with, and ending up in utter disgrace and sacked for committing a criminal offence.

The policeman gave her a hard shove in the back and she obediently stepped forward, following Mike who was making his way out of the room behind the other policemen.

Like a strange caravan of mismatched people, they walked down the stairs, through the splintered and torn doorway and out into the garden.

21

Richard

"Richard?"

"Speaking."

"It's Gonzalo Madraso here from the Heritage Team at the Guardia Civil."

"Yes, of course! What's up?"

"Well, we appear to have two associates of yours in custody. They were apprehended breaking into Victoria Forentin's home in Madrid yesterday evening."

Richard felt his heart thumping unpleasantly as his grip tightened on his mobile phone.

"Who?" he croaked.

"Miss Eilidh Simmons and Mr Mike Telford."

"Ah."

"Yes. There's a lot of anger flying about my department at the moment. It's not looking good at all, I'm afraid. Victoria's in a terrible rage and threatening to sue the Guardia Civil if we don't incarcerate them permanently. My superiors are fuming because they'd already refused your request to interfere with Victoria and they've now discovered Miss Simmons works for Scotland Yard."

Gonzalo coughed apologetically.

"We all know Mike Telford, of course. He helped the Duquesa de Alba recover her stolen Goya only last year. Unfortunately, his methods are very unorthodox and he's worn down the goodwill of my department by crossing several red lines on other art theft cases. We don't understand what Eilidh Simmons is doing mixed up in this because it seems she's a Detective Inspector from the Homicide Branch of Scotland Yard."

"Good grief. What a mess!"

A migraine was beginning to take a hold of Richard's forehead. He lifted his free hand and started to rub between his eyebrows in a bid to stop its pincer-like pain.

"Yes, exactly," continued Gonzalo gloomily on the other end of the line. "It's looking bad. Both of your colleagues are refusing to divulge what they were up to in Victoria's house. Victoria says nothing has been stolen but the intent to steal was there, plus it seems they managed to get their hands on a set of Victoria's house keys. I think we need you to take a trip out here as soon as possible and sort this out or your friends could be looking at some serious jail time."

"Has anyone else from the Guardia Civil contacted Scotland Yard?"

"Not that I'm aware of. We're trying to sort this out in the best way possible. Discreetly. Things could easily get out of control. If the press got hold of this story, for example, you can imagine the scandal for your police force."

Richard blanched at the thought and clenched his mobile phone tighter still.

An unwanted picture of Lionel's irate face appeared in his mind, only to be dismissed quickly. He had to focus on getting this dilemma sorted as soon as possible and not get stressed out. There would be plenty of time to worry about Lionel's reaction to it all later.

"OK. I'll be on the first flight to Madrid that I can find. I'll text you as soon as I've booked it. If you can keep a lid on things until I get there I'd really appreciate it."

Gonzalo laughed without any humor.

"We'll certainly do our best. I think there's more to this than we realize at present, my friend. They don't seem to be at all concerned or guilty. In fact, the pair of them are strangely calm."

"I bet they are," said Richard grimly, feeling his irritation increasing with every passing minute.

After hanging up he booked a flight out to Madrid the following morning, took some Nurofen and spent a sleepless night tossing and turning as he thought about the break-in to Victoria's home.

In the end, he got up, made himself a cup of coffee and took it through to the lounge. Although it was spring there was still a cold chill in the air, so Richard put on the gas fire and lifted his feet up onto his footstool.

As he reclined, semi-comatose, on his armchair he tried to think logically about the situation, which wasn't an easy task given the anger he felt towards Mike and Eilidh's illegal escapade. The reputation of his department depended on him getting the pair of them out of jail without any scandal and he wasn't sure he had much leverage with the Heritage Team in Madrid. There was no way he could get Lionel involved. Regardless of how furious he might be with Eilidh and Mike, Lionel was always loyal to his force and was perfectly capable of causing a major diplomatic incident over the affair.

It seemed from what Gonzalo had told him that Mike, who always seemed to be like a cat with nine lives, had come to the end of his luck as far as the Spanish police were concerned.

However, Richard had known Mike Telford professionally for the better part of ten years and although Mike didn't tell him much about the ins and outs of his work, he did not believe he would break into someone's house without compelling evidence. Deep down he was hoping Mike had not been carried away by Eilidh's outlandish theories. Eilidh could be very persuasive when she wanted to be, he thought, thinking back to the email he had unwillingly sent to Gonzalo on her behalf.

At this point he realized he had started to bite on his nails. Annoyed at his weakness in succumbing to a childhood habit, he got up and went through to the kitchen to get some breakfast cereal. It was only half past four in the morning but insomnia always made him ravenously hungry and he felt he needed the distraction of some food when his mind was going around in circles.

After pouring a liberal amount of milk over his cornflakes, he sat down on his metal kitchen chair and proceeded to chew his cereal.

The calories seemed to be working in energizing his tired mind because it wasn't long before he suddenly remembered Sheila Mackenzie and the bank accounts. He decided he had to ask her again about them because if they managed to trace anything on those accounts back to Victoria, it would give him grounds for asking the Spanish police to turn a blind eye to Mike and Eilidh's misdemeanor. There were too many "ifs" involved in this line of thought but it was all they had left in terms of a paper trail to the painting.

He waited impatiently until it was five o'clock and then rang Sheila's mobile.

"Hi Richard! I've been meaning to call you. I got to work on those accounts after receiving your text messages. You know, the texts you sent me while I was in Stockholm..."

Sheila was not only wide awake, she sounded as though she had been up for some time.

Thinking back to when they were both younger, Richard remembered Sheila was one of those sickening people who appeared to thrive on just a few hours" sleep and who often as a result left their parents broken and shattered in their wake as they grew up into adulthood.

"Brilliant, Sheila. I need anything you can give me."

"Well, as I said to you, they weren't easy to trace. I'm afraid I've had no luck whatsoever with the money that came from the Swiss bank account. I did manage, however, to follow the money trail from the shell company *Pelícano Azul* back to a man called Emilio Cantos Lucado. Based in Madrid. He's got his fingers in many pies. Where do I start? He's a real estate owner, along with several members of his family. Proprietor of several galleries in all the main cities of Valencia, Asturias, Castile and León and Galicia. He also co-owns with a company called Forentin Cristalería a network of well-known designer ceramic shops in Spain, Ceramica Essima. He's taken over and rebranded three hotels in the South of Spain in the last two years. He also..."

"Sheila, that's all wonderful, thank you," said Richard, cutting her short. "Could you possibly send all these details to my email?"

There was an uneasy pause on the other end of the line.

"What? What's up?" asked Richard anxiously. "We won't divulge your sources."

"I know you won't, Richard. But even just writing this all down and sending it to you in an email could place me in jeopardy."

Richard sighed impatiently.

He understood her situation but she also needed to know why he was so desperate for the information she had uncovered. Things were different now from when he had first requested her to look into those accounts.

"Sheila, there's a Detective Inspector from Scotland Yard and a private investigator languishing in a Spanish jail at this very moment and unless I come up with something soon they're going to be charged with breaking and entering Victoria Bretanzos Forentin's home. The information you've dug up could be invaluable in building a case against Victoria, which in turn could help me get them both released."

"Blimey, Richard. Nothing predictable in your line of work, is there?"

"I could happily strangle the pair of them for doing this. I really don't know on what basis they decided to go rogue in the search for Igor's damn painting but I suspect they're both equally guilty. I really need to get them out as soon as possible or else my colleague could end up getting the sack in the best-case scenario or plastered on the front pages of the tabloids at worst."

"OK, OK. I get it. I'm not sending the information by email. I'll get it printed out for you right now and come to your flat in a taxi within the next hour. But Richard... This information needs to be kept confidential and you need to keep my name out of it or else *I'll* be the one getting the sack."

"Of course, Sheila."

"You owe me big time."

"I do," agreed Richard.

"The hen party better be good."

Richard had completely forgotten about his commitment to be Sheila's maid-of-honour.

He sat back on his kitchen chair.

"It will be, I promise."

He didn't care what it took but he was now more motivated than ever to give his friend a fantastic bridal send-off.

Sheila hung up and Richard started to get organized.

He needed to be at the airport in three hours. In the meantime, he had to cancel two meetings and send a message to Lionel Grieves, informing him that he would not be available that day. The latter task was going to be the trickiest and would require some thought because Lionel was no gullible fool and it wasn't going to be easy to pull the wool over his eyes. Richard was still composing his email to Lionel when his doorbell rang.

Without bothering to answer the intercom and still

dressed in his pajamas, he raced down the stairs of his apartment block and opened the door.

Sheila, dressed in a smart red suit and holding a briefcase, was standing in the doorway with a black cab waiting behind her.

"Here you go," she said, handing him an A4 envelope. "It's all in there."

She started walking down the steps and then turned back.

"It might be helpful for you to know that Emilio Cantos Lucado has substantial debts. Having over-extended himself he's teetering on the edge of financial ruin. It should be easy for you to get him to spill the beans. I suspect he'll want to save his own skin and given some clemency he should tell you all you need to know."

"You're a star, Sheila."

"I know," she said, as she walked to the cab and opened the door. She blew him a kiss and in the next minute she was gone.

Richard walked back up to the flat cradling the envelope as though it were a fragile baby, gazing down at it in delight. Against his better judgement, as soon as he was back in his flat he decided to forget all about Lionel's email and the need to get ready for his flight to Madrid and instead opened the envelope, reverently extracting the typed sheets of paper and spreading them out all over the kitchen table.

He was so engrossed in studying them that he was surprised when the taxi rang his mobile to let him know it was waiting downstairs for him.

After asking the taxi driver to wait for him, he threw on yesterday's shirt and rapidly put on his underwear, socks and suit. Then he rammed his tie into his trouser pocket.

Hastily stapling the sheets on his kitchen table together, he shoved the paperwork back into the envelope. He grabbed his briefcase and coat as he exited the apartment and flew down the stairs at breakneck speed.

He hadn't booked a return ticket or packed an overnight bag but his mind was buzzing with the precious gems he had gleaned from Sheila's envelope and it had no space for any other more practical considerations.

He arrived at Stansted only to discover the flight was delayed by forty minutes, but despite this temporary inconvenience he found himself shaking Gonzalo Madraso's hand approximately five hours later in Madrid, outside the Command Centre of the Guardia Civil.

Gonzalo was a tall, elegant man with a kindly face and Richard enjoyed dealing with him on a professional basis. Gonzalo was always courteous and respectful, which was often a balm to the spirit after a bruising encounter with Lionel Grieves. If only all other art detectives were as helpful. Unfortunately, many international art detectives had a huge ego to feed and were often unwilling and reluctant to share any information that might lead someone else to a successful conclusion on an art theft case.

"Good to see you, Richard," said Gonzalo effusively, as he led the way up a flight of stairs. "Come through and I'll introduce you to my Colonel, Alonzo Cabrera."

They eventually walked into a large room in which

there were three men seated, all of them dressed in the green, belted uniform of the Guardia Civil.

Looking round at them all, Richard knew straight-away which man was Gonzalo's Colonel. It had to be the shortest of the three men because he had an air of authority and the others" deferential body language suggested he was the most senior official in the room.

"Colonel Cabrera, this is Chief Inspector Richard Langley."

Sure enough, the little man stepped forward and gave Richard a firm handshake.

Looking at him closely, Richard noted he had the rigid posture of a seasoned soldier, as well as a grizzled, buzzcut haircut and a face that was tanned, lined and worn like a piece of old leather.

Colonel Cabrera turned and pointed to the chairs.

"Let's take a seat, gentlemen."

Richard felt his heart sink.

He had hoped for a chance to speak to Eilidh and Mike before any negotiations on their release began. He felt Eilidh and Mike's version of events might have been helpful in the discussion that was to follow and he wanted all three of them to be singing off the same hymn sheet so as not to arouse the suspicions of the Guardia Civil.

Trust was a fragile thing between international police forces.

Quickly thinking on his feet, Richard tried to esti-mate how much the Guardia Civil would know about *The Spanish Princess*.

He was fairly confident they would have been unsuccessful in extracting any meaningful information from Mike. In his line of work Mike was used to finding himself in unconventional situations, and despite his genial persona he was as sharp as they came.

Richard had no idea what Eilidh would do under pressure but he assumed that Mike, knowing the possible consequences of their actions, might have already primed her for a situation like this one.

He took a seat in the middle of the circle, hoping to show a confidence he was far from feeling.

"Richard, we've a delicate situation here and I'm glad you've been able to come so quickly," said Colonel Cabrera, crossing his legs and clasping his hands together on his lap as he leaned back on his chair. "Victoria Bretanzos Forentin is not a woman anyone would want to cross. She's a well-known celebrity here in Spain and right now she wants to see your Detective Inspector securely behind bars, as well as Mike Telford of course. And the truth is, I'm afraid, that the wheels of our justice system will continue to turn unless you can provide us with some much-needed answers."

"What kind of answers are you looking for?" asked Richard, playing the politician's game of cat and mouse by trying to encourage Colonel Cabrera to be more specific.

The other men in the room shuffled their feet impatiently, knowing fine well Richard was stalling for time.

The Colonel smiled at Richard but there was no warmth behind the smile.

"Come on, Richard. Don't toy with us. The only way your two colleagues are escaping an appearance in court is if you let us know on what evidence or basis they decided to break into Victoria's house. We know Mike Telford. We don't approve of his methods but he never puts himself at risk without good reason. He's refusing to say anything so I'm afraid it's on you to explain to us what the pair of them were up to."

"Right. I understand," said Richard slowly, deciding he had nothing to lose since it appeared that Mike hadn't told them anything.

He took it as a positive sign that the Spanish police seemed to think Mike and Eilidh had good grounds for suspecting Victoria.

If these men had found out the truth about Eilidh and Mike's break-in and realized it was based on non-existent proof and some crazy, hereditary theories, they would have no mercy whatsoever.

"I'm afraid there's further evidence that we haven't yet shared with you," confessed Richard, immediately getting their full attention. "Evidence that links Victoria Bretanzos Forentin to the stolen Greco painting. In order to corroborate this, you'll have to question the man in the middle of it all. He's called Emilio Cantos Lucado and he co-owns a business with Victoria. The Russian police discovered that the money which was wired to Irina Kapitsa for the painting came from a shell company called *Pelícano Azul*. We now know that it was Emilio Cantos Lucado himself who arranged the transfer to Irina's account from *Pelícano Azul*."

Richard picked up his briefcase and opened it, extracting the envelope Sheila had given him that morning.

"I've got here the information that's been uncovered on the financial transactions. I'm afraid I need to protect my sources but they're utterly reliable. The details of this can be checked by yourselves anyway."

He pulled out the neat, stapled sheets from the

envelope and, without saying another word, he passed them to the Colonel.

Earlier on that morning he had made notes on the edges of each sheet so as to highlight certain details but the financial information on them was clear and self-explanatory. It would be child's play for the Colonel to pick up on the implications listed meticulously on each piece of paper.

The Colonel took his time scrutinizing the papers, flicking the pages backwards and forwards for a good few minutes, leaving the others beside him to wait with barely concealed impatience.

Letting out a frustrated sigh, the Colonel finished reading, then reached across and handed the paperwork to Gonzalo.

With a hungry expression on his face, Gonzalo seized the sheets and started to read through them, ignoring everyone else in the room like his boss had done.

"I've been told that Emilio is in a precarious situation financially and if squeezed he'll talk. I suggest you do this as soon as possible," added Richard helpfully.

The Colonel leaned forward.

"Why were we not informed of this? All we were given by yourselves was a bizarre theory about Victoria being a living descendant of El Greco and that a poster tube was sent to her on the day of the murder…"

"Yes. That *was* all we had on her at the time. This latest information has only come to light very recently."

"Can I ask you again why you didn't inform us of it? Would we not have been best placed to deal with this? Instead you've sent a British detective and a private investigator to Madrid and look what a mess they've made of things!"

Richard shifted uncomfortably under the piercing eyes of the Colonel. He hated being put into a tight corner, and lying to a fellow police officer did not come naturally to him.

"We were worried that if Victoria was alerted to the fact she was under suspicion, she might hide or remove the painting, making it harder for us to find," he offered, hoping this would allay the Colonel's distrust.

After a few seconds Colonel Cabrera's taut face eased into a more relaxed expression.

"I can see some kind of logic in that," he admitted. "However, if this Emilio fellow doesn't confess we'll be no further forward I'm afraid."

He turned to Gonzalo, who was still perusing the sheets of financial information with a look of intense concentration.

"Gonzalo!"

Gonzalo looked up straightaway, lifting an eyebrow as he did so.

"Can you please ensure that Emilio is brought in for questioning as soon as possible? He could be anywhere in Spain or even abroad, I suppose, but it shouldn't take too long to track him down. I would enquire at his Head Office, here in Madrid first, and take it from there. Hopefully if he's a busy businessman he'll be tied up in meetings somewhere and won't be expecting us."

"Sí, Señor," replied Gonzalo, standing up with alacrity.

He handed the incriminating sheets back over to Colonel Cabrera and then headed straight out of the room.

The Colonel carefully slid the paperwork back into the envelope and then turned to look at Richard.

"Right," said Colonel Cabrera. "I suggest we go and visit your friends. You'll be pleased to know they haven't been treated too badly."

He smiled wryly.

"We have a good prison system here in Spain. Our tabloid news even reported on a man last year who committed a crime solely so he could get a place in jail. It seems he was living in poverty and wanted to be taken care of in prison, even at the cost of losing his liberty. But of course, there are prisons and prisons... Some are better than others, as I'm sure is the case in your country." He shrugged. "Your friends fortunately have ended up in a local one that we use for our VIP prison population, in other words our political or celebrity prisoners. This prison is where they were going to stay until their sentence was administered."

Richard said nothing.

Despite Colonel Cabrera's assurances, he was pretty sure that Eilidh would not be enjoying her time in jail because no sane member of the police force would like to find themselves on the other side of the divide, setting aside the awful implications for her job too.

As for Mike Telford, it would be of no surprise whatsoever to Richard if he were reveling in the whole adventure.

He knew, though, that Mike's patience would be limited. If he remained incarcerated for too long, Mike Telford was capable of causing just as much trouble as Lionel in one of his tempestuous and unpredictable moods. Mike Telford had deep pockets, powerful backers and knew all about his rights within the British and European legal system. If he became too frustrated or impatient, he could easily end up suing the officers that had arrested him and that would ruffle more than a few feathers in Scotland Yard, especially since he was accompanied by one of their own.

Mike had known fine well what he was doing when he had brought Eilidh along with him as a representative of the British police force, thought Richard. He admired many of Mike's sterling qualities but his self-serving attitude was definitely not one of them. Only Mike could have made use of Eilidh with such sangfroid and forethought, while at the same time deliberately ignoring the considerable risk to her career and reputation.

Richard sighed as he saw Colonel Cabrera waiting for him by the door.

With a polite smile to the other two men, Richard picked up his briefcase and followed Colonel Cabrera out of the room.

22

Eilidh

Eilidh sat at the desk in her narrow prison cell and reread the torn, stained page of her book.

After she had requested an English book to read, one of the guards had brought her the dog-eared *The Mysterious Affair at Styles* by Agatha Christie.

She was astonished that the deceased Mistress of Crime had such an international following because her books were really quite dated now, with no computers or technology in them, just the use of the "little grey cells".

She had been stuck staring at the same page for the past two minutes; somehow, when you were locked away in jail, time seemed to slow down, and consequently she found her actions and mental processes had slackened too.

""Instinct is a marvelous thing," mused Poirot. "It can neither be explained nor ignored.""

Eilidh had no affinity with Poirot, finding him annoyingly meticulous and precise, but she liked that line because she herself believed in gut feeling. She was proud of what she and Mike had uncovered as a result of her persistence and instinct.

Now, though, they were playing the waiting game.

She was sure Mike had been questioned by the Guardia Civil just as she had been, but she was following Mike's instructions to the letter and waiting for a British police representative to appear before she said anything of value to their Spanish counterparts.

According to what she understood from the broken English and exaggerated gestures of the friendly guard who had brought her the Agatha Christie book to read, Victoria was foaming at the mouth with anger at their break-in.

Eilidh smiled to herself.

She could well imagine Victoria's distress and frustration when she found El Greco's painting of the Spanish princess had somehow vanished from her dressing room without a trace.

There was a loud bang as the door to her cell opened and a burly man held out a small plastic tray to her.

Eilidh took the tray and put it on her desk, looking down at the milky coffee and the pastry, or *"la Palmera"* as the guards called it, with trepidation.

"La merienda," he said brusquely, before leaving again.

She decided she should wait until dinner before she ate anything because with very little exercise she was going to end up putting on weight. She was sure this prison, the most luxurious one she had seen to date, would have a gym but her Spanish was sadly lacking in fluency and she doubted the guards would understand her if she asked to use it.

The prison food was also very good.

Recalling the beans, chips and fried chicken nuggets of New Scotland Yard's canteen, she felt a little envy. The Spanish knew how to relish their food and she was happy that not all vestiges of Mediterranean cuisine had vanished in Madrid with the introduction of McDonald's and the cheap, fast food diet currently invading every corner of the civilized world.

Lifting up the hot, ceramic cup, she swallowed the coffee with relish, savouring the sweetness of it. In an antiseptic-smelling, anonymous prison cell, a cup of milky coffee became a thing of luxury.

Only a few minutes later there was a sharp knock, the door swung open again and Richard Langley appeared through the doorway.

Eilidh put down her half-finished coffee and turned around fully to look at him.

The first thing she noticed was that Richard was looking very careworn, his tired eyes were set in dark ovals and his mouth was tight-lipped. He also was more untidy than usual, with his suit trousers badly creased and a careless knot in his tie leaving it hanging at an angle.

His anxiety seemed to Eilidh to be a little extreme but given he had no idea they had discovered the precious painting in Victoria's house, it was understandable he was under strain. He was probably having a difficult time trying to extricate them from their incarceration.

"Hi Richard. How are you doing?"

Richard stared at her in disbelief for a minute.

"Eh, I'm good, thanks," he said politely.

"Actually, I'm not good," he amended quickly,

sounding annoyed. "You and Mike have put me in a hell of a position."

He walked over to the metal bed and sat down heavily on the mattress, the plastic mattress cover rustling underneath him as he did so.

The door to the prison cell was still ajar and Eilidh was sure there was a prison guard waiting on the other side of it.

"Have you spoken to Mike?" asked Eilidh.

Richard shook his head.

"You might be better talking to him," she suggested.

"Oh? And why is that? My first duty is to get a member of our police force out of prison. He can wait."

Eilidh smiled at Richard's stern tone.

"We're both equally to blame. I'm sorry but I took Mike's phone number from your mobile."

"Yes, I gathered something like that must have happened. However, you don't need to tell me that Mike was the one who encouraged you to accompany him on this break-in. This whole venture has his markings all over it."

Eilidh shrugged.

"There's no point splitting hairs." She lowered her voice. "I think before you lose it with Mike, you should know that we were successful."

Richard looked back at her stunned, almost as though he had just been hit by a bullet.

"You were?"

Eilidh nodded and lifted a finger to her lips.

Bemused, Richard stared at her for a moment. Then he took off his glasses and rubbed his bloodshot eyes.

Eilidh could understand his confusion. For so many

months the trail to *The Spanish Princess* had led nowhere and it seemed almost inconceivable now that they had finally come across it.

"I think I'll manage to get the two of you released," he said at last, putting his glasses back on. "After doing some digging on those Russian accounts we've found an incriminating money trail leading almost directly to Victoria. We're just waiting for the Spanish police to interview her accomplice and see if he opens up. Otherwise, things are going to be difficult."

"'*We've*'? I take it you mean your friend Sheila Mackenzie has discovered the money trail?"

Richard glanced away without saying a word, his silence confirming her suspicion.

"What about Lionel?"

"He doesn't know anything yet but it won't be long before he does."

"So, it's Richard to the rescue," Eilidh said, her frivolous words tempered with a note of relief because she knew that watching Lionel at work trying to free them would be similar to watching a cruise ship trying to squeeze under Hammersmith Bridge. In other words, carnage.

"You should be thankful we cracked the money trail or there'd be no rescue on the cards for either of you. If it hadn't been for that you'd be facing a jail term."

Eilidh smiled docilely back at him, making sure she looked as angelic as possible.

In reality, she disagreed completely with Richard's assessment of the situation but she wasn't going to be confrontational and argue the case with him.

She thought it would be terrible publicity for the Guardia Civil and Madrid's Ministry of Justice to put a custodial sentence on a member of the British police force, especially given that the records would show she hadn't actually stolen anything from Victoria's house. She was almost certain that to avoid any embarrassment something would be arranged in order to release her and Mike.

Right then, though, all the arguments for their release were unimportant in the greater scheme of things. They had to focus on what mattered right now and that was recovering *The Spanish Princess* from Victoria's house.

"Once we're out of here," said Eilidh quietly, "we should go back to Victoria's house with the Spanish police. The sooner the better..."

Richard, who had been rubbing abstractedly at his unshaven cheek, froze.

"You left it there?" he asked, looking worried.

"We had to."

"She still has it in her possession?"

Eilidh rolled her eyes. Richard's brain wasn't working with its normal fluency.

"No."

"You hid it?"

"Yes, of course. Thanks to Mike's quick thinking."

"I'll have to have another word with Colonel Cabrera," said Richard, almost speaking to himself, his eyebrows raised in surprise as he took in this latest snippet of information.

Richard turned and gazed out of the small window on his left-hand side, clearly trying to gather his thoughts together, and for a time it was as though he had forgotten Eilidh was even in the room with him.

The light from the window highlighted the dark shadows under his eyes and his pale skin.

He looked exhausted.

Eilidh could see he was also tense with suppressed excitement; it was obvious in the taut set of his shoulders and the fixed look in his eyes. At one point he lifted a hand to his mouth as though to bite a nail and then put it down again.

Unsure what to do while he mulled things over Eilidh glanced down at her book again, trying to find where she had left off.

"Are conditions alright for you here?" Richard asked suddenly, taking her by surprise.

Eilidh looked across at him.

"Yes, all very comfortable here," she replied, disconcerted by his unexpected solicitude.

Richard nodded, pleased.

"Good."

He stood up and stretched.

"I'd best be getting on with pushing this case forward. I take it neither you nor Mike are going to let us know where you've hidden the painting?"

Eilidh shook her head.

Richard sighed, as though this was what he had expected all along.

"Tell them we'll only reveal where the painting is if they release us without charges."

"Yes. I get it. He's trained you well…"

Indignant that Richard would think she was Mike's puppet, she scowled at him.

"I've got a mind too, I'll have you know. Trust is in short supply these days. We need some assurances before we divulge the whereabouts of *The Spanish Princess*. That's all you need to pass on to them."

"Agreed. Let's just hope they don't take it into their heads to search Victoria's house from top to bottom first, though, because if they find the painting we'll be screwed and Igor can kiss his precious painting goodbye."

"Come on, Richard! You're exaggerating. Spain isn't run by some corrupt, autocratic dictatorship. Igor's ownership won't be in dispute. It might make our situation here a bit more precarious and we'll lose our leverage but if that's the way it goes, so be it."

Richard listened to her with a hint of admiration in his light blue eyes.

What was he so impressed with? Eilidh asked herself.

Much to her annoyance she began to feel uncharacteristically shy and self-conscious under his forthright gaze. She became aware she was wearing the short-sleeved, bright orange prison uniform given to her when she arrived and that it clashed hideously with her strawberry blonde hair. She must look an absolute fright.

Richard grinned at her and winked.

"You're right, Eilidh," he conceded. "I'll see what I can do."

As he walked past her he patted her gently on the shoulder, in the manner of a benign relative, and then without another word he disappeared out of the door.

Eilidh wasn't fooled by his paternalistic gesture.

For whatever reason, Richard had undoubtedly developed a soft spot for her and she hoped it could prove useful to her later on because she wanted to ask him for yet another favour.

She had spent a lot of time in her prison cell, lying on the hard mattress with a lumpy pillow propping up her head as she gazed up at the cigarette-blackened ceiling. During the long, tedious daytime hours she had lain there, feet crossed at the ankles, and pondered her job with a clarity of mind that she wholly lacked when she was working within the frenzied chaos of the Homicide Unit at New Scotland Yard.

In the early hours of that morning she had made a momentous decision: she wanted to leave the Homicide Unit to work in the Art and Antiquities Unit. Somehow, for her own sanity, she needed to persuade Richard to put her at the top of the waiting list for any vacancies for a DI in his department.

23

Richard

Gonzalo pushed the buzzer outside Victoria's home for a second time.

The others stood beside him in an awkward huddle as they waited to be allowed into the property.

"*¿Quién es?*" asked a male voice through the intercom, almost inaudible as the dogs on the other side of the fence started barking madly.

"*Es la Guardia Civil. ¡Déjanos entrar por favor!*" shouted Gonzalo.

Seconds later the heavy metal door to the property was opened by a guard in a pale grey uniform. He was impressively burly, with broad shoulders and the muscles in his arms straining against the fabric of his shirt sleeves.

The guard began an impassioned conversation with Gonzalo, which Richard found impossible to follow. Their voices steadily increased in volume and fervor, with the guard towering over Gonzalo and blocking the entrance to the house.

Richard sighed to himself.

It seemed as though they had little chance of retrieving the painting quickly, but then again it wasn't as though they were going to be welcomed back to Victoria's house like the prodigal son was.

Glancing across at Eilidh and Mike he could see they had not polished up on their Spanish during their time in jail. Both were gazing blankly at the fracas at the gate and seemed at a loss to understand what the guard was saying to Gonzalo.

Looking at the guard again, who was waving his hands around with typical Hispanic expressiveness, Richard wondered if Victoria had beefed up her security since the day Mike and Eilidh had broken into her house.

He remembered that on day of their break-in the guard had very conveniently been away from the house. Had that guard had been sacked? He was pretty sure Victoria had a 24-hour watch at her house so someone must have failed her the evening Mike and Eilidh searched her house for the painting.

Unless it was Mike who had arranged for the guard to be absent that day, in his usual devious and enigmatic way. Richard wouldn't put it past him. Mike would see Victoria's guard losing his job as an unfortunate consequence to their break-in but he wouldn't feel a twinge of remorse about it. He was a pretty ruthless man.

Gonzalo was accompanied by another three members of the Guardia Civil, two of whom had driven Mike and Eilidh to Victoria's house in the back of an unmarked car. Technically, they were still under arrest but it remained to be seen if they continued to be so at the end of their visit to Victoria's house.

The heated exchange continued at the gate for

another few minutes until it was interrupted by a woman's voice; shrill, angry and talking at speed.

Immediately, both men stopped arguing and turned to face the newcomer.

Richard assumed that only Victoria in person would be able to command such respect from the two men, given that up until that point they had been oblivious to anyone else around them.

He craned his head to get a better view.

A lady was striding towards them, leaving the front door of the house open behind her. She was a very tall lady, dressed all in white and looking like a glamorous Spanish *gitana* with her waist-long, midnight blue-black hair, black eyes and mahogany skin.

Her beautiful face was somewhat marred by an expression of complete and utter fury, most of which seemed aimed towards Gonzalo.

After exchanging angry words with Gonzalo, she looked past him at the group standing on the pavement and erupted like a volcano.

"You *demonios*! What the hell are you doing here? Have you no respect or integrity? How dare you come back to my home after what you did to it!" she screamed, so angry that spittle could be seen coming out of her mouth.

Mike stared boldly back at her, a look of haughty disdain on his face.

Eilidh, meanwhile, seemed taken aback by the amount of emotion swirling around the entrance to Victoria's house.

Richard didn't blame her.

The dogs" excitable barking had joined in the general cacophony. It was not what anyone expected in

such an upper-class neighborhood and Richard reckoned they were providing the neighbors with enough
gossip to keep them going for weeks.

Victoria, her eyes flashing magnificently, turned to
Eilidh and then shouted out what they could only
assume were Spanish swear words at her. Her words
were incomprehensible to the English speakers but
seemed to horrify the Guardia Civil members, who
stood frozen to the spot with their mouths dropping
open.

Eilidh watched Victoria with a fascinated and wary
eye, as though she was expecting her to burst into
flames at any moment.

Feeling protective, Richard began to walk round to
her side but at that precise moment, Victoria, hissing
something in Spanish, lunged towards Mike and Eilidh
with her arms outstretched, her fingers bent over like
claws.

Victoria's guard, looking shocked, grabbed her by
the waist and pulled her back.

As Victoria wrestled with her guard, who was
trying to reason with her, Gonzalo quickly pulled out
the search warrant from his briefcase and held the
document right in front of her face.

Victoria stared at it for a minute and then deflated
like a burst balloon.

She looked up at Gonzalo, her face confused.

"¿Por qué?" she beseeched.

Nobody said anything. They were all assuming the
question was a rhetorical one.

Shaking off her guard, Victoria turned to look at
Mike and Eilidh.

As she glared at them comprehension began to

dawn in her eyes. She sneered, a ghastly grimace that narrowed her lips until they were two thin lines stretching across her cheeks.

"So, it is here? You hid it here?" she asked them in English.

Neither Mike nor Eilidh bothered to answer her question.

With renewed confidence and holding the search warrant close to him like a protective shield, Gonzalo pushed past Victoria's guard and walked on into the garden.

All the others soon followed suit.

Victoria hung back, making sure she walked right next to Eilidh and Mike, all the while darting malevolent glances at them.

What a bully, thought Richard to himself, unimpressed by her behaviour.

If she thought she could intimidate Mike Telford, she could think again. Whatever else people could say about Mike, there was not a single person who could cast any doubt on his courage. Rumor had it that three years ago, when the Dutch police cornered a gang of international art thieves inside their base in Amsterdam, Mike had placed himself directly in the line of fire in order to stop a Van Gogh painting hanging on the wall from getting damaged by any stray bullets.

They all walked into Victoria's hallway and then turned towards Mike and Eilidh, awaiting further instruction.

"We'll need the keys," said Mike, looking back at the guard who was hovering at the entrance of the house.

"I have keys," said Victoria, watching him closely. "Which key are you looking for?"

Mike turned and stared at her.

"I think you know which key we need, Victoria," he said calmly.

Victoria flushed under her dark skin and said nothing.

"And," Mike continued. "If you accidently happen to lose the keys, we can always leave the Guardia Civil to wait here until we find a way to enter the dressing room. But I'm sure you wouldn't want it to get to that stage."

Mike smiled at her, then turned and walked to the staircase.

He led the way up the stairs, assuming, quite rightly, that Victoria would not be able to resist seeing where the painting was lying hidden and would therefore be following in his footsteps.

Richard wondered when her infatuation with the painting began. What had fuelled her desire to own *The Spanish Princess*? To put at risk her reputation and future for the sake of a picture painted hundreds of years ago?

Richard, following behind the crowd of people making their way along the landing, marveled at Mike's ability to find his quarry. He was like a sniffer dog, hot on the scent, when pursuing missing artworks. In such an enormous house how had he managed to locate the hidden masterpiece? One day he would have to ask Eilidh to give him the full story.

As he came into the main bedroom he saw a door at the far end was wide open, leading in turn to another carpeted room with cupboards in it.

He assumed the room connected to the main bedroom was Victoria's dressing room. It looked as though there had been no need for keys this time. Maybe Victoria had given up locking the room after the valuable painting had been removed by Mike and Eilidh.

There was no sign of Mike, Eilidh or Gonzalo, so Richard assumed they had already slipped into the adjoining room.

Two policemen had stayed behind in the bedroom and were holding Victoria by the arms, one on each side.

Ignoring her captors, she was muttering to herself as she tried to see and hear what was going on in the other room. Richard thought the others were wise not to let Victoria see where the painting had been hidden. Victoria was so volatile; it was anyone's guess what she would have done if she caught sight of it again.

Richard walked into the dressing room and watched, intrigued, as Mike and Eilidh pulled back the carpet and underlay. He then saw them trying to lever up a couple of loose floorboards.

Finding the floorboards reluctant to shift, Mike went to one of the cupboards and grabbed hold of a coat hanger. He twisted the hook on it until it was bent at an angle and then knelt down to try and pry up the floorboard once more.

Soon afterwards the floorboard tilted upwards with a complaining creak. Mike pulled it away from the floor and tossed it to the far corner. He then lifted the next one using his bare hands.

Gonzalo and Richard bent down to look into the crevasse but they couldn't see much because both Mike and Eilidh were in the way. The pair of them had their heads together as they reached into the void with their hands, desperately searching for the hidden painting.

"Yes!" shouted Mike, pulling up the top of a rolled-up canvas after an anxious, heart-stopping minute.

He slid the coiled canvas out of the hole in the floor and then laid it tenderly on a flat piece of carpet.

Eilidh laughed as she watched him, delirious with relief.

Richard and Gonzalo, caught up in the excitement, stood riveted as Mike gently opened out the old canvas.

When at last the painting was lying fully exposed on the floor, Princess Micaela Catalina stared up at Richard for the second time that year.

Mike looked up at Richard and winked.

"Well, what do you think, my friend? Another goose chase or the real deal?"

Richard smiled.

"I'd be willing to bet it's the real thing," he said.

"Well," said Gonzalo, letting out a big breath. "I think this is incredible. Mike, fantastic work keeping this hidden. We must put this somewhere safe. It should be taken to the Prado as soon as possible. Even with just a few days lying under this floor there could be some damage done to the painting. Let's take this to the car and get going."

He turned to Richard.

"You're welcome to join us, Richard."

Richard shook his head.

"No, I think we need to get Mike and Eilidh officially discharged first."

"Oh yes, of course," agreed Gonzalo distractedly, returning to practical matters with a bump. "I'll call for more reinforcements. We need to get Victoria to the police station too."

Gonzalo took his mobile phone out of his suit pocket and started making calls from the other side of the room.

His colleague, the third Guardia Civil policeman, remained standing next to the painting, keeping a close eye on it while his boss dealt with his administrative duties.

Richard saw that Mike and Eilidh, sitting back on their heels, were gazing down at the painting as if they couldn't believe their eyes. Success was sweet and he was reluctant to interrupt their big moment but it was time to go. The painting was safe now.

"Guys, we should head back to the Guardia Civil Headquarters and sort out your release," said Richard.

"I'm not leaving until I see Gonzalo drive off with the painting safely tucked into the back of his car," asserted Mike, looking up at Richard. "As a matter of fact, while we're at it, I'd like to ask Victoria a few questions."

Eilidh snorted with derision.

"I'd like to see you try," she said to Mike.

"I know it's unlikely she'll answer them but I'm still going to try. I don't like unresolved riddles," said Mike firmly, a look of stubborn determination on his face.

He stood up and, without another word, walked back through to the main bedroom.

Richard and Eilidh stared at each other for a few seconds and then both rushed to follow Mike out of the room, leaving the painting on the floor and Gonzalo watching them in bemusement as he held his mobile to his ear.

In the main bedroom, Richard saw that Mike had gone and seated himself on Victoria's bed. The first thought that crossed Richard's mind, when he saw Mike perched on top of the bed's fancy, white lace quilt, was that this was a foolish move because it was only going to rile Victoria even more. She was not going to want to cooperate and answer his questions if provoked in this way; after all, nobody would want their arch-enemy sitting casually on their bed.

He glanced across at Victoria. She was watching Mike from the other side of the room with a speculative glint in her eyes.

Victoria turned to the policemen holding her.

"*¿Puedo sentarme?*" she asked them, gesturing towards the bed.

To Richard's surprise it seemed she wanted to sit down too. However, he could see that both the men who were holding her weren't keen on the idea.

"*Déjale,*" said Gonzalo authoritatively from the doorway.

Not looking too happy about the order, the two policemen released her from their grip.

Victoria walked over to the bed and sat down next to Mike.

Close but not too close.

The two Guardia Civil policemen, meanwhile, made sure they were standing right next to her, unconvinced after the scene downstairs that Victoria was to be trusted.

Gonzalo had disappeared once more into the dressing room, no doubt to finish his calls and gloat over the painting.

"What is it you want to ask me?" asked Victoria in a

quiet voice, all the time staring straight ahead to the dressing room door.

"Well, where do I start?" said Mike with his usual bonhomie. "I've a lot of questions. How did you find out about the painting? It wasn't registered on any database."

Victoria smiled wistfully.

"I've had what you could call an obsession with El Greco since I was a small girl," she admitted. "Probably ever since I was a young girl of six and I was told by my father about our family's ancestry and links to El Greco. My father was proud of his ties to the famous artist and the Spanish princess... After my father died El Greco became an icon for me and a link to my past. I've visited and viewed every painting by the artist in Spain and, of course, I'm a regular visitor to the El Greco Museum in Toledo."

Victoria lifted a hand to her face and began to wipe away tears that were starting to make their way down her cheeks. Richard noticed her hands were trembling. It seemed to him the woman was on the brink of a nervous breakdown and was in need of some psychological intervention.

Accepting a tissue proffered by Eilidh, Victoria cleaned up her face. Afterwards she held the crumpled tissue in a clenched fist on her lap.

"Two years ago, I was invited to a dinner party in London at Irina's house," continued Victoria. "A friend in London, who sells our glassware, knew Irina and thought I should meet her. From a business perspective only. Irina was well connected in Russian society and we are always looking to break into new markets with our glassware. During the dinner party I managed to spill some red wine on my dress and Irina took me to her bedroom, to change into a dress of hers while the maid fixed the stain on mine. I straightaway recognized El Greco's work on her bedroom wall."

"Irina told you that it was by El Greco?" asked Mike curiously.

"No, she had no idea," said Victoria, moving further back on the bed and hugging her knees to her. At the same time, she bent her head and rested it on her knees. She was now staring sideways at Mike's back but there was no animosity in her face. "But I was instantly sure of it. I've spent a lifetime studying his work. I offered her some money for it right then but she said it wasn't hers to sell. She had to ask Igor. A week later she called me and told me Igor wasn't going to sell it. It had sentimental value to him. I asked her if she could confirm with Igor if it was painted by El Greco. Apparently, Igor wasn't happy with the question and refused to tell her. Anyway, we left it at that."

"*You left it at that*?" repeated Mike.

If only, thought Richard.

"Of course, I couldn't get the painting out of my head," said Victoria, ignoring Mike's interruption. "I was so excited because I was certain the portrait was of Catalina Micaela. Both the artist and the princess were ancestors of ours, their birth line comes down directly to me. I planned to wait a while and then ask Igor again if I could buy it from him. Give him an offer he couldn't refuse."

"What happened to change Irina's mind?" asked Mike.

Victoria lifted her head at his question.

"The Russian mafia got to her. They were going to

pay her to steal the painting and she felt she had no choice but to do so. But she was already wanting to start a new life without Igor. My friend in London was a confidante of hers and told me Irina had begun a relationship with an art restorer in London. She was head over heels in love with him. Irina decided she had no choice but to do what the mafia wanted her to do. Don't ask me how they found out about the painting. I've no idea..."

She sighed to herself.

"Maybe one of them had been in their flat or maybe the artwork was noticed when it was transported to Britain from Russia. Who knows? They could have seen it when it was getting restored. Or perhaps rumours about the painting were circulating back in Russia. Either way, Irina got greedy and decided she was going to get me to bid against the mafia for the painting. If I was able to pay up she'd get the painting delivered to me that month. I paid a deposit and then paid the rest when I received the painting in the post... I honour my commitments."

"Emilio Cantos Lucado paid the money, didn't he?" asked Richard.

Victoria nodded.

"Yes. I didn't explain what it was for but I've been keeping his business afloat for a while now so he didn't have any choice in the matter."

"We have three deaths chalked up to this painting," said Richard. "The mafia also know they were sold a fake, so they'll be searching for the authentic painting now too. Max is dead but they might've had a confession out of him before he was killed... Victoria, I don't fancy your chances against them. The Russian mafia have a big foothold here in Spain."

Victoria was unmoved.

Judging by the expression on her face, she seemed unafraid and oblivious to the consequences of owning a painting wanted by the Russian mafia. Or maybe she just wasn't taking anything in.

"You have kids, don't you?" demanded Mike, turning to look back at her.

Victoria glowered suspiciously at him and nodded.

"You're safer in a Spanish prison and without the painting, if you ask me."

"You don't really believe that," said Victoria scornfully, her lips curled. "I've heard of your reputation. You love these works of art. You put yourself at risk to retrieve them. You know what art can mean to people and so you'll know what that painting meant to me. Yes, you can lock me up but in my heart that painting belongs to me and as long as I live I'll work to get it back again."

Mike shrugged his shoulders.

Richard could see he wasn't going to waste his breath explaining his thoughts to her. Mike knew that he was dealing with someone mentally unstable and had accepted he would never be able to reason with her.

Richard estimated the amount of prison time Victoria would get for the theft. Not long enough in his opinion. Who knew where her infatuation would carry her after a few years in jail?

At that moment four policeman turned up at the bedroom door, appearing slightly bewildered. Gonzalo came back through to the main bedroom and spoke to them in quick Spanish, explaining what the situation was.

The two men who were still standing next to Victoria bent down and muttered something to her.

She stood up, they put a set of handcuffs on her and, unresisting, she was escorted out of the room and down the stairs.

Gonzalo followed them out. Richard was certain he was going to fetch a makeshift crate from his car so he could transport the painting to El Prado.

The atmosphere in the room lightened after Victoria had gone. It wasn't pleasant for any of them to see someone in the grip of a such a strong obsession and watch as her hopes and aspirations crumbled before her very eyes.

Loosening his shoulders, Richard drew a deep breath of relief.

Eilidh, meanwhile, had her back to the room as she inspected the canvas hanging on the bedroom wall.

Mike stood up and stretched, as though shedding the events of the past hour in the manner of a dog shaking off water after a plunge.

He then glanced at his watch.

"Hmm. Two o'clock. Well past lunchtime. Any chance of stopping at a restaurant on the way back to the Guardia Civil Headquarters, Richard?"

Richard smiled.

"I don't see why not. Gonzalo?" he asked as Gonzalo walked across the room carrying a large, plastic crate and a pair of gloves.

"Yes?" replied Gonzalo, turning around before entering the dressing room.

"Can you ask your men to make a pit-stop at a restaurant on the way back to headquarters?"

Gonzalo glanced across at Eilidh and Mike and laughed.

"Yes, of course. I'll catch up with you all back at headquarters once I've dropped off the painting at El Prado. There's a good restaurant called Luna Illuminante on the Gran Via that many of us go to. I'll tell them to take you there."

He turned to two of the policemen and explained what was required of them.

They nodded and accompanied Richard, Mike and Eilidh out of the house and into the sunlit street.

The dogs had quieted, the guard waved at them from his portal and the strange occurrences from earlier that day seemed like a dream that had evaporated under the warm Spanish sunshine.

24

Eilidh

Vivaldi's music echoed pleasantly through Room 8 at El Prado. So as not to drown out the general chit-chat the small orchestra was positioned at one of the doorways into the room as they plied their instruments.

The room was colorful as it was filled mostly with women and they were all wearing gorgeous dresses in every shade of the rainbow. Like a kaleidoscope of butterflies, they moved around the large space, greeting and meeting.

On the walls, paintings by Juan Sánchez Cotán, Ribera and El Greco looked down benignly on the women as they ate hors d'oeuvres and drank champagne.

Eilidh smiled at her partner, one of the two men in the room.

Igor, dressed in a tux, was swallowing his champagne and chatting vociferously with Isabel Perón. They were both staring with considerable interest at a painting on the wall.

Smaller than the other paintings in the room, it

nevertheless stood out because of its bright and vivid colors. Princess Catalina Micaela, seated on her turquoise chair and dressed in her amber-orange gown, was pulling her weight amongst the renowned and revered paintings in the room.

Her knowing dark eyes pulled the observer in, gleaming black against the startling white of her face. The amorous hunger in her face remained undiminished centuries later as she held her pose for the smitten artist.

A small plaque beside the painting named it as *The Spanish Princess* and gave a brief background to the painting and the inscription on the back of it.

Eilidh turned and looked behind her, searching for the man who had organized this event.

At the far side of the room and looking unusually smart in his tux was Richard, surrounded by a group of women who were creased over laughing. Perhaps they were finding Richard as funny as she did…

Sheila Mackenzie, dressed in a beautiful silk, sea-green dress, was giggling at his side. Eilidh was pleased to see her looking so happy. Richard had been stressing for weeks over her hen party but with some help from Isabel and Igor he'd made it an event to remember.

Actually, with a little help from her too.

The itinerary had been arranged between the two of them, during lunch breaks back at New Scotland Yard. Looking at her watch, Eilidh noted that the flamenco dancing was due to begin in twenty minutes" time.

The highlight of the evening, though, was going to be a gourmet meal served in Room 12. Room 12 was an enormous room filled with many of Velázquez's best-known paintings.

Eilidh had enjoyed planning the meal. Small, battery-powered candles were going to be festooned around the tables (no one in their right mind would allow real candles inside El Prado), tasteful flower arrangements were placed between the paintings and subdued music would be playing in the background out of several speakers.

The seating plan was going to cause controversy.

Numbers were going to be picked out of a box for seat placements, so with the exception of Sheila and Richard as well as herself and Igor, all the guests were going to have to follow a random number to their place at the table. There was going to be no girly cliquishness tonight.

It had to be said El Prado had been extremely obliging in providing the venue for Sheila's hen night. This had a lot to do with Igor's generosity; Igor was allowing his cherished El Greco portrait of Catalina Micaela to be shown in the gallery on permanent loan.

Sensibly, Igor had realized that there were too many competing interests out to steal his treasured painting and at least in El Prado the painting would be closer to the artist's lifelong home and, of course, safe.

Maybe, just maybe, he'd been a little moved by Victoria's story. Could he relate to her passion for the painting? Eilidh did wonder. At least here in El Prado Victoria would one day be able to look at her ancestor.

Nevertheless, Eilidh didn't put it past her to try and steal the painting again…

All of which brought her to thinking about her new job.

Taking advantage of Lionel's good mood and with Richard's support, she had requested a transfer to the Art and Antiquities Unit. Much to their mutual astonishment, Lionel had agreed to it.

It was possible, of course, that he'd been only too happy to shift a burnt-out detective, who no longer had any interest in homicides, to a less controversial department. Anything for an easier life tended to be Lionel's motto at Scotland Yard.

When he heard the news, Abdul had grinned at her and said, "Told you you were too soft for the Homicide Unit, Si." Then he had surprised her by giving her a hug and saying, "We'll miss you."

She knew she had a lot to learn and Richard had already started piling art history books on her for home-time reading. It was surprisingly enjoyable learning from Richard. He was patient and, more importantly, always enthusiastic about the subject so he never grew bored of explaining or repeating facts to her.

"Having fun, Eilidh?" asked a familiar voice at her elbow.

Eilidh looked up into Richard's kind face and smiled.

"Yes, of course. You did Sheila proud tonight."

"It was a team effort, I would say," said Richard modestly.

He scanned the hall and then looked down at his watch.

"We still have ten minutes before the flamenco starts. Fancy a sneak peak at the Velázquez room?"

Eilidh glanced across at Igor, who was still deep in conversation with Isabel Perón.

Igor, catching her eye as she gestured towards Richard and the other room, winked and nodded at her.

"Let's go," said Eilidh.

She hooked her arm in Richard's and the pair of them made their way to Room 12, where no doubt Richard was going to indulge in pointing out to her the features he most liked about Velázquez's paintings.

They were both going to miss the flamenco dancing but neither of them cared.

Acknowledgments

Most books I read have pages of acknowledgements at the back of them. However, for this book the thanks simply go to my husband and the friends and family members who have encouraged me.

A Look At Book Two:
The Chagall Cello

When Detective Chief Inspector Richard Langley and Detective Inspector Eilidh Simmons are tasked with investigating a stolen Botticelli painting from the home of a former slave trader—at Penrhyn Castle in Wales—three brutally murdered bodies are discovered in Hampstead Heath, London.

One victim appears to have been tortured with pieces of broken glass and has in his possession a cello with two Chagall paintings hidden in it—stolen during the Night of Broken Glass in Nazi Germany.

As dedicated detectives work together to track down the original owners of the Chagall paintings and uncover if the murders are part of a revenge killing, a plot more intricate than anyone thought possible begins to unfold... And no one is safe.

AVAILABLE OCTOBER 2022

About the Author

Bea Green grew up as the daughter of a British diplomat and a Spanish mother. She spent every summer at her grandfather's olive tree farm in Andalusia. She graduated from the University of St Andrews in Scotland with an MA in English literature and currently lives in Edinburgh with her husband and two daughters.

Printed in Great Britain
by Amazon

16499310R00196